black truth

KRISTIN MAYER

Black Truth
The Twisted Fate Series
Copyright © 2016 by K. Mayer Enterprises, Inc.
Book cover by JM Walker with Just write. Creations
(https://www.facebook.com/justwrite.creations/)
Interior design by JT Formatting
(https://www.facebook.com/JTFormatting/)
Editing by Nichole Strauss with Perfectly Publishable
(https://www.facebook.com/perfectlypublishable/)
Editing by Janine Weathers at Write Divas (http://writedivas.com/)

Black Truth / Kristin Mayer – 1st ed.
Library of Congress Cataloging-in-Publication Data
ISBN-13: 978-1-942910-15-2

VISIT MY WEBSITE AT
http://www.authorkristinmayer.com

To Mom,
I love you infinity factorial. Never forget how strong you are. I'm
thankful each and every day to have you in my life as my mother.
Kristin

Chapter One

My supposedly dead husband stood before me.

He was alive.

The asshole who'd caused havoc in my life was here. He'd torn me apart emotionally.

"Willow." He sounded concerned. He took another step forward with his hands out in front of him. "Willow, please let me explain."

He took another step, jolting me out of my shock. Fear ebbed back in its place.

I remained speechless as the man I'd come to known as Tack took another step toward me. How were they the same man? Alex was cold and callous. Tack was warm and caring. Examining every part of him, he was exactly the same—dark hair, green eyes, built.

Alex had manipulated me… again.

Hurt and anger raced through me like an explosion, and a metallic taste filled my mouth. I wanted to scream, but the words caught in my throat.

He took another step forward.

I retreated by the same amount. On the phone, he'd had an Irish accent. Now the accent was gone. I felt sick. The man who had betrayed me. Tricked me. He was married... with a kid. I took another step back, not wanting to hear anything from his mouth. Lies. All of it would be lies.

Instinct kicked in and I pushed the panic button on my ring Trent, my security advisor, had given me minutes before he'd left my hotel room.

"Willow. I know what you're thinking. Let me explain." He still held his hands out and his voice was gentle. The old Alex was back. The one before the war and the night we made love and created the baby I was carrying.

My head spun.

The door to my hotel room busted open. Trent, Andre and Peter came in with their guns drawn. Alex's hands went up higher as Trent repositioned himself in the room. I backed up farther as Alex trained his eyes on me.

"Let me explain. I'm not Alex."

Trent came to my side as the other two spread out. Gently he guided me behind his body.

Alex watched his every move.

"Are you okay, Willow?" Concern etched Trent's voice, which caused his Irish accent to become more pronounced.

"Yes. No. I don't know." I turned my attention back to Alex, stuck on his earlier words.

"What do you mean you're not Alex?" My heartbeat pulsed through my ears as adrenaline raced through my body.

Alex's hands remained in the air. "I'm Gabriel Alexander Thompson. The man you married was Alexander Gabriel Thompson, my twin."

"Twin?" There were two of them? *Two.* How was that

possible?

I turned to Trent who fit the part of a military man with his dark-haired crew cut and lean muscular body.

Trent turned his tense expression on Alex. "I didn't find a record of a twin."

Andre lowered his weapon. He was the giant bodyguard who'd saved me in the car accident that put Carson on life support.

"Andre, I did not give the order to stand down." Trent's voice was deadly.

The tension built as Andre kept his gun lowered. At Trent's nod, Peter turned his guns on Andre.

My eyes widened, and I stopped breathing as I waited with bated breath to see what was going to happen next. The door opened and another security guard with his gun drawn entered.

"Move toward the door, Willow. Slowly."

Inch by inch, I took a step back, following Trent's lead. Everyone watched each other. Alex looked nervous as he watched me.

Andre's large booming voice rang through the room. "Hear him out, Trent. I served with him. He's telling the truth!"

Andre was in cahoots with Tack. That explained how Tack was able to get into places with extremely tight security. When I had asked him about having an inside man, Tack avoided my question since he promised to never lie to me.

My breaths were coming faster as my heart accelerated to an unprecedented pace.

Alex or Gabe, or whoever the hell he was, took a step forward, but stopped at the sound of Trent's gun cocking. The other security guards cocked their gun as well.

Doing the unthinkable, Andre stepped in front of Alex. "He's not going to hurt her."

"I don't take fucking orders from you, Andre." Trent's voice turned icy.

"I know you fucking don't. All I'm asking is that you stand down. Hear him out."

I stood frozen in place.

Trent backed us up a little more. "Willow, when I say open the door, you run to the suite with the guys. Okay?"

"O-okay." Fear wanted to claw its way in, but I refused to give into it.

Slowly, Alex stepped to the side and became a target again. "Willow, hear me out. You're pregnant with my baby. Not Alex's. Mine. That night before Alex died, you were with me. I'm the man you fell in love with. Not Alex. Me. I left and Alex tried to take you from me. Think about it. You felt something different that night."

How was this happening?

Twin.

Gabe.

Alex.

There were two of them. The room spun a little. "I feel dizzy."

"Trent, don't let her fall. Get her a seat." Alex took another step forward. "Damn it; tie my hands behind my back. Whatever you need to do, but don't let her fall."

My head swam a little more and I leaned into Trent.

"Peter, throw both this fuckwad and Andre some ties to secure themselves." The command was given from beside me.

Peter threw the zip ties to both men and they complied quickly.

"Peter, if they move, shoot to injure."

"Yes, sir."

I leaned into Trent's side as he took me to a wooden dining room chair with a leather seat. My breaths came even faster.

"Breathe with me, Willow. Long deep breaths."

I followed Trent's lead, slowing my breaths considerably. I was not able to take my eyes off Alex as he tracked me the entire time.

"Will you get her some water, Trent? I don't want her going into shock. Not with all the stress she's been under and being pregnant."

Pregnant. I was carrying this man's child who wasn't the man I had been married too, but was the man I thought I had married. My head hurt. This was a cluster fuck. Honestly, with my mind trying to comprehend what had been going on, I wasn't sure what to think. Still, my eyes weren't able to leave Alex's. A water glass appeared before me.

"Take a sip, sweetheart," Alex said, imploringly.

Without thinking, I complied. The room was coming back into focus. A few minutes passed as I glanced around the room. No one moved.

"Please, Willow. Let me explain." Alex's words pierced me. They were honest and heartfelt.

Trent asked, "What do you want to do?"

Taking another tentative sip, I looked at the man seated on the floor. His emerald eyes were soft. Concern and love filled them. I wanted to have him taken away, but this was Tack. This same man had been there for me through so many ups and downs. There were too many times he'd had a chance to hurt me in the last month or get what we believed Alex was after... my trust fund.

I took another sip of water as everyone waited for me to

answer. Finally, I asked, "Trent, can we clear the room except for the three of us? Is it safe?"

Weighing his options, Trent thought for a second. He pointed to Peter. "Take Andre out of here. I'll deal with him later. I want a three-man team outside the door. Secure Alex to the chair across the way. Before you leave, search him. I won't take any chances with Willow's safety."

Carson's parents put us up in one of their hotels to be closer to the hospital since the car accident. I was thankful Nonno slept with earplugs and a sound machine since he was in the other room of this suite. On top of that, he was a deep sleeper.

Alex gave Trent a serious nod. "Good. Her safety is all that matters. But my name is not Alex, it's Gabe."

A warm shiver went through me. This man cared for me. It was evident, but I was leery. Regardless, Tack had played me emotionally and physically.

Following Trent's instructions, Peter patted down Gabe.

"I don't have anything on me." No one responded while he was escorted to the chair across the room. His wrists and ankles were zip tied to the armrests and legs. Peter was a little rougher than was probably necessary, but Gabe remained quiet. The men filed out. Trent stood to the right of me with his gun drawn.

I took another sip before speaking. Surprisingly, my voice came out stronger than I felt. "Explain what you are talking about."

"When we met, it was unexpected. I was on an extended leave from the military. From the moment I saw you, something clicked. My world forever changed." Gabe watched me.

I nodded. "I remember."

A small smile crept on his face. "It was the only time I'd

wished I'd never enlisted in the Marines."

I sucked my lip between my teeth remembering our time under the tree where he'd said something similar. This man was different from the one I'd been married to for a short time. Was a twin possible? Or was he still playing me? I wanted to believe I hadn't fallen in love with a monster.

He sighed. "Without any notice, I was given a mission that restricted all communication. There was no time to tell you. When I got back, I read your e-mail stating you'd moved on, were shutting off the e-mail account, changing your phone number, and to never contact you again."

"I didn't send that." My hand went to my mouth.

Gabe shifted minutely and slightly winced. "I know that ... now." He took a deep breath. "Almost six weeks ago, I was discharged from the military. I didn't re-enlist. I tried to stay away, but that lasted about a week before I had to see you. I needed to see if you'd moved on. What you were doing. Our feelings had been too strong to ignore. I was angry and irritated with how you were able to discard what we had. None of it made sense. So, I came to your house." His tone turned more clipped.

I tried to imagine what he saw.

Pausing, Gabe worked his jaw as a vein in his neck popped. He took a second to look down at the floor, visibly trying to calm down. "When I stopped by, I parked down the road. I wasn't sure if I wanted to confront you. Then I saw you with my supposedly dead brother."

The words grew terser and he swallowed. "One more step and you would have seen me. But you yelled at him and ran to your car. I knew then by the look on your face you had no idea. I don't know how I knew. I just knew." Gabe shifted again and I felt his frustration at not being able to move. Tied to the chair he was like a caged animal.

"What happened next?" I asked.

Again, it took Gabe a few moments to speak as I watched him flex his hands a few times at his sides. "I knew the bastard had set this up. You hadn't written the e-mail. When I got it, I had been blinded by the hurt. When you drove off, I was still processing. My brother was living the life I was supposed to live. I needed to know more, so I followed you to your hotel. In the lobby you cried as you checked in. All I wanted to do was tell you who I was. I—"

"Why didn't you, Gabe? Why didn't you tell me then what was going on?" My tears nearly sprang free but I held them back.

Hurt mixed with anger flashed through his eyes. "I had to make sure you were okay. Instinct told me to investigate Alex and figure out his endgame before I made myself known. I came to your room. When you opened the door, the situation spun out of control and I lost myself in you."

From the moment I'd opened the door that night, our chemistry had taken over. We were hungry for each other. Our bodies were desperate to unite. I thought we were finding our way back to each other. But, was it possible we were simply finding each other again?

There was too much missing information. "Di-did you kill Alex?"

He shook his head. "Part of me wanted to. It took every ounce of control to confront him after I left the hotel. I found him downtown and intended to let him know the shit ended here. He took off down the street away from me. A black van intercepted him up and sped off like he was being kidnapped. I investigated. The plates weren't registered. Then, he turned up dead. I couldn't reveal myself to you until I knew what was going on."

My breathing had increased again, so I took another sip of water and a deep breath. It was still hard to wrap my mind around the fact that there was a Gabe *and* an Alex.

"You never told me you had a twin." The words were accusatory with bite to them, which I thought were deserved.

Gabe's jaw moved back in forth. "I thought he was dead. I watched him drown in a river when we were thirteen years old. That was the other reason I held back when I first saw you. My brother was supposed to be dead."

Dead.

The words resonated within me. "Why wasn't he?"

"That's something I'm going to have to ask my mother." The words became a deadly omen as Gabe's jaw set. A muscle ticked in the side of his neck as his arms flexed.

"Did you get along?"

"No, I hated him along with my mother." His words were spoken with conviction and lingered in the air.

When we'd dated, I'd never met his mother. Gabe said they were estranged and it was too fucked up of a story to go into. He'd promised to tell me everything when he returned. With Alex's PTSD diagnosis and erratic behavior, I never pressed the subject of his mother. I knew his father was out of the picture from Gabe telling me so one night in bed.

The situation hit me and again I forcefully asked, "Why didn't you tell me who you were after Alex's death? Why did you trick me? You played me!" I nearly shouted the last sentence and took a few steadying breaths. Per the doctor's orders, I was to remain calm. As the reality of the situation sank in, all I wanted to do was yell and cry at the same time. This situation was proving to be a challenge.

Gabe looked down for a second and a sigh left his lips.

9

I was on the brink of breaking. When he met my eyes again, I felt the connection I had with Tack—the same one I felt when I first met Gabe. They were one in the same. My head hurt.

Gabe reiterated, "No one knew I was a twin. I needed that to remain a secret while I figured out exactly what Alex was up to."

"I wouldn't have told." Anger bubbled up and I felt as if I were trapped in a maze, unable to get straight answers or make sense of what had happened.

"I know you, sweetheart. I know you better than I know my own self. Your anguish had to stay real. If I was there, the people watching you would know there was something wrong. You were being watched by the police. You were being watched by Harley. You were safer not knowing until—"

"The accident," I said, finishing for him. Harley had been Alex's accomplice in the Botticelli theft.

Gabe flinched at my word. "Yes. Fuck, I nearly died, thinking I'd lost you."

Warm squishiness returned to my stomach as I absorbed his words. Watching Gabe, I knew his words were the truth. I felt it in my gut.

"Cut him loose, Trent."

Trent stepped to my side. "Willow, are you sure?"

I looked at Gabe. "Talk like Tack."

Gabe's dark eyebrow quirked. "I want you to believe me."

The voice and the Irish accent were a perfect match to what I'd heard on the phone all those times I'd spoken to Tack as he protected me from a distance. I was drawn to him like I'd been to Gabe when we'd first met.

Trent looked at me with confusion. "Who is Tack?"

I kept staring at Gabe, who was looking straight at me. "The day I went to the station and learned Alex was an undercover cop, Gabe, who I knew as Tack, put an envelope in my car, which lead me to Cocktails. After that we saw each other at random places or we talked on a burner phone Gabe had given me. He spoke with an Irish accent." Weariness crept in as the adrenaline rush left my body. For now, I wanted to get away from this situation.

There was a touch of hurt on Trent's face. Through everything, we'd become close in a brother-sisterly way. I knew we'd be talking about this more in-depth later. "He had multiple opportunities to hurt me, Trent. Multiple."

Gabe's intense face relaxed.

Exhausted, I continued, "Cut him loose. He was in my room undetected. He called me to let me know he was here and wanted me to see who he was. He never put up a fight and stepped around Andre to make himself vulnerable."

After stowing his gun, Trent pulled out one scary knife. "If I even think you're up to something, Gabe, I won't ask any questions."

Meeting Trent's stare, Gabe answered him calmly, "I would never hurt Willow. I'd die for her. I love her."

Whoa. My hands trembled slightly. I set the glass down on the table. Abruptly, I stood, wanting space. "I need to rest. I'm going to go lie down for a bit."

This was all too much, and I needed time and space to think. With Gabe's admission of love, I had been shoved into territory I wasn't prepared to face yet.

Bed. Thoughts. Sleep. That was my priority for now.

"What do you want me to do with Gabe?" Trent asked.

Both men watched me as I answered, "Whatever you think is safest."

That was all I had left in me. Quickly, I rushed to the door.

"Willow." Gabe's voice halted me before I entered my room. My name was spoken like a prayer.

For a moment, my eyes closed as his voice penetrated that place only he was able to. *Do not show your vulnerability, Willow.* I straightened my shoulders and turned to him.

"This is too much for me right now. Gabe... you deceived me repeatedly over the last month. I'm pregnant with your child. You have a twin. You went under a pseudo name of Tack who I felt something for, too. You promised you wouldn't lie to me. But deceit is the same thing."

"I'll make this right." The words from Gabe were a vow that bounced around and took root inside of me. He had spoken similarly to me before he had been deployed and when he was Tack. I gripped the door handle to restrain myself from running into his arms and feel his comfort.

I nodded and thought, *I hope so.*

Trent watched our exchange. As soon as the door closed, I leaned against it and let out a long breath I had been holding. The familiar charge was there between us. Even through the door I felt Gabe on the other side. There was no doubt this man was not the same man I'd been married to.

He was most definitely the man I'd fallen in love with.

Chapter Two

I tossed and turned through the night. It was still hard to wrap my head around it all, but in some ways, many of Gabe's choices made sense.

Alex played the PTSD and guilt card well when he weaseled his way into my life. Thinking back to it all, Alex talked and walked like Gabe. He had been Gabe except for his soul, which he masked. My soul knew Alex wasn't Gabe. The feelings that had been there with Gabe and Tack were absent. That was why I had second thoughts.

I touched my stomach; thankful this child belonged to the man I fell in love with versus the monster I married.

But I was still hurt and furious that Gabe had taken away my choices with his antics. Gabe said it was to protect me, but there had to have been an alternative to the deceit. A twinge pierced my heart. Tack was there for me. When I needed someone the most, he had been there. That was hard to ignore.

The pregnancy.

Gabe had known I needed him. Inexplicably, I loved him.

But, I was terrified of being hurt again. When I saw him this morning, I would have to reinforce my walls until I was able to sort through the mess.

All this time, Gabe knew he was going to be a father—that my child would not be fatherless. During one of our phone conversations, I had expressed this fear of my child not having a parent like me. He hadn't said anything except that I would be a wonderful mother. My life had been turned upside down over this last month, leaving a path of destruction in its place.

Seeing the time, I realized we were heading to the hospital to see Carson in an hour. My heart physically ached not having my best friend to talk to about this mess. He hadn't known about Tack, but I needed to tell him. Maybe verbalizing what had happened would help me get my head straight.

I glanced to the door, knowing I needed to eat. *Gabe may be out there.* What was Nonno going to think? Was he awake? Probably, which meant it was time to get up. Swinging my feet over the edge of the bed, I contemplated food versus chancing who was in the main part of the suite. I wasn't ready to face Gabe yet even if Trent had let him stay. But at the same time, I hoped he hadn't left.

First, I needed a shower. The heat from the water seeped into my muscles, relaxing me. All too soon, the shower was over, which meant it was time to face the music. At some point, Gabe and I were going to have to talk.

Maybe it will just be Nonno and me.

Dressed in jeans and a T-shirt, I wiped the steam away from the mirror and made sure my blond sloppy bun looked okay. The cuts and bruises from the accident were fading, but still present, and I had dark circles under my eyes from the lack of sleep. I was a mess. I'd rest later when we came back from the hospital.

I headed into the suite, wondering where Trent made Gabe stay last night. Or maybe he was gone. I knew Gabe wasn't going to be far with how protective he seemed to be of the baby and me. A small part of me wondered if he only stuck around to see if I was pregnant. A sigh left me. I knew that wasn't true, but I needed to protect my heart.

Voices came from the kitchen. I paused to listen before rounding the corner. Trent was speaking about the schedule. I bumped into a lamp and the noise was easily heard.

Silence ensued.

Shit.

It was time to make myself known since my not-so-suave entrance had given me away. I rounded the corner and found Trent and Nonno at the table sipping coffee. Tingles raced across my skin and my eyes gravitated to the stove where Gabe was flipping pancakes—one of my favorites for breakfast. He paused his movements and took a deep breath as if preparing to face me.

Do not focus on how good his low slung jeans and T-shirt look on him.

He took two pancakes off and put them on the platter. The muscles flexed under his shirt. I was frozen in place as I thought about our first date. Pancakes were the meal he'd cooked for me after we made love for the first time in my apartment.

I longed to run into his arms and hear how everything was going to be okay. But, I had to keep my distance. *Stay strong, Willow.* The game had changed. Now, I was pregnant and I needed to make sure I understood his intentions.

Gabe pulled the remaining pancakes off the griddle and turned in my direction where I was still rooted like a fool. There was concern written all over his face. I forced my gaze to the counter. The room was deathly quiet.

"Morning, Willow. How did you sleep?" Gabe said, halting my perusal of the room.

I felt the gaze of Nonno and Trent on me from behind. It was awkward to say the least. It was hard to miss as Gabe swept his gaze over me with a pained expression. I still looked rough.

"Morning. Not very good," I responded rather despondently, hoping to keep my emotions hidden.

He nodded and watched me. I broke eye contact.

Part of my body screamed to be near him, but I ignored it and focused on my grandfather instead as I turned my back to Gabe. Some of the realities in my life were now falsehoods. What Gabe and I had been was real. The night before Alex died was real. The manipulations of love I thought had happened hadn't. My head hurt. Having my feelings for Gabe reignite caused tears to pick my eyes. But the hurt won out. I rolled my neck to release some of the tension.

Nonno gave me a smile as I walked to him and gave him a hug. Was he okay with everything? I held onto him a little longer than normal, needing a connection to normalcy. His white hair was a little unruly this morning, which brought a smile to my face.

"Glad you could join us, baby girl. Gabe and Trent filled me in on what happened last night."

Well, that was one way to address the huge ass elephant in the room. I tried to brush it off casually, but I still wasn't sure how I was going to tackle this problem.

"Yeah, it was eventful to say the least."

Apparently, Nonno was okay with what had happened, and Trent seemed fine that Gabe was here. I was a little shocked at how amicable everything was. What had Gabe said to them while I was sleeping?

Trent nodded my way as I took a seat next to him. Nonno sat at the end, which effectively kept Gabe from sitting next to me. I turned to Trent as I tried to block out Gabe as he walked over with the serving plate.

"Do we have any new leads?" I asked cautiously.

Gabe set the pancakes on the table. I knew they had bananas in them from the delicious smell. Banana pancakes happened to be my favorite. I bet there were nuts in them, too. He took a seat directly in front of me. His green eyes never left me. Maybe sitting beside him would have been the better choice.

I was a nervous wreck not knowing how to act with him. There was still so much left unsaid between us. So many questions. With him directly across from me, it was hard to miss his watchful eyes. I shifted my body toward Trent, who set his coffee cup down and took his time to answer now that everyone was silent again

Finally, Trent responded, "We're going to keep investigating Jack De Luca and see where that leads."

Jack De Luca was involved in the Alex saga in some way. We believed Alex was part of the reason De Luca had been arrested for murder. De Luca was rumored to be more mobster and less loan shark, but that was simply a guess. Apparently, the case against De Luca had been dropped because all the witnesses ended up dead. Burned. Like Alex and Commander Taylor.

"Anything else?"

Trent shook his head. "Not really. Gabe and I have similar notes. The biggest difference is Gabe was able to make some headway on the cryptic notes Alex left on the papers you gave me."

Until now, the papers my housekeeper, Mildred, found hadn't been of much use. I'd given a copy to Gabe and the originals to Trent to decipher. These same papers confirmed Alex had been the one to steal Dad's Botticelli.

I blurted, "Do you have fingerprints?" I'd never noticed that Alex's fingerprints had been removed. Because of the PTSD, we rarely touched. The only time I remembered holding hands was when we said our vows in Vegas. Otherwise, I might have noticed they had been burned off. It had been hard to isolate the match.

If Gabe wasn't Alex, he would have fingerprints. I raised my eyebrow.

Gabe smiled. "I do. Does anyone have a pen?"

Trent handed him a pen he had with his files and shifted toward Gabe.

With ease, Gabe snapped the pen and rubbed some of the ink on his thumb before rolling it on the notepad. Meticulously, he went through all of his fingers before sliding the notepad back. "Run them. Do whatever you need to do to make Willow feel more at ease."

Damn him. I wanted to be furious with everything that had happened. Hell, I *was* furious. No doubt Trent had run them already, otherwise he wouldn't be so at ease with him.

My stomach growled. The sound of the plate scooting toward me brought me to look into the watchful emerald eyes of Gabe.

"Here. They're your favorite, banana nut."

I knew it. "Thanks." Another wave of warmth spread through me as I grabbed the plate and applied a liberal amount of syrup.

He gave me a beautiful smile. "You're welcome."

This was getting off track. At some point, I turned my attention back to Trent, not wanting to lengthen my conversation with Gabe. "What does the cryptic text mean on the papers?"

"It was a meeting location and time on the day Alex died. It was in an old abandoned warehouse. Essentially, a dead end. Gabe visited there."

Nonno kept switching his gaze between Gabe and me.

Before I could blurt out something else out, I took a bite of the pancakes. Flavors burst across my tongue. "These are delicious."

Everyone agreed as they tasted their pancakes.

I kept my focus on my pancakes, aware of Gabe's stare. Having a gulf between us was uncharted territory. My heart longed to be in the protective arms I remembered. Suddenly feeling a little nauseous, I pushed a piece of pancake around my plate.

"Why do you think Alex faked his death when you were young?" Thinking of everything had my appetite abating. I chanced to look up.

Running his fingers through his hair, Gabe took a deep breath. "I'm not sure. But I plan on paying my mother a not so pleasant visit soon." There was venom in his voice.

My eyes grew wide. I'd delve deeper into the mother situation later. With Nonno being here, the last thing I wanted was him on edge. So, I asked a different question, "Are you going to go back into hiding so people don't know you're a twin?" I wasn't sure what I wanted the answer to be and that scared me insurmountably.

"No."

It was the same as always. I was drawn to Gabe and talking to him was as natural as breathing. "Then, what are you going to do?"

"Protect the woman I love."

Love.

That wasn't past tense. This was too much. Way too much. Too fast. Abruptly, I stood not knowing how to respond to his statement. It was like a grenade tossed into my camp without any warning.

"I need to get to the hospital. I'm up first this morning to see Carson." Quickly, I kissed Nonno on the cheek.

"Willow, you should try to eat a little more," he said.

"I will, Nonno, at the hospital. I don't want to be late. Francesca's turn is after mine." My heart still hurt because of what had been ruined the night of the accident. Carson had planned to propose to Francesca. It was such a mess.

Nonno squeezed my hand. "Okay, baby girl, I'll see you later. Chris and Mildred called to check on you. I told them you were sleeping and would phone them later." Chris, our gardener, and Mildred, our housekeeper were like family.

"Promise me you'll eat something."

"I promise, Nonno."

Trent stood as did Gabe. My eyes grew big. "Are you coming, too?"

Gabe watched me wearily before he answered. "Yes. I need to make sure you're safe after that accident. I've never felt so helpless in my life. I'm not making the same mistake again. If it takes us longer to figure this mess with me out in the open, so be it."

There it was again—the no holding back. Gabe was always raw and honest with his emotions like Tack had been. Even in front of Nonno and Trent, Gabe confessed his love.

"What about the police? They think you're dead. There are no records of Alex being born." I knew it was a lame excuse to keep some distance between us.

As expected, Gabe had an answer. "We'll cross that

bridge when it's time."

I half expected Nonno to say something, but he gave me an encouraging smile. Even Trent was at ease with it. This was maddening and puzzling at the same time.

"What changed your attitude? Last night you were ready to take Gabe out. This morning you're sipping coffee and going along with all this." I said to Trent in front of Gabe.

"We talked."

My voice rose. "That's it? You talked?"

"Yes, we talked. I understand his reasoning, though I don't agree with it." Trent remained calm and collected.

A headache loomed in the back of my head. "Which was?"

Nonno's hand touched my shoulder and I jumped. "I think that's something you and Gabe need to discuss when you're ready, baby girl. Right now, go see Carson. I get that you're mad. I would be, too."

I was stunned. "Do Bennett, Marie, and Francesca know about this mess?"

I could only imagine what Carson's parents thought about this situation.

Gabe winced at the tone of my voice. Good, he needed to be affected.

"They do. Gabe met Bennett and Marie last night. They're going to tell Francesca when she wakes up," Trent replied,

Turning back to Gabe, he stood there with a little hurt in his eyes. I was torn, not able to close the gap between us. Instinct made me want to walk into his arms, but he'd slept with me without protection and hadn't disclosed the truth. Yeah, I was pissed. Though, I would never regret the baby. A child was never something I would view as a mistake.

A wave of nausea hit. My stomach lurched. This wasn't good. *Morning sickness.* As fast as I could go, I ran to my bathroom, barely making it. Footsteps approached as I emptied my stomach contents.

"Is it morning sickness?" Gabe was here and he rubbed soothing circles on my back.

My body craved him. *Don't think like that, Willow.*

"Please stop." I managed between heaving.

Immediately, the hand retracted and he sighed. "What can I get you?"

Remaining silent, I waited to see if I was done. Nothing else came up. I flushed the toilet and wiped my mouth. With jerky movements, I yanked out my toothbrush and vigorously scrubbed my teeth.

After spitting, I rinsed before I responded. "Nothing. I think you've done enough."

As I tried to walk around him, Gabe touched my elbow. I ignored the heat from his touch.

"Willow, please. We need to talk."

On a dime, I turned and let it all out. Everything I felt spewed. "I get that you want to fix whatever we had. I get it. I feel it, too. Hell, even with you as Tack, I was drawn to you. But, Gabe, you slept with me. Impregnated me. And never told me anything. You knew I thought Alex was you and you said nothing. Making banana nut pancakes doesn't fix it. Not even close. You may have won over Nonno, which I have no damned idea how you managed that, but he's not the one who has to be okay with what's happened. That's me. If you're coming this morning, you can ride in a separate car."

It felt good to get this all out in the open.

When I tried to leave the bathroom again, Gabe managed to get in front of me, effectively blocking the door. He grabbed my shoulders, and I tried to ignore how the energy between us intensified.

"We still have it, Willow. We are not the past tense."

I tried to wrench out of his grip, but he refused to let me go.

"I'm going to be there for you, for our baby. Yeah, I fucked up. Majorly fucked up. After I thought you broke up with me, I started to believe that our relationship had been one-sided. It broke my heart thinking I was never going to have you again—have the family we talked about. I love you with my entire being. Not past tense. I love you."

My lip trembled. This was too much.

"Sweetheart, imagine what it was like coming back to some fucked up alternate reality with you married to my brother who was supposed to be dead. I was mad. Confused. The first chance I had to get you alone, I wanted to confront you. But when I saw you, I realized you had no idea what was going on. And then we happened. Like we always do. I honestly lost all coherent thought when you put your arms around me. Until you told me you might be pregnant, I forgot I hadn't used protection. We'd stopped using protection before I'd left. It never crossed my mind.

"After we made love, you gave me insight into what my miserable asshole of a brother had done to you. You even said it felt like old times. Your body knew I wasn't Alex. I wanted to tell you. Shit, Willow, you have no idea. But, I needed to confront Alex first. I was coming to tell you that night. But, Alex turned up dead."

He took a deep breath and closed his eyes for a moment. "What if someone was after you next? The best way to protect you was to remain a secret. No one knew we were twins."

Tears broke free as they streamed down my face. The sincerity of Gabe's words rung true. I understood in some weird way. Gabe cradled my cheeks with his hands and wiped away my tears with his thumbs. I leaned into his touch, relishing the love I felt.

"And now you're willing to let everyone know you're a twin?"

"Someone chased you down with a Hummer and ran you off the fucking road. Your best friend is in a coma. There was nothing I could do. Nothing. I've never felt so helpless creeping around a hospital and trying to get news about the only two people who have ever mattered to me—you and our baby. I was scared shitless. As soon as you could handle the stress, I decided to tell you. So, yeah, I don't give a fuck if anyone knows I'm a twin. The only thing that matters is keeping you safe, our baby safe, and getting Carson better so he can be a father."

A sob erupted from me, and Gabe pulled me into him.

"Shh… We're going to figure this out. I'm not going to rush you. I know you need time to process what's happened, but I'm not going to hold back my feelings. You'll never doubt or wonder how I feel."

Chapter Three

B eep.
  Pause.
  Beep.
Pause.

The sound of machines in Carson's ICU room created a rhythmic background. I sat next to the bed, holding Carson's hand as I had the first time I visited him after I woke up. I glanced at the clock. My two hours were almost up and I had hardly paused as I filled him in on everything—mainly my feelings for Gabe, which were all over the place. One minute I was pissed and the next minute I was in love. Then I was good with things, and then I was furious. A ping-pong ball bounced around less than I did. It was maddening and only soured my mood.

And worst of all, I hated how indecisive I felt.

The ride here with Gabe had been less awkward, but still not *us*. This new dynamic was hard when my body wanted to curl into him like old times, but my mind wasn't that forgiving.

"I wish you were awake so you could help me work through this tangled mess."

No response.

I felt so deflated. I knew it was from my restless night and the debacle.

I sat back. "Carson, it doesn't make sense why there were no records of Gabe's twin. I mean, Trent would have found a twin if there had been a record." When was Gabe going to talk to his mother? I wanted to be there when he did. I needed to see this part of his life.

"Carson, I don't know what to do. The attraction and feelings are still there. I can feel them beneath the surface and that scares me. On the one hand, he deceived me. On the other, he tried to protect me with how he handled things. Us sleeping together and me pregnant was unexpected." I cradled my forehead with my free hand. Sitting back up, I asked, "What am I going to do?" Tucking his shoulder length blond hair behind his ears like he did on a regular basis, I willed Carson to come back to me.

Nothing.

At least the bruises and cuts were turning purplish yellow like mine versus black.

Staring at him, I imagined what he'd say. *Willow, just give it time to see what you want to do. Follow your heart. I'll support you regardless. Nothing has to be decided today.*

I moved my hand back to his. "Please, Carson. Come back."

I stared at the monitors, wishing there was something, anything to give a sign he was improving.

Nothing.

My watch timer went off. It was time to leave. Francesca

would be here in five minutes. Kissing his forehead, I whispered, "I have to go now. Francesca is about to come in. I miss you, Carson."

A single tear slipped free and I blinked the rest away. In silence, I left the room. It was more than deflation I felt, it was defeat. Our worlds were falling apart and Carson hadn't awoken. Was that a bad sign he wasn't going to? I wanted to scream in frustration from all the suffering Alex caused.

It was because of him, someone was after me.

It was because of him, Gabe and I were hurt.

It was because of him, Carson's child may not have a father.

The only reason I wanted to bring him back from the dead was to ask one question. Why?

I shook my head. *Remain positive, Willow.* Drowning in all the negativity wasn't going to help. It would lead to more negativity. I refused to give up hope. ICU felt desolate and empty of life. I hated the feeling—especially today since I felt more off than normal. Was it the hormones? I wasn't sure. Maybe I needed rest.

I opened the door and walked into the waiting room, which felt just as sterile. Francesca was at the desk waiting for me, and I put on a smile I wasn't feeling. The last thing I needed was my mood to affect her. Francesca needed all the support she was able to get.

"How did he look?" The hopefulness in her voice was hard when I was unable to report anything new. But, there was an expected deep sadness in her chocolate brown eyes. Francesca had her hair in a ponytail and she looked exhausted. The doctors continued to monitor her after she'd fainted a week ago.

I hugged her and cheerfully responded, "He looks good. I

talked his ear off about everything."

She touched my hand with hers and gave it a squeeze. "I heard about everything. If you want to talk, let me know. We could eat ice cream or something together."

Maybe talking with Francesca would help. We were getting close, but I wanted her to feel like she was able to ask me for anything. She was family simply because Carson chose her. Francesca was alone with her father disowning her when he found out about the pregnancy.

I squeezed her hand. "I would like that a lot. My mom always said ice cream solved everything."

"I agree with your mom." Francesca held her hand over her stomach. "It's a date. I can't wait to tell Carson about our plans. The door buzzed. I'll see you later."

"Tell him I'm going to get his favorite, peanut butter chocolate fudge."

She laughed. "I will." She disappeared behind the door with a little more pep in her step.

With the click of the lock, the cold feeling returned. I felt Gabe before I saw him. He was near, but didn't touch me. Which agony was worse, keeping my distance or wanting him close? I was a mess.

"How is Carson?"

Since our talk this morning, things had been somewhat better, but now an irritation sizzled beneath the surface I hadn't realized until I heard his voice.

"No change." My clipped tone sounded bitchy. Part of me wanted to crawl into his arms and never let go, but then the other part wanted to scream at him. Reliving it all with Carson reopened the fresh wounds. I needed to settle on where I stood and get my attitude in check. But, I felt like I had whiplash and was ultimately... betrayed. I loved Gabe and distance was my only defense right now.

Marie approached after finishing her conversation with Trent, who stepped back into the bay that housed the elevators. "How's my boy? Any change?"

Since I was now first on the visiting list, I was asked the same thing by every person each day. It was hard. Giving her the same smile I gave Francesca, I repeated my answer. "He looks good. I talked his ear off about everything."

Marie responded, "I think he's looking good, too. Any day. I can feel it."

We hugged. I hoped it was sooner rather than later. The one thing I was certain of, if Carson was still here he was fighting his way back to us.

"I'm going to get some coffee while Francesca is in there. Bennett is meeting me. Would you like to come with us?"

Exhaling, I felt weary. "I think I want to go back to the hotel. I'm tired."

"Sounds good, sweetheart. Get some rest. It's been"—she glanced to Gabe before finishing—"tense."

That was an understatement. Gabe came to stand beside Marie and searched my face before she spoke to him. "Promise me you are not going to hurt Willow any more than she has been. That's the last thing she needs for the baby or her." There was more ice in Marie's voice than I'd ever heard before. Generally, her kind demeanor won out.

Gabe positioned himself to face her. "I promise you I will never hurt her again. I swear it."

There was that blatant honesty that stripped me raw. Gabe continued to reveal his feelings to everyone important in my life. It unnerved me to have so much out in the open while still trying to determine how I felt. I was speechless.

Marie looked at him. "I hope you mean it." She then gave

me a smile. "I'll see you at the hotel. Call if you need anything."

"I will."

After Marie left, we were alone again. I headed to the elevators without a word, not wanting to have a discussion at the moment. As we entered the white corridor, Dr. Byrum stepped off the elevator. "Good afternoon, Ms. Russo. How are you feeling?"

"I'm a little tired. I just saw Carson. We're about to head back to the hotel." I knew I sounded bad.

He switched into doctor mode. "Have you been sleeping?"

"I didn't last night."

Gabe watched the exchange intently. Dr. Byrum typed a note on his phone. "Can you come by my office first thing in the morning?"

My nerves were a little on edge. "Absolutely. Is there something I need to be worried about?"

"It's simply precautionary. Rest this afternoon. I want you to avoid stress if at all possible."

My eyes went to Gabe unintentionally. Our eyes locked and Dr. Byrum's gaze followed. He held out his hand. "I'm Dr. Byrum."

"Gabe Thompson. Willow's—"

"He's... uhh... the baby's father," I interjected a little too loudly, knowing Gabe, he was about to label us something I wasn't ready for. My mind was barely hanging on and the emotional roller coaster was only adding to my problems.

What was wrong with me?

With an arched eyebrow, Gabe watched me from the corner of his eye as I focused on the doctor's gray hair. There were a couple of hard shakes before Dr. Byrum released

Gabe's hand. "I haven't seen you before."

"An oversight on my part."

The doctor nodded. "The last thing Ms. Russo needs is stress."

"Understood. Willow and the baby's health are my highest priority."

Seemingly satisfied with his response, Dr. Byrum continued to the nurses' station. He had been my OB/GYN while in the hospital. Idly, I wondered why he was up in the ICU. "I'll see you tomorrow, Ms. Russo."

"Thank you, doctor."

The air grew awkward around us as Trent approached. Closing my eyes, I reopened them. "Are we ready?"

Trent pushed the button to call the elevator. "Yes. Peter is pulling the car around."

"Sounds good. What happened to Andre?"

The elevators dinged and the door opened. Trent pushed the lobby button after we entered. "He's on suspended duty."

"He made the right call and you know it." Gabe was beside me.

The doors closed, only heightening the animosity in the elevator. I ignored it and waited for Trent to respond. "I get you two were tight in your black ops unit. But, Gabe, this is my security team. Not yours. I can't have people I don't trust in charge of someone's life. Back the fuck off."

Black ops? That sounded a little more dangerous than the military. Too tired to delve into that at this moment, I filed that piece of information away for later.

As we descended, the vein in Gabe's neck pulsed as he took in Trent's mask of steel.

The doors opened. No one moved. This was ridiculous. The doors closed. I reached forward to push the button to keep them open. Gabe was about to say something. I touched his stomach, and he broke his standoff with Trent. "Please, don't. I want to go back to the hotel."

Gabe softened. "Yes, let's get you back."

The tension was still thick as we exited the elevator. I massaged my temples as the car pulled up.

"Willow, what's wrong?" Gabe's worried voice brought my eyes up to look at his.

"I need to sleep some. I'm tired. I feel off."

He opened the car door. "I won't argue with Trent anymore in front of you. I shouldn't have done that. Let's get you to the hotel."

With a light touch, Gabe put his hand on my back to guide me into the car. I refused to acknowledge the little jolts of electricity I felt where his hand rested. Trent slid into the front seat before the car took off.

To distract myself from Gabe, I watched people on the sidewalk, walking their dogs. Still, I was acutely aware of the man beside me. The car stopped at a stoplight.

Gabe leaned in and his shoulder brushed mine. His voice was low. "What happened? I thought we made a little bit of progress in the bathroom this morning."

I let out a deep breath and turned, not expecting him so close. Frozen, I searched his eyes. Gone was the irritated man in the elevator. This was the man who looked like he'd die for me, and he left me breathless. He waited for me to respond. I wanted to tell him how I felt, but I was scared.

The car resumed as our eyes searched each other's. I cleared my throat and responded, "We did. I thought we did. I told Carson everything and it all irritated me again. My emotions feel like they're all over the place. I want to punch something one minute, cry the next, and then I was fine."

"Willow, you're pregnant. It's completely normal."

"Have you researched pregnancy?"

"From the moment you told me you might be pregnant in the closet at Cocktails, I started reading. If you were, I needed to be prepared."

I rolled my neck and leaned my head back. "I wish you had told me who you were. Things might be different."

My eyes were growing heavy as I felt his hand on mine. "Me, too."

I was too tired to respond or take my hand away as I drifted off to sleep.

There was movement and I barely woke, not wanting to leave my peaceful slumber. I was in Gabe's arms with my head against his chest. The vibrations of Gabe's voice soothed me even though I knew I should pull away. "Let me get her in bed and then we can review the schedule for the next week."

"The lab will be coming by to take the DNA sample," Trent whispered.

A door creaked opened. "I'll be back as soon as I get her situated. We have other things to discuss." There was an edge to Gabe's voice.

What was wrong?

"Gabe, I've granted you more concessions than you deserve. Don't push it."

His arms tightened around me. "Not in front of Willow." There was no arguing with his tone.

I buried my face deeper in his chest, wanting to escape.

Doors opened and no one else spoke. I let the sleep creep in again. My limbs grew heavier. Blankets rustled before I felt cool sheets, and I snuggled into the bed. I'd thank him later.

Lips pressed against my forehead. "I love you, Willow."

Without thinking, I answered as the sleep continued to claim me, "Love you, too."

Chapter Four

It was early evening when I checked my phone after sleeping most of the day away. I lay in bed in the elegant beautiful room, but I was ready to be in my own bed at home.

I couldn't hear anyone. Total silence.

Hopefully, Trent and Gabe had worked through their pissing contest. I wasn't in the mood to play referee nor should I have to.

I shifted and listened again. Nothing.

I felt the urge to paint. It had been too long. Maybe that was why I felt off balance. The canvas was my way of coping. Since the night Gabe and I conceived our child, it was hard not to paint or draw with all the inspiration I felt.

It had been the same when I met Gabe, until Alex came into the picture. Just thinking about it felt like a nightmare. A terrible one at that. After I married Alex, all my inspiration stopped and then Dad died. One of our last conversations was about my block. He had said the block would eventually lift. He was right.

My stomach growled, alerting me that I had not eaten most of the day. If not for my hunger, I probably would have holed up in my room for the remainder of the evening.

Even though it was quiet, I knew Gabe was out there.

As I pushed the navy comforter aside, I thought of how I ended up in bed. After hopping in the car, I remembered Gabe saying he wasn't going to argue with Trent anymore. Then, I was out like a light. Deep down I knew Gabe put me here.

My stomach rumbled again. A light bit of nausea came as well. It was definitely time to eat.

Exiting the room, I saw Gabe in a chair, bent over as he looked at a file. I hadn't made a noise, but he looked up, probably sensing me as I always did him.

A huge grin spread across his face. "Did you sleep well?"

"I did. I feel a million times better." It was hard not to smile back.

"Good. You look much more rested. I was worried."

Nervously, I tucked a piece of hair that had escaped my bun behind my ear. This was the first time we'd been alone besides the emotional bathroom incident.

He stood. "Are you hungry? I ordered some food not too long ago and have it in the warmer. Bennett and Marie stopped by to see if you needed anything."

Bennett and Marie were some of the most caring people I had ever met. They were going above and beyond to make sure Francesca, Nonno, and I were taken care of.

"That sounds good. I'm starving actually." Gabe set toward the kitchen. I called after him. "Where's Trent?"

A few cabinet doors opened and closed in the kitchen. "He went with the technician to take my DNA to the lab. A man named Nathan is outside. Do you need something?"

DNA? This was news to me. "No, just curious. Why did

you give him your DNA?"

A few moments later, he handed me a tray. As Gabe removed the dome, the succulent aroma filled my nose. "I ordered you tomato soup and a grilled cheese sandwich. You told me once you always ate this when you were sick."

He remembered.

My mouth salivated as I took a bite of the cheese that was still warm. "Oh my gosh! This is delicious. How did you remember?"

Gabe cocked an eyebrow. "There isn't a moment I've forgotten with you. I remember everything about you, Willow. Absolutely everything." His words silenced me and I simply nodded. Fact was, I hadn't forgotten anything about him either. "It's good to see you eat. To answer your earlier question, they're using my DNA against the finger you received. Since we're twins, there should be a match."

I shuddered at the memory of opening the box with the finger after I'd been to the art gallery. The memory of the aroma would never leave me. It was imperative I focus on something else before I became sick again. "Do you think isn't Alex's?" If not, then who's? Panic ebbed its way in as the possibilities sped through my head.

"Willow." He paused, but I kept staring forward, thinking about it.

Alex may still be alive? He was burned.

How was he alive? Would he come back?

Gabe crouched in front of me. "Willow, look at me."

The command in his voice brought my head up.

"I'm leaving no stone unturned, sweetheart. None. I want to make one-hundred-percent sure. I examined the remains myself after I broke into the coroner's office. I confirmed the dental records matched mine since Alex doesn't exist technically in the system."

Words from the police came to me. "The police said it was only a partial match."

"Yes, but the part that survived the fire matched my dental records. It's common for twins to have the same records. The only difference would be if Alex had some work done I hadn't, or vice versa. I'm sure inconsistencies would be found if we had his full dental record."

Thank goodness. I closed my eyes and calmed my racing heart. Alex was dead. He was burned. There was no reason to worry about him. However, the police thought Gabe was dead. "How are you going to tell the police you're still alive?"

He cleared his throat. "They never recorded the death. To everyone else I'm still alive. The entire precinct under Commander Taylor was corrupt. I think the commander may have known we were twins. If they recorded the death, the military would have been notified."

"And that's the other reason you're doing this test."

"Yes." Unease crept back in my mind. "Willow, let's wait to see the results. Alex was involved with some nasty people. He might not have wanted me to know because it would lead me back to you."

True.

I pushed the thoughts from my mind for the time being. When we got the results back, I would worry if need be.

Gabe sat about three feet away from me on the couch and shifted to face me. "I need to ask you something."

I swallowed a bite. "Okay."

His hands tapped his knees. "Can I go to the appointment with the doctor tomorrow? I get it if you say no, but I do want to be part of every aspect of this pregnancy."

Honestly, I hadn't thought about Gabe being present. Until now, I had forgotten about Dr. Byrum. This was something I wasn't able to deny him. "I'm fine with it, but you have to leave the room when I'm dressing."

"Deal. Thank you." Visibly he relaxed.

The conviction in his voice helped assure me that he was in this for the long haul. The last thing I wanted was for him to worry about being a father. "I want you to be part of this baby's life. I won't keep you from him or her."

He watched me and I looked away, afraid of revealing too much. I touched my stomach, wondering how I would be able to do this if we weren't able to work things out.

"Willow, I'm not going to ask you to be away from our baby. Ever."

My eyes shot to his. How had he known I was worried? We were connected on such a level that I shouldn't have been surprised.

He continued, "The last thing I want you to worry about is not being with our child. I won't ask you to give up any time."

"What?"

His hands flexed like he wanted to reach for me. "I do not want our baby to be away from his or her mother. Everything that happens will be because you want it to. The only exception would be to keep you guys safe."

Needing the connection, I reached out to touch his arm. "I promise to keep you involved in the decisions. This is your baby, too. Gabe, I'm trying. It's a lot for me to work out."

"I understand. I never was worried about you keeping the baby from me. I know you. And you know me. We'll figure it out."

He did know me. I knew him, too. But I never could have imagined this scenario between us. Things felt a little too intimate as I pulled my hand back. "Can I ask you a question?"

Scooting a little closer, Gabe turned his palm up inviting my hand. "I'm an open book to you now. You can ask me anything and I'll answer."

"What did you do to get Trent on your side?"

He chuckled and shook his head as he combed his hand through his hair. "I told him the truth."

Truth. What truth? I was intrigued. "Which was?"

He locked his eyes on to my lavender ones. Again I felt the charge. "What all happened. How madly in love with you I still am. How I would die before I let anyone else harm you."

"Gabe..." I wasn't sure what else to say. That happened a lot around him.

He scooted a little closer, but kept space between us. "I'm not rushing anything. I know it seems like it, but I want to be honest with you. I'm not pushing you to say anything back. But... I will never hold anything from you again. You're it for me, Willow. I'll wait forever."

I needed a change in subject even though the walls around my heart unwillingly crumbled some more. There was a lapse in talking as we got lost in our thoughts. Mine went back to simpler times with Gabe and me. I took another bite before asking the next thing on my mind. Gabe said he was an open book, guess it was time to see how true that was. "When are you going to see your mom?"

The warmness left his features as he raked his hand through his dark hair. "It depends on what the doctor says tomorrow. I can't leave until I know you and our baby are okay."

It was hard resisting the urge to reach out and take his hand. I wasn't sure how he would take my request, but if we were being honest with each other, I needed to be part of this. All of this. "I need to ask a favor of you."

"Anything. I mean it. If you need something, all you have to do is ask. I know you tend to be independent, but I'm here and I'm never leaving again."

I took a deep breath. He wasn't going to like my request. "I want to go with you to see your mom."

The color drained from his face. "No, absolutely not. I will not subject you or our unborn child to her. I can't. I won't. I refuse."

Clearly there was a lot more to this story. Maybe I needed to try another tactic. Something told me I needed to be there for Gabe when he went. And after his reaction, the feeling grew stronger.

I set my tray aside before I asked, "Why weren't there any records of Alex?"

"Shit, I never wanted my past to affect you." He let out a deep sigh. There was unimaginable pain and anguish from Gabe. "It's why I was evasive about my family when we first got together. That decision fucked us over. That was the only subject I held back from you. I never wanted my mother to mess with anyone I love."

The turmoil passing over his face was heartbreaking. My parents had been loving and cared deeply for me. It was unimaginable to me that a mother would intentionally mess with someone her child loved. The closest thing I had to a sibling was Carson and he would never hurt me as Alex had Gabe.

I wasn't able to stop my hand when it found his. "Please tell me. She won't affect the baby or me. But, I need to know. If you want for there to be an *us*, there can't be any secrets."

Without any hesitation, Gabe said, "My mother had a home birth. I don't know why. And I don't know how. I have no idea who my father is. Mom never would tell us any details. Anyway, Alex was kept a secret. For as long as I can remember, Mom and Alex were always close. They had an unexplainable bond I never felt with them. They acted and thought alike. I was never like them. A constant outsider."

It was because Gabe was a good person.

He leaned back in the chair and exhaled another long breath. The pressure on my hand intensified minutely like I was his lifeline. "Mom loved when Alex pretended to be me. Until school, I was kept in almost isolation from the world. In first grade, she messed with my outside life. With a lot of practice, he got to where he could imitate me perfectly. Until he got it right, she kept food from us. Randomly, Mom kept me home from school and sent Alex, who had mastered being me."

I saw the torment of reliving the memories. "Anytime I received a beating for anything she felt I needed it for, Alex went to school for me. She knew exactly how to hit me. The marks would fade after a few days. Normally Thursday night I got them and was fine by Monday."

Gabe shifted forward, clearly uncomfortable. "I was terrified to tell anyone. Mom threatened I would get the worst beating of my life if I did. Every day when I got home, I had to give a detailed recap of my day. Alex memorized it. It was the most fucked up situation."

Gabe closed his eyes for a moment. He continued with venom in his voice, "They made my life hell. At thirteen I'd had enough. I threw everything I owned in my backpack and took off. Mom was frantic. Alex was cursing at me. I was a little faster, and he wasn't able to catch me. We got to the river and I ran across a fallen tree trunk that acted as a bridge. I refused to look back. The screaming continued, but all I cared about was getting away. As I crested the hill, my mom's shrill scream changed. I sensed it was something bad. Without thinking, I turned around, wary it might be an antic. No one was coming after me. Mom was on the bank screaming while Alex splashed around. The tree trunk had fallen in. Without thinking, I ran to the bank. Regardless of what they'd done, I wasn't able to let someone die. Before I got to Alex, he disappeared under the surface. I dove in but wasn't able to find him." A shudder ran through Gabe.

I rubbed my thumb in soothing circles on his hand, needing him to know I was here for him. This was more terrible than I imagined. Why would a mother do this to her child, or children in this case? Gabe flipped his hand over and intertwined his fingers with mine. It felt right to connect in this way. My tension eased slightly from his touch as I placed my free hand on my stomach, unable to fathom what he'd gone through.

"What happened next?" My voice was barely above a whisper.

"Mom screamed I was a murderer. I swam back to the side of the river I came from, got out, and ran to my backpack on the hill. I never looked back.

I lived in the woods and went to school until a mechanic offered me a place to stay in exchange for work. The teachers never asked questions. We were in a poor school. He died shortly after I enlisted. He was a good man. I'll never forget his kindness."

I scooted a little closer. "Did you ever see her again?"

All of the emotion left his eyes as he focused back on me. I hated seeing his normally vibrant emerald eyes dead. "From time to time, she would park at the school and simply watch me when I left to get on a bus. I changed my routes constantly. When I left for the Marines, I lost track of where she lived. Honestly, I didn't care. When I met you, I never wanted my past to taint my present."

"Gabe, I can't imagine. Do you know where she is now?"

He moved his shoulder to where it touched mine. Our interlinked hands moved to his knee. "I tracked her down last month. She's in a different town now—Eatontown, New Jersey—under a different name."

I laid my head on his shoulder, knowing he needed more connection. "I'm so sorry you had to deal with that. I can't even imagine."

"I'd do it all over again if it led me to you."

For now, I let my guard down and my heart talk. "That was the best day of my life, too." Gabe kissed the back of my hand and I felt the love. I had missed this feeling. Pressing my luck, I knew my earlier request was imperative. "Promise me you won't go see her until we agree on whether or not I'm coming."

His eyes grew wide when I glanced up. "You still want to go after what I just told you?" He stood breaking the connection. "Why?"

I grabbed his hand. "Because I think you need me there. You haven't seen her for nearly fifteen years."

"I don't want you near her." I went to protest and he raised his hand. "I'll agree to talk about it before I go. I want us to work through things. I want you to trust me again. But, I'm not going to change my mind."

Maybe there *was* hope for us. My anger continued to ebb. "All I ask is for us to come to an agreement."

Gabe settled back on the couch beside me. "You're different since this morning and the hospital."

"How's that?"

"Less distant. Not that I'm complaining. I hated the distance and thought I might have lost you. What changed?"

It felt good to clear the air. Hopefully, it would allow us to get back to normal. "We're having a baby together. I don't want to fight with you. What we have is deep. It's unexplainable. But, I'm not ready to put a label on us. Not yet."

"I deserve that. But, you're not saying *no* to an us, right?"

A small smile crept on my face. "No, I'm not. I'm saying give this time. Give me time. I still feel deceived."

Lips pressed against my forehead. "I'll take it. I shouldn't have slept with you until I told you the truth. I took away your decision."

"You did." My hands touched my stomach. "But, I can't regret the blessing it gave us."

He put his hand on top of mine. "Me, either."

Chapter Five

"Ms. Russo?" The nurse in blue scrubs caught my eye.

"Here." I stood and walked to her.

Gabe was behind me. His mere presence was driving me mad. His outdoorsy scent was so close, and I was having a hard time concentrating. This morning while I reflected on how delicious he smelled, he had asked me the same question three times before I heard him. Yeah, I was nuts. He was then worried something was wrong, which I played off as nothing. Hopefully, my brain had stopped malfunctioning.

"Good morning, Ms. Russo. Right this way." The nurse was a petite little thing that came only to my shoulders.

After last night, things between Gabe and me were lighter—more natural. It scared and delighted me at the same time.

The light-gray walls had an ominous feel as we walked in silence to a little area with a scale and chair. "We'll get your blood pressure and weight first before I show you to a room."

"Sounds good. Thank you."

I caught a glimpse of Gabe's unshaven face and looked away at a picture of flowers on the wall. The closeness of yesterday invaded my mind. His smell. The way his warm body felt.

"Ms. Russo, is everything okay?"

"What?" Oh hell, I had done it again.

The nurse looked perplexed and Gabe's eyebrows pinched together. "I just asked how your evening was."

I needed to focus. "It was good. I rested a lot."

"Good."

Gabe watched me intently. It was going to be hard to keep my thoughts in check and my mind focused. Last night, I'd fallen asleep on his shoulder as we watched some action movie. I barely remembered the opening scene before falling asleep. Sometime later, I'd been barely jostled as he carried me to bed. The moment was innocently sweet, and I found myself excited to see him again.

From the blankets on the couch, I knew he'd slept there. Nonno was in the guest room and Gabe was offered one of the other rooms on the floor, which he declined.

It was near impossible to ignore the love fighting to the surface. We all had our imperfections and made mistakes. Gabe was trying to right his and his brother's wrongs. It was a heavy burden to take on.

His fingers brushed against mine and I smiled as we waited for the nurse to get what was needed from her station. Around Gabe, happiness was contagious. Always had been.

The nurse pointed to the scale. "Ms. Russo, would you please step on the scale?"

I pointed at Gabe. "Turn around."

He rolled his eyes while I stepped on. I was small, but there were some things a man did not need to know.

The nurse took my vitals next when I sat in the chair. "One-twenty-three over sixty-two. Your blood pressure looks good. Let's get you into a room."

As we walked to the room, Gabe's fingers brushed against mine. I loved the little shocks of tingles I felt every time we touched.

The nurse pointed into the room. "The gown is on the table. The doctor will be in once you've changed,"

"Thank you." The nurse walked down the hall as I nervously waited at the door.

He winked at me and then gave me a beautiful smile. "I'll wait here. Let me know when you're ready."

I walked in, closed the door, and tried to wipe the smile off my face. Gabe was here. We were having this baby together. It was what I had wished for so many times while married to Alex. A part of me felt guilty for not realizing Alex wasn't Gabe. It felt like I betrayed Gabe in some way. It was a complicated web of emotions to untangle from.

I hadn't realized Alex wasn't Gabe. "How was I so stupid?"

"Did you say come in?"

"No!" I squeaked. "Not yet!"

Quickly, I dressed in the gown and took a seat on the table. I took a few calming exaggerated breaths. *Get yourself together.* I looked down at the thin material. *Geez, I'm practically naked.*

Three quick raps brought me out of my thoughts. "Willow, are you ready for me to come in? Is everything okay?"

"Yes, come in." Gabe opened the door and strode in looking magnificent. I was in deep, deep, deep shit with my thoughts. Then it hit me. "Sorry, I forgot to tell you to come in."

He deadpanned, "Thanks. I looked like a creeper hanging outside your door and listening to make sure I hadn't heard you."

I died laughing as he leaned against the counter near the bed, imagining his ear to the door. Then he folded his arms, bringing my attention to his muscles.

Oh. My.

The fitted blue T-shirt and worn jeans caused inappropriate thoughts to swirl faster. Oh shit, I was in over my head. He shifted and his jeans tugged against his thighs just right.

My word.

Focusing on the pattern of my pale-blue gown, I tried to think of something… anything to fill the silence.

"What are you thinking about?"

"How huge you are." My hands went to my mouth and my eyes shot to his. "Wait. No. I mean you're bigger. I mean big. Your muscles look big. I mean your muscles!"

Silent laughter shook his solid frame as the door opened and the doctor entered. My face felt hot with my blush. What in the world was happening to me?

"Morning, Ms. Russo. You're looking rested." The doctor greeted us with morning cheer.

Focus on the doctor, Willow.

Plastering a smile on my face, I answered, "Thank you. I think I slept most of the day yesterday." I chanced a glance at Gabe who winked again. The heat only intensified on my cheeks.

No looking at Gabe.

Dr. Byrum made a note in my chart. "Good. Continue resting." Laying the chart aside, he asked, "Would you like to see if we can see the heartbeat? At almost six weeks we won't be able to hear it, but might be able to see it."

"I would love to." I looked at Gabe. "Do you?"

"More than anything."

More than anything.

I took a closer look at Gabe as he intently watched the doctor who flipped buttons on the ultrasound machine. He chanced a glance at me and froze when our eyes met. There was pure joy on his face. I returned the same look.

He was here. Safe. My Gabe came back to me as he'd promised under the oak tree in the park right before he was deployed.

"Come back to me."

"I promise. I'll always come back to you."

Those were the words he'd said. And he had kept them. Dr. Byrum cleared his throat and broke our gaze. We'd been caught and the heat returned to my face.

"Okay, Ms. Russo, lie back."

Gabe stepped away from the counter and grabbed my hand as the doctor put a condom on the wand for the transvaginal ultrasound and squirted lubrication on it. Ugh, the noise was less than pleasant.

"This may be a bit uncomfortable."

"Okay."

The doctor stared intently at the screen as he moved the wand around.

Gabe's lips were at my ear making it a little less unpleasant. "That doesn't look very big. I know big was on your mind a second ago."

"Stop it." I wanted to smack him and refused to look his way.

"Pardon. What did you say?" The doctor looked from the screen to us.

I died of mortification as I knew the red deepened in my

cheeks. Gabe wasn't covering for us as he remained silent. He was definitely getting smacked later. "Gabe was telling me how excited he was to see the heartbeat."

The doctor seemed satisfied and turned his attention back to the screen as I widened my eyes at Gabe in silent scolding. Of course, I only received a playful smirk in response. So many ways things felt like they had before he left. And it was faster than I expected despite the many walls I'd constructed around my heart.

"Do twins run in either family?"

Both of our heads snapped toward the doctor. I knew where this was going.

"I had a twin," Gabe said as he touched my shoulder.

"It was too early to see before, but there are definitely two heartbeats. Congratulations!"

A tear crept from my eye. "There's two?"

Gabe's hand found mine as the doctor confirmed it again.

"Are you sure?" His voice was a little more distant as he watched the screen. He'd lost a little bit of his color.

The doctor pointed to the screen and described what the different parts meant. "Yes, I'm positive."

All I was able to do was stare at the two little fluttering dots. Those babies were inside me. Growing. They were alive. They were survivors. We'd nearly lost them in the car wreck. Two.

Dr. Byrum turned off the screen and removed the wand. "Ms. Russo, it will be imperative that you continue getting rest. I'll want to increase your folic acid. I have a colleague I'd like to refer you to who specializes in twin pregnancies. The morning sickness may be more intense as well, and you may experience more spotting. Don't be alarmed. Call Dr. Jamiston or me and we'll check everything out. I have some reading material for you at the front desk. Don't let it scare you."

Scare me. Oh my gosh! There were two babies. Two. And everything the doctor had said was so fast, it was hard to process. The thought was beginning to sink in. They were going to outnumber me.

"Ms. Russo?"

I nodded still in shock. "Okay. I can do this." I was definitely giving myself a needed pep talk. Two. There were going to be two. "Yes, I can do this."

Gabe crouched down beside me and raised my hand to his lips while he placed his other hand on my stomach. My focus turned to him. "We can do this, Willow. I'm here."

"We," I repeated, feeling some of the nervousness decrease. Gabe was here. He wasn't the nightmare of a husband I thought I had. This was real.

Dr. Byrum made a few more notes on a pad of paper. "I'm glad to see you supporting Ms. Russo, Mr. Thompson."

"I wouldn't be anywhere else." Gabe stood.

The ripping noise filled the room as the doctor tore off a piece of paper. "Here's a prescription for a stronger prenatal with additional folic acid. If you'd like, I can let Dr. Jamiston know you'll be calling."

"Please." I knew I sounded off, but enough together to keep the doctor from pausing and asking additional questions.

"And for at least a week, I'd like for you to abstain from sexual intercourse. Everything looks good, but with you and the babies being in distress during the accident, I don't want any additional stress on the uterus. It's merely a precautionary measure."

My head whipped from Dr. Byrum to Gabe repeatedly as I sat up. "Um, I'm not having sex. No sex for me. That won't be an issue."

Dr. Byrum's eyes dipped to my stomach for a second. Obviously, the babies were in there because of sex.

"Well, I had sex. But not now. Not anymore. No plans for sex." I yanked my hand from Gabe's grasp and cradled my face in my hands. "I need a redo to this morning. I'm calling Gabe big. I'm spouting craziness about sex." My head shot up. I had said that aloud. Oh my gosh! "Can we pretend none of this conversation happened and that I know to abstain from sex?"

Dr. Byrum tried to maintain a professional decorum.

Gabe was barely holding it in.

Dr. Byrum cleared his throat and said, "That will be fine. I'd still like to see you next week to make sure you're happy with Dr. Jamiston."

"Sounds good."

Dr. Byrum left and Gabe followed with him. I heard Gabe speaking to the doctor but wasn't able to make out what was being said. Thankfully, I was left to rein in my self-induced humiliation. When it rained, it poured. Apparently I suffered from severe word vomit during pregnancy. This was going to be a long nine months. In the mirror, I looked at my flat stomach. Two babies. It was hard to imagine there were two babies growing inside me.

When I finished dressing, I touched my stomach again. The story of Gabe's mother still lingered. "I'm going to love you both equally."

Knock.

Knock.

Knock.

"Willow. Everything okay?" Gabe sounded a little worried.

"Yes." My voice was small.

"Can I come in?"

"Yes."

"What's wrong, sweetheart?"

Sudden tears were on the cusp of falling from the concern and love in his voice. I wasn't alone in this. My babies were going to have a loving father. Gabe was beside me in a flash.

I shrugged. "I don't know. I was fine. Then you asked. And then tears. These damn hormones." He brought me to him with his strong arms, and I welcomed the comfort as my face sank into his chest.

"Willow, everything is going to be fine. We'll figure it out. You won't have to do this alone."

"I know. I believe you. It's a lot at once and unexpected."

"It is."

Wiping away the tears, I centered myself and changed the subject. "It's almost my time to see Carson."

Gabe interlaced our fingers. "Let's head upstairs. Do you want me to call Dr. Jamiston to set up an appointment while you're there?"

I wasn't going to have to do this on my own. The realization started to sink in. "That would be great. I don't have anything scheduled over the next week I can't rearrange."

"Sounds good. I'll see what they have available and coordinate it with your schedule to see Carson."

Carson. I needed my best friend now more than ever with everything that was going on.

Chapter Six

Later that afternoon, I lounged in the living room of the hotel room and read a new historical novel about the Medici family. Since I was a little girl, I had been obsessed with the Medici family. I loved hearing stories about them and devoured any reading material on them.

I took a sip of my orange cinnamon tea.

The family intrigued me with how they had the foresight to preserve the art that was a defining factor in the Italian culture. They had preserved my dad's painting *La Primavera* by Botticelli. It was because of them we had that beautiful piece of art that now was on indefinite loan at the Uffizi.

The worst of the physical injuries were behind me, which I was thankful for. In places I was tender. The deep purple was almost gone and back to normal. I thought about Carson and how his bruises were almost the same color as mine. His body was healing. Today it was easier to look at him as some color had returned to his cheeks. Francesca and Marie agreed with my assessment.

My appointment with Dr. Jamiston was scheduled for the day after tomorrow. They'd gotten me in earlier than expected. It still seemed surreal I was having twins, but the idea was slowly becoming my reality. It was going to be double the trouble.

Finishing a chapter, I watched Gabe stare intently at the pictures and notes sprawled across the coffee table. Earlier, I saw a few from the car accident and I quit looking, not ready to face that memory so graphically. The metal screeching still haunted my dreams. Gabe had offered to look at them somewhere else, but I insisted he stay. I wanted him near me.

I craved the feeling of being home when he was nearby. Thinking of home, I asked, "When do you think I'll be able to go home?"

He paused writing on his pad of paper. "I'd like to talk to Trent about making a few security upgrades if you approve. I think we should add a few infrared cameras along with some sensors. Rotate the security a little more frequently."

"Whatever you need to do, tell Trent."

He nodded and went to say something but closed his mouth.

I knew it was about where he was going to stay. I felt safer with him near. To put any doubts at ease, I said, "If you want to stay at the house, you're more than welcome."

Gabe's tension released. "I'd like that. I'll work with Trent. When do you want to go back home?"

"Whenever you and Trent think it's best. I know with Carson's situation it's probably easier to stay here, but I'm ready to be back in my bed and in my studio. I need to paint." With all the emotions swirling inside, I knew this would help me sort through it some.

He leaned forward. "Give me a little bit. I promise—"

A knock at the door interrupted him.

"Willow, Gabe, it's Trent."

"Come in," I called over the sofa.

After we'd returned to the hotel, Trent had left to catch up on some work in his room a door down. One of the other security guards, Matt I believed, was outside our door in the interim.

The key card reader beeped and Trent came in. "I just got off the phone with the lab. We'll have the DNA results by tomorrow."

Gabe sat back and closed the file he'd been working on. "Good. Have you found anything else?"

"No. But, I came to a decision about Andre."

My eyes darted between the men. I liked Andre but had to respect Trent's decision for his team. I hoped Andre could stay.

Trent leaned forward. "Andre is back on under the condition that he never pull a stunt like that again. I understand you two have a history—a close history. If I suspect anything, he's gone. I will not tolerate insubordination when someone's safety is in my trust. Understood?"

"Understood." Gabe relented easily enough. "Willow is the only reason I went to such extremes before."

Trent sat back. "As long as we're clear."

Whew. That seemed to go pretty well and Andre was back. Playfully, I stage-whispered, "I'm glad he's back. I missed him."

Laughing, Trent looked my way. "I figured you would be."

The earlier conversation about the DNA brought on the same worries I had before. "What if the DNA doesn't match?"

The fingers running along Gabe's scruff was the response

I received. He was probably thinking about the best way to approach this situation. "Why send you a message with Alex's ring and someone else's finger?" My eyes widened and Gabe put his hand on mine. "We'll cross that bridge if we have to. Remember, it's only precautionary."

The thought of Alex still being alive was horrifying. I released my bottom lip I was chewing. "But you suspect..."

Gabe gestured to the papers on the table. "There's too many unanswered questions. I suspect there's more to the story."

Of course there was.

Trent looked at the papers sprawled across the table while I took a sip of my tea, hoping to curb the nerves doing jumping jacks in the pit of my stomach. Tipping his head, Trent asked Gabe, "What are you looking at?"

Gabe glanced to me. "Later."

Now, I knew there was more. Not knowing was worse at this point. "Go ahead."

A few seconds passed before Gabe turned a picture to face us. It was of the ravine we'd rolled down in the accident. I refused to look away. Gabe held up another from on top of the ravine looking toward the tree line with a road just beyond. The last moments with Carson were crystal clear and a shiver ran through me. Trent and Gabe focused on me.

As Gabe put the picture away, I pushed him to continue. "I'm fine. I need to know. I'll worry about it if I don't know."

He hesitated.

"Please don't keep me in the dark."

I knew he was unable to resist my plea since he promised to never keep something from me again.

Gabe pointed to the pictures. "It doesn't make sense to me. I was so caught up with Willow being hurt, it wasn't until this afternoon when things were calmer I was able to look at these with fresh eyes."

I set my tea aside. Gabe paused, assessing me from head to toe, and I forced myself to remain outwardly calm though I felt this was about to get worse.

"The note in Italy said they wanted what was owed to them. Then the note in the art gallery said they were coming for her. If something happens to Willow, all her money goes to charity and they can't touch it. From all accounts of the accident, whoever was behind the wheel was on a mission to push them down the ravine. The location of the attack was designed to accomplish precisely this."

Trent sat back and muttered, "Oh fuck."

My eyes darted back and forth between them. "What does that mean?" I shook my head. "I mean... I... I know it means they wanted me..." I wasn't able to say it. The word had too much finality.

Gabe looked at me. "I think we are dealing with two different sets of people."

I felt the blood drain from me as I whispered, "And they want two different things."

No one responded.

It was true. Not only were we worrying about someone kidnapping me, but also someone trying to kill me.

Trent picked up a few of the pictures, looking at them with new eyes. Gabe came and sat on the couch.

This was terrible. Worse than I imagined. Who wanted to hurt me? Why? What had I done to elicit such an emotion from them?

I felt Gabe's finger under my chin as he brought my lavender eyes to meet his green ones. "I'm not leaving your side. Our children will be born with all this shit behind us. No one is going to hurt you."

"I hope so." My voice lacked conviction.

"I swear it."

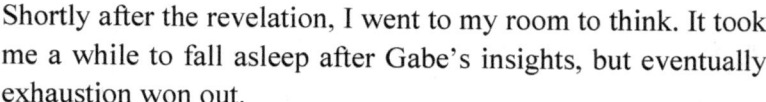

Shortly after the revelation, I went to my room to think. It took me a while to fall asleep after Gabe's insights, but eventually exhaustion won out.

After I woke up from my nap, I was still nervous what the future held and scared what this new player's end game was. One thing I prided myself on was being a good person. To want to kill someone seemed as though it would have to be something so terrible it would drive a person crazy.

I gasped. "Candy."

I threw the covers away and ran to the kitchen.

Gabe was sipping coffee at the kitchen table. "Hey there, sweetheart."

"Does Candy know about me?"

He walked up to me and put his hands on my shoulders. "I don't know. While you were sleeping I made a list of possible suspects. She's at the top."

"Of course you already thought about it."

He removed his hands from my shoulders and placed them on my cheeks. "I've thought of nothing else since I had the realization. Nothing. Trent's team is on it."

His eyes moved to my lips and I felt myself lean in closer. "Do you think it's her?"

"I don't know. We're looking at Commander Taylor's men. They may be holding a grudge for him. I'm not sure. Jack De Luca is still at the top, even though nothing else has turned up on him that connects him to the accident or notes.

It's almost like he's being framed to take the fall for this. From the charges that were brought up, threats like this don't seem to be his style. They are all interconnected somehow; I just don't know what the common thread is besides Alex." His forehead moved closer to mine. "I'm going to keep you safe." His hand moved to my stomach. "And our babies. I'll figure this out."

"I know you will."

Our lips moved a little closer when the door opened and I took a hasty step back, breaking the connection. Nonno walked in and it felt like I had been caught doing something naughty.

"Hey, Nonno." My voice was a little off as I thought about Gabe's mouth being close to mine.

"Hey, sleepyhead. Glad to see you're awake. Let's sit. My old legs are tired."

The chairs made noise as we scooted them out. I sat next to Gabe. He smiled into his cup of coffee. I knew it pleased him having me near. It pleased me. During our breakfast the other day, I had barely acknowledged him.

My lips turned upward as Nonno looked between us. "How'd the doctor's visit go?"

Gabe remained silent and looked at me to answer. No one knew about the twins yet. Was I ready to share? A slight tip of his head told me Gabe was leaving it up to me. "The doctor said everything looks good. He wants me to keep resting."

"I'm glad to hear it. I've been worried about you and the little one. It's going to be a special day when I get to see my great-grandchild. Your parents would be so happy."

Happiness filled my heart. "Yes, they would. I can't wait to get home and start planning the baby room. I found the paintings Dad made for me when I was a baby before the art show. I plan on hanging them in the nursery."

Plus, it would be nice to have a project on my hands to occupy my time. Maybe a mural on the wall.

Nonno cleared his throat. "Speaking of home, I've decided to return to mine."

Alarm shot through me. This wasn't part of the plan. "Nonno, I don't think that's a good idea."

He held up his hand. "I've spoken to Trent and Gabe about this while you were sleeping. We are going to take the necessary precautions. Trent has a friend who is going to head up my security."

"Nonno..." I turned to Gabe, seeing Nonno was resolved in his decision. "Don't you think he should stay? He should stay, right?"

There was someone out there trying to kill me. I wanted everyone I loved close to me.

Gabe leaned forward and took my hand. "For safety? No, I don't as long as the necessary precautions are taken. We're working on you getting home, too."

When Gabe put it like that, it made it a little less scary. I ran my fingers through my hair when Gabe leaned over. "I'll be in the hallway if you need me so you and Nonno can talk."

"Okay." I wasn't sure if I wanted him to leave as I watched his retreating back.

The door clicked. My eyes were transfixed on it as I thought of what to say to Nonno to convince him to stay. There was another reason I was afraid for him to leave that scared me to admit.

"Nonno, why are you leaving? I don't want you in danger. How were they able to get the precautions done so quickly?"

He reached his hands across the table, and I put mine in his. "You need this time with Gabe, Willow." I started to argue when he held up his free hand. "Hear me out, baby girl."

I nodded and he continued, "I hadn't met Gabe before he was deployed. All I knew was Alex. And it was hard to see what you're father had seen between you and Gabe. Your dad said you were two spirits completing each other. In the couple of days I've watched you two, I see it. And I think you need this time to find your way back to each other. I've spent a lot of time talking to Gabe. He's a good man. I can sense it. You're on the cusp of finding each other and I don't want to be in the way. I can't be in the way."

Wow, his words were beautifully frightening. The connection was intense.

I closed my eyes and whispered, "I'm scared, Nonno." That was another huge reason I wanted him to stay. Being alone with Gabe, truly being alone with him, meant that we were going to be alone... together. My heart was terrified of getting hurt again.

"Love is scary." He paused and I opened my eyes. "Follow your heart, Willow. I'm not saying you should end up with Gabe. All I'm saying is open yourself up to it. You guys are having a baby together. I know the circumstances around how you became pregnant are questionable. I don't agree with what Gabe did and he knows this. I can't imagine what he's been through either. Alex did a number on everyone."

I pulled my hands back and played with the edge of the placemat. "There's a part of me that feels like I betrayed Gabe."

Nonno watched me with his all-knowing eyes. "And this is why you're keeping your distance from him?"

"Yes. Part of it. I'm trying to stay away... unsuccessfully."

He cleared his throat. "That's why it's best that I leave.

It'll give you two time to figure things out and follow your heart. Willow, I don't think you betrayed him. But, I'm not the one you need to tell your thoughts to."

I knew this was true—all of it. Sometimes the truth was scarier than a lie. "Thank you, Nonno. I needed this talk."

"If you need anything, I'm a phone call away, baby girl."

Nonno was my rock and I was grateful I still had him in my life. "I love you, Nonno."

"Love you, too."

Chapter Seven

Nonno left and I sat on the couch, collecting my thoughts alone. What had only been a few days felt like a lifetime. So much so fast.

The door opened, but I continued to face forward with my unfocused eyes as I thought about my conversation with Nonno. *Open up my heart. Allow myself to be happy.* I knew Gabe was sorry for what had happened. If I had to deceive someone to protect them, would I?

Unequivocally, the answer was yes. Gabe had made those decisions to protect me until he was able to piece together the mess Alex had brought into my life.

He settled in the chair across from me. "And then there were two."

"And then there were two," I echoed with a grin on my face, remembering the first time we were alone. On our first date, we'd met in a restaurant and closed the place down. When we were the last two people there, Gabe had said those exact words.

It was weird. I knew Gabe intimately, but suddenly I was nervous.

"Do you trust me, Willow?" he asked, his voice questioning as if he were afraid of the answer.

"Yes." I was shocked at my lack of hesitation. But, then I knew it was true, I trusted Gabe fully.

My quick answer pleased Gabe as he stared at me with a gorgeous smile. "I'd like to do something different, if that's okay?"

That seemed like the perfect idea. "I'd love that."

He held out a piece of fabric. "Will you put this on? I want it to be surprise. The men are helping me with something I don't want you to see."

A surprise. I loved surprises. I stood and turned. "Will you put it on me?"

It would have been easy to tie the fabric over my eyes, but I wanted to feel his touch.

"It'd be my pleasure, sweetheart." His hot breath was at my ear.

I remained silent, hoping he would kiss me just below my ear. He covered my eyes and secured the black cloth behind my head. Then I felt his fingertips on my neck. They lightly trailed down my arm.

The cloth was thick and completely blocked any residual light.

Involuntarily, I leaned into his chest. His lips came to the top of my head. "Thank you, Willow. I'll never take your trust for granted. You'll never have to doubt my feelings for you."

A warm shiver moved through me as his hands trailed farther down. And then on a squeal I was lifted.

"Gabe!" I gripped him tightly.

"I don't want you tripping."

I cocked my head to the side even though I wasn't able to see him. "Admit it, you wanted to hold me."

"True. But, I think my excuse works so I don't scare you off."

I laughed. "I like your excuse, too."

A door opened and closed, which caused him to shift me only momentarily. We entered what I assumed was the hallway. There were footsteps behind us, which was probably the security team. Gabe's outdoorsy scent smelled like home as I laid my head against him. His heartbeat was a little fast. Maybe he was as nervous as I was with Nonno's departure and the paradigm shifting between us rapidly.

I was following my heart and it was leading me to Gabe.

Thank goodness, the doctor had taken sex off the table. With my desire and naughty thoughts on the rise, that limitation was a very good thing indeed. We needed to take things slower sexually with everything else moving at light speed.

Our chemistry had proven time and time again that we were near uncontrollable around each other. The same night we closed the restaurant down on our first date, we slept together. It was unstoppable the moment we were alone. Just like the night Gabe came to my hotel room.

The ride down to the first floor was quiet. The only sound was the elevator. The doors dinged open and we were on the move again. I felt the sun on my face as we exited. There was distant chatting and a few laughs from what I assumed were guests coming and going. A car door opened and then I sitting on plush leather seats. The seat coolers were on. "Let's get you buckled up and away we'll go."

The buckle clicked. No one said a word. It sounded like someone had shut the trunk, too.

"Do I get any hints?"

"No, 'cause you'll figure it out."

I jutted out my lip and I felt his finger press against it.

"Patience, sweetheart. It'll make the surprise that much better, I hope."

The car took off as I felt Gabe intertwine his hands with mine. "Who's driving?"

"Andre. He insisted."

Into the dark, I called, "Thank you for driving, Andre. Means a lot. Welcome back."

"No problem, Ms. Russo. Just doing my job."

Though Andre had kept a fundamental piece of information from us, I knew he had done it to protect me. Fate had stepped in, having Andre work for Trent. All this had happened before Gabe and I dated. We were meant to be together. Or at least have a fair chance at being together.

I felt the car turn left, but had no idea where we were. "Hey, Andre. Want to tell me where we're going?"

In response I only received a deep chuckle. Figures. Gabe came into the picture and everyone seemed to follow whatever orders he gave. At times it was maddening, but he had that effect on people. Gabe squeezed my hand when the car slammed on its breaks and I jerked forward.

No. No. No! Not again! Panic ensued over me. *Was someone hitting us again?*

Someone was after me! They wanted to kill me!

It was dark! I needed light!

My breathing sped up. My fingers clawed at the blindfold. "Gabe, I need to see!" It wouldn't come off. "Gabe!"

Immediately, the blindfold disappeared and I stared into his eyes. "Shit, Willow. I wasn't thinking." Gabe cradled my cheek. "Take a deep breath with me."

I followed his instructions.

"Exhale."

I blew out the air. We repeated this until I calmed.

"Better?"

"Yes, much."

Gabe turned fractionally to Andre and nodded.

Andre called from the front. "I apologize for the abrupt stop, Ms. Russo. Everything is okay."

"Thank you, Andre." There was a tremor to my voice. The car moved again and I exhaled.

Leaning on Gabe's shoulder, I held onto his arm. "I can't do the blindfold, but I can close my eyes."

He brought me closer. "If you need to watch, you can."

My heart fluttered at his words. Any time I was concerned he placed my needs above all else.

"I want to be surprised."

Being in Gabe's embrace helped chase away the bad memories of the car crash.

The rest of the ride was smooth as I felt the car move through the city. The speed picked up on what I assumed was the interstate. The warmth from his body was lulling me into a near sleep when Andre parked the car.

"Wait right here. Andre is in the front seat. I'll be right back."

"Come back to me soon."

"Promise."

Those were the same words he spoke to me while under the tree and before he was deployed. Gabe was a man of his word and had come back for me.

The door opened and closed. Silence ensued. Then the trunk popped open.

I spoke, knowing Andre was still here. "I know helping Gabe caused you some issues, but thank you. I believe you made the right decision."

"Ain't no thing, Ms. Russo. You remind me lot of a person I once knew. She was a good person. One of the best."

"Who?" I asked.

"That's a long time in the past. Sometimes that's where all that belongs."

The door opened before I could probe any further. "Are you ready, sweetheart?"

"Yes."

He lifted me as I kept my eyes closed. I heard children laughing in the distance and I had a feeling where we were. "You know don't you?"

The smile on my face must have given it away. "You brought me to our park."

I felt him kneel and gently place me on the ground. My fingers touched a quilt.

"Open your eyes, Willow."

Beside me was a brown wicker basket opened and brimming with food. My eyes shot to Gabe. "You planned all this?"

"I did with the help of the hotel staff. When you were talking to Nonno, I pulled it together."

He had done all this. For me. He was here. Alive.

I threw my hands around him and placed my head in the crook of his neck. How could I have ever thought this man was Alex? The thought tore at me. I should have pressed more for answers when I knew things weren't right.

"Thank you. I love it. I needed this more than you could possibly know." Being with Gabe like this was as natural as breathing and free of awkwardness.

We sat and a sense of déjà vu came over me. I spied our tree trunk and ran my fingers over our initials. "I came here after I visited the police station. I needed a connection to life before the war."

"I know. I followed you."

Gabe's hands came on top of mine as I traced the letters. I drew my knees up and rested my head on them. Our eyes met. "How were you able to follow me without me seeing you? I can always sense when you're near. That sense left when it was Alex, but it was there with Tack."

"You have no idea how happy that makes me. But, I think you did sense me." My brows scrunched in confusion. "I was the old man in the precinct, the old man in the Boboli Gardens, and the old man at your art show. We connected each and every time. You weren't able to stop staring some of the time, but I believe the appearance threw you off."

My eyes widened. "I remember them." Each time I had felt something, but my mind had failed to make the connection. "Wait. Were you the man at the Uffizi?"

"I was. I needed to be close to watch. Are you upset?"

I thought about this for a second. It was all part of the deception. But, he was there. I sensed it. "How'd you get the rose and note into the room with the Botticelli?"

He gestured with is free hand. "I blended with the cleaning team. Then became the old man. Being the obvious is sometimes the most unexpected."

"Hide in plain sight."

"Yes."

We watched each other, taking in the moment.

"What did you do in the military?"

"Black ops. Secret missions."

I shifted to lay on my side. Gabe followed suit. "I figured it was something like that."

"It was."

We were mere inches apart. The lawnmower in the distance added the perfect ambience to our picnic. It was summer and I loved it.

Without warning, I blurted, "Do you think I betrayed you? I feel like I did."

He stroked my cheek with his thumb. I closed my eyes to his soothing touch, but it was worrisome he hadn't answered right away. I kept telling myself Gabe was entitled to his feelings.

"Open your eyes, Willow. I want you to see mine when I answer you."

I opened them.

"I don't think you betrayed me. Not in the slightest. Alex is a different story. Words can't express the amount of hate I feel for him."

It was hard to process family hating each other when I had a completely different experience. I leaned into his touch.

"I'm in love with you, Willow. I have been since I first saw you."

Tears pooled in my eyes while his burned with honesty.

"Don't let that keep you from me. Please. The only time I've ever misled you was with Tack. And that was the last time. I'll never give you a reason to doubt me again."

I touched the scruff on his face. I liked the coarse feeling against my skin and imagined it dragging across my sensitive breasts. Oh man, to have it across my nipples. *Stop it, Willow. I need to keep a clear head through all this.*

"I know you're thinking about us."

There was no denying it. "I am." I cleared my throat ready to put my feelings out there. "I still love you, Gabe. I never stopped."

Those words felt right as I spoke them, but I was terrified. I had been here before and things had fallen apart not long after.

A huge brilliant smile spread across his face. "Sweetheart, you have no idea how happy that makes me."

"But... I'm scared."

Please don't let this be a repeat.

He kissed my hand. "I'm scared, too. I'm afraid after wishing to have you back for so long this will all be a dream. But, I can promise you this, I will never lose you again. Never."

His words addressed my fear. But, it was still terrifying to allow love to take such control. "I hope so."

Gabe scooted closer. "Oh, baby, I promise. Just like I promised I'd come for you, I promise I will protect your love for me."

I lay down and stared up at the sky, letting his words penetrate my thoughts. "That's all I want."

"Willow, I want to kiss you."

Turning, he was closer than I anticipated. The warmth of his breath brushed against my lips. "I would like that."

Without hesitation, Gabe pressed his lips to mine. It was sweet and familiar. I wanted more. Craved more. As I was about to open my mouth to let him in, he pulled back. "I don't want to push my luck and rush you. Let's take this slow. The wait will make it that much sweeter."

"Or drive us crazy." I half laughed.

He winked at me. "That, too."

Moving to his back, he motioned to me to move closer. "I can't believe I didn't recognize your touch when you kissed me as Tack."

"I had to be careful. It's why I kept contact to a minimum. The accent kept you from making the connection."

It was amazing what our cognitive reasoning did to our

thoughts. "You kept your familiar touch from me."

He wrapped his arm around me. "Yes. I had to change all that. I couldn't stand not having you touch me, but I had to keep it controlled. It was so fucking hard. I want you to know that. I hated doing that to you."

The sincerity was overwhelming as he held me. I melted. "I know." It was time to move past the deceit. "What would you think of Carson and Francesca as the godparents to our children?" My throat tightened, hoping that I had the chance to ask him.

"I think that's a wonderful idea."

"Me, too."

The words hung between us. There was a slight breeze and the warmth of his body was the perfect balance while I snuggled into his side. "Have you thought of any names?"

"For the babies?"

"Mmm." The deep rumble in his chest was sexy.

"I haven't. Have you?" Honestly, I hadn't. I was still working on getting used to being pregnant with twins.

"No, but I have something I want to propose."

"What's that?" The steady thud of his heart brought me closer to him, and I wrapped my arm around his middle.

"We each have a boy and a girl name. We don't tell the other. You name the first baby, I name the second one," he answered.

I raised my head and looked at Gabe. He watched me intently and gave me a loving look. This was to build strength between us. Not knowing what the other one picked, but trusting it was something we'd each like.

I loved the idea and added, "No telling anyone. I don't want it to slip."

"So you like the idea?"

"Yes, I love it. It has a beautiful meaning behind it."

"I agree." He trailed his hand down my back as we relaxed in perfect harmony.

"When are you going to tell everyone about the twins? Was there a reason you didn't tell Nonno tonight?"

Laying back down, I pressed the palm of my hand to his heart and the tattoo of the swords crossing each other. "I don't know why I didn't say anything. I knew you left it up to me, but I wanted to wait." It didn't feel like the right time. It was unexplainable like it had been with how fast I trusted Tack in the beginning.

"I'm fine with whatever you decide, sweetheart. For now, we'll keep it between us."

Escaping for the evening was the perfect suggestion to rekindle our relationship.

"Are you comfortable?" Gabe methodically rubbed my feet.

"Mmm..."

We were back at the hotel in our pajamas. Currently, I was being treated to a foot massage. It was amazing. I never wanted it to end. My eyes drifted close.

There was a knock at the door

"Shit."

Gabe's curse brought a chuckle from me. I knew he wanted me to rest.

"Let me see who it is."

"Okay." My words were still sleepy as I stayed on the pillow.

The door opened followed by whispering.

"Willow, Francesca is here."

Sitting up, I saw Francesca standing in the doorway with a tub of ice cream. "Oh, I'm sorry. I wasn't thinking. I'll come back later."

"No, please come in. I spy with my little eye some ice cream."

Francesca giggled. "You do."

Gabe gave me a wink. "I'm going to check in with Trent. You girls have fun."

I motioned for Francesca to come in as I called, "Oh, we will."

The apprehension left her face as she walked to the navy couch and handed me a spoon. "Do you like mint chocolate chip? I thought it might be nice to have some girl time." Dark circles still rimmed her eyes.

Unless Francesca brought Carson up, I wouldn't. Maybe a little escape from reality like Gabe had provided me would help her.

"I love it. Great choice."

She popped off the lid and we both dug into the ice cream. The minty flavor mixed with chocolate burst across my tongue.

"This is amazing." I almost moaned.

She took a bite too. "I needed this. I wish I could be left in the dark until I know everything is okay."

"I understand." Everyone needed something different to cope.

We sat back, put our feet on the coffee table, and set the tub of ice cream between us.

"How are you doing, Willow?"

I took another bite. "I'm hanging in there. Things are progressing with Gabe."

"Ooh la la." A giggle came from Francesca.

I clarified. "We're taking it slow. I mean obviously"—I gestured to my stomach—"we've raced through a few milestones, but I like the place we're at."

Francesca's hand came on top of mine. "I'm so glad. I can see how much Gabe loves you. I overheard him talking to Trent this morning in the hallway. He told him to do whatever it takes to keep you safe."

A tear left my eye and I wiped it away, moved by how Gabe kept proving he loved me. It's all I ever wanted. "Sorry. I can't seem to control the tears at times."

"Me, either. I feel like a leaky faucet most of the time."

We laughed. "Me, too. Plus my word vomit is atrocious."

"Word vomit? I don't understand what that means." She looked at me with a raised eyebrow. Even though Francesca spoke fluent English, sometimes she wasn't able to follow slang.

I took another bite. "It's like my filter to my mouth has gone. This morning in the doctor's office, I was thinking about how built Gabe was. More so than before he was deployed. I told him he was big and that I liked him big."

Francesca sputtered and laughed. "You did not."

"I so did. Then I continued the nightmare by telling the doctor I was not currently having sex with Gabe standing right there like I was a virgin."

Francesca dropped her spoon as she held her stomach and laughed. "I'm so glad I did not get word vomit. I'm becoming a carnivore. Red meat is all I can think about."

We put our spoons back in the ice cream. "Here's to pregnancy."

Chapter Eight

"**M**orning." I shuffled into the kitchen where Gabe stood at the stove, cooking. His low-slung lounge pants, messy hair, and T-shirt were not helping my thoughts stay on the straight and narrow.

I will keep my mouth shut. I will keep my mouth shut.

With expert skill, he flipped an omelet.

I am so screwed.

"Morning. How'd you sleep?" His deep voice was sexy as hell. Always had been.

"Really well." I motioned to the couch where blankets were strewn to the side. "You know you can sleep in the room Nonno was in. You would get a better night's rest."

He sprinkled some cheese on the omelet before sliding it on a plate and pouring more egg batter into the pan. "I slept perfect, knowing you were okay. Unless it bothers you, I would prefer the couch."

Last night I had debated whether to call Gabe on my phone from my bedroom to hear him talk. When he had been

Tack, there were many nights I wasn't able to sleep. To help, he read to me, which chased away all the nightmares.

"No, it's fine." He glanced over his shoulder and there was no missing his quick appreciative glance at my body.

I was wearing silk shorts with a camisole. The appreciation brought delight to me.

Gabe added some peppers to the pan as I came to stand beside him.

"I feel bad you're cooking all the time. I need to set my alarm to get up one morning and cook that bacon quiche you love."

He pressed a quick kiss to my cheek. "I like cooking breakfast for you. Grab your omelet before it gets cold. Mine will be done in a second."

As soon as I grabbed the plate, the smell of eggs hit me out of nowhere. It was raunchy and I gagged. Normally, I loved eggs, but this was foul and rank. It got worse as I tried to breathe through it. My stomach turned. This wasn't going to end well. I knew what was coming as I dashed to the bathroom. The stench followed me as if it had permanently soaked into my skin.

My cracker I'd eaten was lost as I heaved into the toilet.

Morning sickness. I hated it. More heaving. It was as if I had food poisoning from the smell alone.

Gabe kneeled beside me with a warm cloth as I flushed the toilet. There was a dull ache in my stomach after retching.

"What triggered it this time?"

I wiped my face and muttered, "Eggs."

"No more eggs. Check."

A small giggle escaped. "That's probably wise to start a checklist." I stood and tossed the cloth into the hamper. "I'm going to stay in here until we leave for the hospital. I don't think I can stand smelling it again."

I gagged thinking about it and closed my eyes tight. *Think about something else.*

"How about some crackers and ginger ale?"

My stomach was raw, but I needed to eat something. The thought of either wasn't causing any additional nausea. "Yeah, I'll try it."

Gabe took off and I shut the door behind him to keep the smell out. I sniffed my clothes and swore there was a faint egg aroma.

I'm going to be sick. Oh my gosh!

It was like I had some sort of super sniffer. I gagged again. Hurriedly, I stripped off my pajamas and threw them into the hamper like they were toxic.

"Here you go. A plate of crackers and—"

I spun around. Naked. I felt the heat creep over my skin.

Gabe took me in, swallowed hard, and tried to look at my face, but his eyes kept drifting down. My arms instinctively covered my breasts.

His face remained blank. "Willow... we... I... the doctor said no sex right now."

Kill. Me. Now. Apparently my body was taking over since I had put my mouth on lockdown.

This had to be explained. "I... uhh... I was changing. I smelled eggs on my clothes and stripped. I wasn't asking for sex. No sex!" My sentence ended on a near squeal. My word vomit wasn't over yet. Of course not. "I don't mean no sex ever. I love sex with you." My hands flew to my mouth. "Why can't I stop?" I muttered. Pregnancy was stripping every ounce of dignity I had left as my hormones took over.

Gabe set the plate and drink down.

Would I still be sexy even pregnant?

Reemerging, Gabe held a white terry cloth robe out and helped me put it on. "For my sanity, let's get you covered."

Tears pricked my eyes. *His sanity?* Was I that horrid looking already? What was wrong with me? Word vomit, tears, horniness... all in the last two minutes.

Averting my eyes, I tightened the sash on my robe. "Thank you. I wasn't thinking when I tried to get away from the egg smell and stripped down."

A finger came underneath my chin raising my gaze. "You have nothing to be ashamed of. Hell, Willow, I want you so bad. If I thought I could control myself, I'd want you naked all the time. But we can't. The doctor said not for a week. And I don't think we're ready for that step. But, I want nothing more than to make love to you while you are pregnant with my children. Every. Single. Day."

"You don't think I'm hideous?" A tear slipped free and then the dam burst and I cried. I wasn't showing, but I felt off.

Gabe wrapped his arms around me.

"I'm a mess. I've never been this emotional."

"You're pregnant, sweetheart. It's messing with your hormones." I felt his lips press against the top of my head. "You're perfect. All I ever want is you. I love you."

"Love you, too."

I wrapped my arms around his waist, loving the muscular feel. Oh, how I'd missed Gabe all these months. He caressed my back and the soothing motion calmed me.

"I'm trying to keep my distance physically from you."

"Why?" I knew the answer was obvious, but I needed to hear his thoughts.

The depth of his stare penetrated my soul. "Because, I need to know you want to be with me and not because of the chemistry."

My heart clenched at the pain in his words. This was the effects of his childhood. Plus, I had been all over the place emotionally and giving mixed signals. I wanted him, then I was scared or aggravated. Mentally, I told myself I needed to decide fully. Right now, I had only one foot on the path and one foot off, which wasn't fair to any of us including our unborn children.

I squeezed him tighter. "We're both holding back."

"We'll get there."

And I knew we would.

Guiding me to the bed, Gabe placed the crackers and ginger ale before me. Thankfully, there was no smell associated with either.

"Here, eat some of this."

Mercifully, I took a small bit of the cracker. "Thanks. I may dub this the breakfast of champions."

He chuckled. "If it keeps you from getting sick, it'll earn that title. Hopefully, this subsides after the first trimester." How much had Gabe read on pregnancy? I'd read quite a bit since I found out. From Gabe's comments, he had been reading as much as I had.

"After we stop to see Carson, I was wondering if we could run home. Just for a bit, not to stay the night."

Gabe touched my leg, and I felt the familiar warmth that was like a drug. His fingers retracted and I stilled his hand.

"Please don't. I want your touch." I wanted to put both feet on the path. Yes, it was terrifying, but all the same, love was worth the risk.

The heat from his hand returned. "Trent stopped by. Marie and Bennett want us there to meet with the doctors this morning regarding Carson."

The cracker dropped on my plate. "Wait. Why? Is there

something wrong?"

"Not that I know of. Don't stress. If Dr. Byrum sees you, he may bring you back to the hospital."

I took a deep breath, picked up my cracker, and took a small bite. "Do you think it's an update?"

"It could be. I suspect they're going to update the options."

Options. There was only one option I wanted, which was to bring Carson back. What other options were there? Take him off life support before he was ready? Absolutely not. Thank goodness Bennett and Marie were levelheaded, and I wouldn't have to worry about them doing something radical.

A few days ago, the doctors indicated Carson wasn't strong enough to breathe on his own yet. Had something changed? Was it for the worse? Better? I hated vague meetings with doctors. It was much better to get right to the point.

Gabe's fingers on my cheek brought me out of my spiraling thoughts. "Let's wait to worry until we hear from the doctors. All we can do is focus on the facts."

He was right.

"How's Francesca?" I asked, worried about her. Now, I was even more grateful we had spent time together last night. We had laughed and left all of the worries from our lives behind. Time had flown until eleven when we simultaneously yawned. Two pregnant women staying up that late was a miracle with how much sleep we now required. It had been worth it.

"They aren't mentioning this to her until we get there due to the stress. Bennett and Marie are worried."

We all were. Right now, Francesca's baby kept us connected to Carson. Knowing a piece of Carson thrived lifted our spirits. When Carson came back to us, the first thing he would ask about was the baby. It was imperative we kept her positive. "Why didn't you wait to tell me about Carson?" Carson had to be okay. He had to be.

Gabe wrapped an arm around me, and I leaned my head on his shoulder.

"Because one, that's not how I want our relationship to be—neither do you. And two, because you're strong. If I thought it would jeopardize the health of you or the babies, I would have waited because I know that's what you would want, too."

There was more than physical chemistry between us. Together, Gabe and I were complete. Apart, things weren't as good. The last six months had proven that. I hadn't felt alive again until I'd spoken with Tack.

"I feel like things are changing back to the way they used to be. I hope I'm right."

Looking up, I set the plate aside. "You are."

His lips crashed onto mine. I moaned into his mouth as his tongue took over. My lower stomach clenched as my hands roamed to the hem of his pajama pants. I wanted to straddle him for that sweet friction.

In a flash, Gabe released me and stepped at him a few feet away.

Why was he over there?

"Six days." His chest was heaving.

"Six days?" What the hell was he talking about?

"We can have sex in six days."

Oh shit, the doctor's orders. In a defeated sweep, I fell back on the bed. "I want a second opinion."

The bed dipped and I felt Gabe's hand on my stomach. "It'll go by fast."

I raised my eyebrows and called bullshit.

"Okay, it's going to be hell."

The next six days *were* going to be hell. Having Gabe's scent this close caused irrational thoughts to come into my mind. The doctor wanted complete abstinence. I looked at the time. We had about an hour before we needed to leave. "I'm going to take a shower and get ready. I need to let my stomach settle before I eat anything else." A perfect distraction from what I really wanted.

"Good idea. I'll take an ice cold one myself."

A small giggle escaped. Gabe was just as affected as me. "We can suffer together."

"And then have that much more pleasure."

Just the thought had me clinching in my lower region again.

Taking the plate with the crackers, he followed me into the bathroom. "Try to eat some more when you get out. I'll be waiting."

"I will."

I turned on the shower, and the room quickly filled with steam. After Gabe left, I took off my robe. My reflection in the mirror caught my attention, and I stared at my stomach, wondering when I would see a baby bump. The babies were so small.

After showering, I got ready quickly and tried to stop worrying about what the doctors wanted to talk about. At least my sexual frustration had moved to the back burner.

We were approaching two weeks with Carson being non-responsive. I feared the two-week mark. For some reason that felt monumental.

My phone vibrated. It was Francesca.

Francesca: Thanks for last night. Can't wait to do it again.

Me: Me, either. It was fun. I needed it.

Francesca: Me, too.

She must not know about meeting with the doctors. I still had a few minutes to burn. To pass the time, I picked up the room and made the bed. When it was finally time to go, I entered the main living room to get my purse on the chair by the door. I hoped the egg smell was gone.

Gabe was near the door, freshly showered, and as I paused to appreciate the sight, a slow lazy smile crept on his face. "What are you thinking about?"

"How lucky I am to have you in my life. How lucky we are to be getting a second chance together."

Without warning, Gabe cradled my face. "I am the luckiest man alive. I don't deserve you, but I'm too selfish to let you go."

The thought of Gabe letting me go wrecked me. I threw my arms around him. "Don't say things like that."

His arms came around me. "But I don't deserve you. I didn't leave you and know that I never will." And it was true, he hadn't but I knew what it was like to not have him in my life. I held him tighter. "Sweetheart, I shouldn't have said it like that. I'm never leaving you. Ever."

"I like the sound of that a lot better."

Part of me knew I had overreacted, but the last thing I wanted were those types of thoughts in our minds especially since we weren't able to connect on a more intimate level. Relationships needed all aspects to thrive.

We were meant to be. Fate meant to bring us together. I wasn't going to tempt it.

Chapter Nine

My palms were sweaty as we stood in Carson's ICU room. Gabe was behind me with his hands on my hips, anchoring me. It was taking everything in my power to stay strong and not freak out. For the next few minutes, the life of my friend hung in the balance.

Carson had to pull through.

Francesca clutched my hand, only adding to my nerves. She was barely hanging on, too.

The room was quiet except for the doctors prepping to take Carson off life support. It seemed too fast. I wasn't prepared for what the doctors told us today—none of us had been.

In Carson's legally-binding will, he had a stipulation to turn off life support after two weeks.

We were at a crossroads on day twelve with two days left.

If we waited two days, nothing could be done except to take him off. His parents decided to take the doctors' suggestion to take Carson off life support today to see how he does. If there's a sign he's fighting, it might buy us time to file a motion to extend the life support due to a clause in his will.

When no signs of life have been shown...

When Carson woke up, we were having a serious talk about his timeframe and lack of specifics. Two weeks. That was no time at all for a serious injury.

The doctor made one more note before turning to Carson's parents. I wasn't sure how, but they managed to get Gabe and me on the list to be in here though I wasn't considered immediate family. Francesca squeezed my hand harder. I leaned into Gabe. Never before had I felt so helpless.

"We're going to turn off the life support now. We'll record all actions. If Mr. Whitmore's life signs drop below a certain threshold, we will put him back on. Are there any questions?"

Bennett held Marie close to his side. "No questions. Thank you, doctor."

All of our eyes were filled with unshed tears. It was important we remain strong. Prior to this we each took a few moments to be alone with Carson. I'd used my few minutes to tell him to fight. Five minutes had not been long enough.

The silence descended on us once again. As the doctor reached for the button, I tensed. Gabe's thumbs made small comforting sweeps that reminded me he was here. A slight tremor racked my body.

Please be okay.

Click.

Life support was officially off. The pressure on my hand tightened as I held my breath. My eyes were glued to the heart rate monitor. I tried to remain calm and keep my stress levels low.

Beep.

Four seconds passed.

Beep.

Four seconds passed.

I breathed a sigh of relief as this continued. My eyes were transfixed on the monitor. Carson's heart was beating on its own. Was this enough to show the courts if we needed to? I hoped so, but doubted it.

Beep.

Five seconds passed.

Wait. Had I counted correctly? My heart sped up. I felt Gabe's right hand flex. He caught it, too. I wasn't wrong. There had been a delay.

Beep.

Six seconds passed.

No. No. No! Francesca stiffened, having caught onto the longer interval. This was not happening.

Beep.

Eight seconds passed.

"Fight, Carson! Fight!" I blurted into the room. My voice jolted those around me, but it was the least of my last concerns as my words felt echoed off the walls.

Beep.

Ten seconds passed.

I took a step forward, releasing Francesca and out of Gabe's hold. "You have a beautiful future ahead of you. Fight, Carson! Don't let this beat you! Fight, damn it, fight!"

Beep.

Twelve seconds passed.

Behind me, Francesca's quiet sobs stole my attention for a brief second. Gabe was holding her. He gave me an encouraging nod. Marie clutched Bennett. "Carson, we need you! Keep fighting! Your baby needs you! Don't leave that precious baby!"

A loud sob tore through the room. I wasn't done. I was not letting my best friend go.

Beep.

Ten seconds passed.

"Yes, keep fighting! You have this, Carson. Fight for your baby!"

Beep.

Eight seconds passed.

Excitement filled me. His heart was picking back up and his lung function was improving.

Beep.

Five seconds passed.

We were nearly to the same vitals where we began. I touched his foot. "I knew you could do it. Keep pushing through the fog, Carson. Don't stop! We're here waiting for you when you wake up."

Beep.

Four seconds passed.

The doctors checked the monitors as his heart rate steadied for several minutes. I kept my eyes focused on the green numbers as I counted and kept up the encouraging words. Taking his hand, I gave it a gentle squeeze. "You've got this. You've got this."

Another sniffle caught my attention. Francesca was silently crying into Gabe's chest like Marie was Bennett. I met Gabe's eyes and they were filled with love for me.

We were going to survive this—all of us.

The doctor cleared his throat. "This is very good news. We will keep monitoring him closely and wait for him to wake up."

Relief filled me. Carson was going to wake up. He had to.

Gabe stepped out into the hall with Trent. Francesca was asleep with her head on my lap. I stared at the wall, eyes out of focus. We had muted the TV long ago. The stench of old coffee filled the room. Luckily, my stomach was able to withstand it for now.

I checked the time. Twelve hours had passed. Every hour that went by was a good thing. The relief was immeasurable. Throughout the day, we took shifts sitting with Carson as permitted by the doctors.

I was exhausted as late evening approached. Throughout the day Gabe had been attentive, making sure Francesca and I ate. Earlier I had closed my eyes to rest but jolted awake at a nightmare of Carson not waking up. The feeling of loss had been too great to shake for some time. I had crawled into Gabe's lap where he slowly coaxed it from me. Fortunately, telling someone helped.

From what Gabe had said, we would be leaving for the evening soon. Marie and Francesca were staying the night, which was good. Two was the max that could comfortably stay in the room.

"How are you doing? It's good news about Carson. Twelve hours," Trent said. I hadn't noticed him walk up.

I gestured to the seat to my right. "It is good news. Each hour that passes without any complications is a good thing."

A soft snore left Francesca as I finger combed through her hair. Trent glanced around the room before he settled into the seat. He was in a worn T-shirt and jeans. All of the security detail were dressed in casual wear today. It helped them to blend in.

"You're a good friend, Willow. Marie told me what you

did."

Emotionally, it had been tough yelling at Carson to fight. Pure adrenaline and instinct had driven me to do it. I hadn't cared what people thought. All I wanted was for Carson to be here. He's my best friend. I can't lose him. We need him.

"I had a sister once. We were close like you and Carson."

Once. Had. These were more clues to Trent's tragic past. Trent always revealed little insights of his past at the most unexpected times. While I was in the hospital he had told me about growing up in the impoverished parts of Ireland. After his parents died, he was adopted by a couple in the States within a year. Shortly after, his adoptive mother died from cancer and his adoptive father killed himself.

Trent had no one. And I wanted to bring him into our family.

There had been no mention of a sister. "Was this in Ireland or the States?"

He looked away focusing on the same wall I had been when he walked up. "States. She wasn't my biological sister. After Irene died from cancer and Arlo killed himself, Lily and I were inseparable. Irene and Arlo were my adoptive parents."

Lily.

Were.

I hated the past tense.

I placed my hand on top of his. "You don't have to talk about it."

"I know." Again, he focused on the wall and I remained quiet. Trent liked to go at his own pace. "Lily's grandparents took us in. They were kind, but older. Raising two teenagers was hard, but they pushed through. Then Nana got sick. It was ovarian cancer like Irene. It was devastating to watch her fade away each day."

Trent scrubbed a hand down his face while his haunted eyes glanced my way. "The day after Nana died, Lily came up to me and gave me the sweetest hug. She told me she loved me and that I was the best brother a girl could ask for. We ate some sandwiches I'd made. She seemed okay. Sad, but okay."

I closed my eyes bracing myself for the next part of the story. The part that made their relationship past tense. "Lily gave me another hug and a kiss on the cheek. Said she was going to rest upstairs. I didn't think twice about it. The last couple of days had been exhausting with Nana's burial and taking care of Papa. I fell asleep, too. When I went to check on her, she wasn't in her room. I knew something was wrong when I read the note on her bed. It said, 'I can't take the hurt anymore.' Frantically, I searched for her. I found her in the bathtub. She'd slit her wrists. I couldn't find a pulse, and she'd been dead awhile."

"For what it's worth, I'm sorry." The story gripped my heart. It slew me to hear about such a strong man nearly brought down by the memories of his past.

"I wish I had fought for her like you did Carson."

"Trent."

He stared forward, not looking at me.

"Trent."

Finally, he focused on me.

"You did fight for Lily. You stayed by her side and loved her. She needed help."

"I should have seen it."

"You were only a child yourself."

He cleared his throat. "Thanks for listening. I shouldn't have put that on you." Share time was over. The memories were locked away somewhere deep.

I shifted slightly. "I'm glad you did. Our past allows us

the foresight to know how to help people when they're barely hanging on. While I was in the hospital you came in to sit when everyone was gone. You gave me hope with your positive attitude and determination. You're strong, Trent. It's admirable."

Trent furrowed his brow and fought to remain in control of his emotions.

Gabe walked up and took in the scene.

Trent stood. "You're a lucky man, Gabe."

"That I am."

Trent grabbed his phone and looked at the caller ID of an incoming call. He flexed his jaw. "It's the lab. Let me take this somewhere private. I'll be back."

My eyes widened. *Please let it be a match to Gabe's DNA.* It felt terrible wishing someone was dead.

Marie and Bennett had just walked in after being with Carson and the doctor and stopped beside Gabe who watched Trent's retreating back. I knew Gabe wanted to follow Trent. Anytime something came up about Alex, Gabe's demeanor hardened.

Marie gave Francesca a concerned look. "It's time for us to go back for the evening. How is she?"

"Tired. She fell asleep about thirty minutes ago, but wanted me to wake her up when it was time go back in for the evening."

In sleep, Francesca's worry lines were gone. Hopefully being near Carson through the night helped. I knew it would have helped me if it was Gabe.

Gently, I nudged Francesca. "Hey, sweetie. It's time you go back to Carson's room for the evening."

Popping up, she glanced to Marie. On a yawn she asked, "Any changes? Is he still okay?"

"Yes, darling, he's doing fantastic. Better than the doctor had anticipated."

Thank goodness.

Francesca stood anxious to see for herself. "That's so good. Let's head back there."

Exchanging hugs with everyone, I said to Marie, "Please tell Carson I miss him and I'll be back tomorrow."

"We will. Night guys."

They disappeared from the waiting room. "And then there were two."

I leaned into Gabe and echoed. "And then there were two."

He wrapped his hands around me, bringing me closer to him. It felt good to lean on someone and just exist for a few stolen moments. The last rays of light were disappearing beyond the horizon through the window. We turned when we heard the footsteps behind us.

Trent took a deep breath. "The finger wasn't Alex's."

Chapter Ten

W hile we drove from the hospital to the hotel, I stared into the night, feeling numb.

The finger wasn't Alex's.

Whose finger was it? How had the fingerprint matched the one from the theft of the Botticelli? When was this ever going to end? It seemed like never.

We had made a tremendous step forward with Carson only to be shoved back again with the test results.

Why? Why? Why? I wanted to scream. But instead, I sat in the back of the car hardly moving or speaking. Gabe sat beside me with his fingers trailing up and down my arm. Briefly he'd pause on my wrist. He was taking my pulse.

We pulled up to the hotel. I barely noticed the opulence because of the haze I felt.

Of course, there was still a chance that Alex was dead. But, I doubted it. The coroner's report stated the finger was missing on Alex's charred remains, which was why I hadn't worried so much about the results.

Trent had explained that originally the lab thought it was Alex's, but they found traces of someone else's blood. Digging deeper, Alex's blood had been transfused into the finger. It was complicated and the lab had nearly missed it. That was why there had been a delay in the initial findings. It was so messed up.

Someone... probably Alex... put an immeasurable amount of work into this. Or someone had Alex and wanted us to think he was dead.

Why?

I looked at Gabe. He was not the same as the man I'd married. There was no doubt in my mind. For the last six months Alex hadn't been able to hide the evil lurking beneath the surface. He got off on scaring and fighting with me. While Gabe pretended to be Tack, and even now, his only concern had been me.

Why put all the effort into letting us think it was Alex when we already had a body that matched Gabe's dental records? Were the partials used because that was the only part of Alex that matched Gabe? Alex had to pull his teeth from his mouth and put them in this man's. Or someone pulled them. I shuddered at the thought.

The elevator ride to our floor was quiet. The tension between Gabe and Trent was palpable and had been since the hospital. While Bennett had said good-night to me, they'd stepped away for a brief conversation.

Gabe unlocked the hotel room door and it clicked open. Mercifully, we were back to my home away from home.

"Night, Trent."

"Night, Willow."

Before Trent closed the door, he said, "I think it should be Willow's choice."

My eyes darted between the two men as fury rolled over Gabe. "Trent, I'm warning you. Don't."

The darkness in Gabe's voice wasn't something to mess with, but Trent stood his ground. "I'm here to protect Willow. Finding out the truth protects her."

Without another word, Trent turned and left. Both men radiated irritation. "What was that about?"

Gabe clenched and unclenched his fists several times as he in his reaction. He was giving nothing away. "Willow, I don't want to go there. I need to think some things through."

Now, I was getting irritated. This morning we had bridged the chasm between us. "Gabe… you're the one constant I have right now. Don't make me second-guess you. This morning you said our relationship was not about hiding things from each other. Let's not lose the ground we've fought so hard to gain."

He was silent as he stared into my eyes. The fact that he was debating on telling me something Trent believed I had a right to now had me boiling.

Enough!

If he wanted distance, I'd give it to him. Abruptly, I took my phone out to dial Trent.

"Willow?"

"Is there another room I can stay in?"

If Gabe was able to get more agitated, he managed to do it. He plucked the phone from my hand. "Willow won't need another room."

He clicked off the phone.

"You cannot—"

He took a step forward and I stood my ground. "No, you cannot, Willow. There is a fucking lunatic on the loose and you are not changing rooms because of some temper tantrum. I was going to tell you what Trent referenced, but I just needed to think it through."

There was a knock at the door.

I went to the door as Gabe called my name. I opened it to Trent.

"Everything okay?"

The last thing I wanted was to leave during our argument since Gabe and I were in the process of working through it. Looking over my shoulder, Gabe appeared furious but remained silent.

"Yes. Everything's fine. I'll call if I still need the room."

I shut the door and stormed passed Gabe to my bedroom.

"You're not staying somewhere else."

I got in his face. "I don't need you censoring what I hear. It's not your place. I'm not your wife, Gabe."

Wife. I said wife. Oh shit. I hadn't meant to throw that out there like that. We weren't ready. The heat of the moment had me word vomiting again.

He turned and combed his fingers through his hair. "For fuck's sake." Pacing five agitated steps, he turned and faced me. His eyes were blazing. "You and I both know I would marry you in a heartbeat if I thought you were ready for that next step."

My fingers knotted nervously with each other. "I know. I don't know why I said that."

"What do you want from me, Willow?"

"Honesty," I said.

He took a step.

"Loyalty."

He took another step.

"Love."

He closed the gap with his last step bringing him within

inches touching me. The heat from his body penetrated mine. I finished with one thing I wanted most. "To be yours."

"I have been honest except for misleading you with Tack." He cradled my face. "There is no one I am more loyal to, Willow. No one. You're it for me." His head dipped down. "I love you so much it hurts." He pressed his lips against mine and I leaned into him. "You are mine. No one else's. Ever. Only mine."

He kissed me again and I deepened it, wanting—no, needing— more. He lifted me off the floor, and I wrapped my legs around his waist. I was in Gabe's arms. We were each other's forever. His tongue commanded my mouth as I gave myself to him. My back found the bed and I tightened my grip on him. His desire pressed against my core and I moaned at the slightest bit of friction.

And then he was gone. "Six more fucking days."

I threw my hand over my eyes. "I want a second opinion. For real. I hate this."

Gabe's jaw was clinched tight when I reopened my eyes. "I don't care if the world is coming to an end, six days from now nothing is keeping me from you. Nothing."

A tremble resonated through me. "It'd better not."

Gabe stood across the room and I patted the bed. "I won't bite. Promise."

Having him near me and enduring the sweet torture was better than being kept from his touch. Gabe was still tense as he lay beside me. I molded to his side, and he wrapped his arm around me.

"Hell, you make me lose my mind, Willow."

"We could do something for you?" His head reared back like I was crazy. "There's no reason for you to suffer, too."

In a fluid movement I was flipped on my back and his

face came within inches of mine. He tasted me, then nipped my lip. "When we come, we come together."

The intensity was off the charts as Gabe held me in my place.

"But—"

"No but. Together."

"Together."

He reversed our positions. We still hadn't discussed Trent's comment. I wasn't going to let it go, but for now I wanted to be in Gabe's arms.

Without any prompting, Gabe shared. "I was going to talk to you tonight about what Trent was hinting at. I thought it would be best after you rested for a bit. It's been a long damn day. And you're still dealing with the DNA news. I get you're strong, Willow, but I have to protect you at the same time."

I sat up and looked at Gabe who put his arm behind his head. His muscles caused the shirt to fit snuggly across his biceps. I played with my fingers. "Do you think Alex is alive?"

"Yes."

I froze and my blood went cold. Hearing someone else confirm my thoughts made what we were dealing with monumentally worse.

"I think Alex wanted me to think he was dead. To him, that will make everyone more vulnerable with him being able to imitate my movements. I'm already working with Trent on how his men can identify me. I'm sure he accessed my dental records and used only the matching teeth. Sometimes twins have identical teeth, too. Alex figured I would have the finger tested and he infused his blood. I don't know if he or Jack De Luca sent you the note in Italy. Hell, they might be working together. Or Alex may be setting De Luca up. From what we can tell, none of De Luca's men have followed you or showed any interest."

"Then why send the finger? Why would Alex risk blowing his cover?"

Gabe dragged a hand down his face. "He's so fucked in the head, I can't even begin to imagine what's going on. I think he was sending the note to draw me out. I was untraceable. Alex has no idea about the skills I've acquired since being on a black ops team. I can blend anywhere. He needed me vulnerable. And through you he drew me out."

It was true. With Gabe being Tack and the old man, he had blended better than I'd imagined, changing his accent.

My mouth was dry. "What if he slips back in? What if I think he's you? I need something to identify you. Alex had Gabe's tattoo. Somehow, he'd known. I can't go back there. I don't want our babies near him." I stopped as my voice became thick.

Alex was a terrible man. I never wanted to be near him again. And now he was alive and playing with our lives like dolls. With all that we had against us, I was terrified someone would slip through the security team. Fear seeped in as all the ramifications hit me. No wonder he had refused to let me go anywhere. Gabe was not letting me out of his sight.

In a fluid motion, Gabe knelt in front of me, grabbed my hips, and pulled me closer to him. I wrapped my legs around him.

"He won't get near you. Alex was only able to sell his deception because I hadn't told you I was a twin. He's a sick bastard."

"He was sick."

"Trent said the finger print was also from the crime scene of the Botticelli theft. If it's not Alex's, whose is it?"

Gabe closed his eyes before opening them. "Either Alex

wasn't there during the theft and orchestrated it or this person was a third accomplice. Smudges are hard to isolate if you don't have an example. If Alex killed this guy, he might have placed the papers in your house on purpose. I don't know."

I closed my eyes. Living with Alex had been a nightmare from beginning to end. Every day had been misery. When Alex died, I had truly mourned Gabe.

I nuzzled into the crook of his neck. "What do we do now?"

"We have two options. Wait for him to make his move or force him to make his move."

I wanted it over. This was probably what Trent was referencing. Gabe had needed his time to work out how to tell me. "How do we force him to make his move?"

"Go after the only two things Alex holds dear."

My hand went to my stomach as I leaned back, only putting a little space between us. "His child."

"Yes... and our mother."

I remembered the picture Mildred gave me in a stack of papers she found. I had found it while Carson and I had been at Martha's Vineyard, which led to my night of drinking. I hadn't known for sure I was pregnant then but would forever regret getting so drunk. In the picture, Alex looked like he genuinely loved his son as he held him. But still... this was a *child* we were discussing.

"Gabe, I can't bring an innocent child into this. We can't lower ourselves because of Alex."

"Sweetheart, I would never hurt a child. I want to emotionally hit Alex. It will throw him off guard. Once, I stood up to Mom. I had her pinned against the wall the last time she beat me. Alex lost it. Completely lost it and crumbled. All rational thought left him. Alex is watching us. I know it. And he will know we visited his kid."

Gabe put his hand over my stomach. "I would never put you in danger."

But we were already in danger. I knew this. Gabe knew this. Trent, too. It was why Trent had pushed Gabe to tell me sooner rather than later. "I know you wouldn't. I'm sure that's why you want to think through Trent's suggestion. But, Gabe, I want out of this nightmare. If we did see Alex Junior, what would your brother do?"

"I think he'll go to my mom. We haven't put any men on Mom's house yet. If we do and Alex sees we've caught on, he might go deeper. It's going to piss them off when I turn this game around on them." If Gabe's mother was as attached to Alex as it sounded, she was not going to like us messing with her favorite son.

"What can I do?"

The wrinkles came back full force. "I'm trying to think of an alternative. That's why I wanted to wait so that you're not involved."

"What does Trent want me to do?" My mind was trying to think of what I would be able to do.

"Offer to teach art lessons at Apple Blossom. It'll give you one-on-one time with his kid."

To Trent's credit, it was a brilliant idea. It would be easy to check my credentials. Technically, my marriage to Alex was a fraud and there wasn't any record. I imagined that whoever married us in Vegas probably wasn't a true officiant but part of this elaborate scheme. I pushed the trepidation aside and found the courage to move forward.

"Let's set it up. The sooner the better."

Chapter Eleven

It felt good to head to my house around lunch. This morning I had visited Dr. Jamiston. He echoed everything Dr. Byrum had stated. No sex for five more days to be safe. The risk had been mitigated, but due to continued distress, they wanted to play it safe rather than sorry. It was going to be torture. Luckily, I had been able to keep all my thoughts to myself.

This morning we saw the heartbeats again. It was something I would never tire of. All of my blood work came back normal. In a week, I would be cleared as long as I kept my activities within reason, rested, and nothing concerning happened. I felt completely fine.

A few houses sporadically stood on the beach like small castles commanding their kingdom. My house was toward the end.

At least my body was healing nicely and the yellow bruises had faded a little more. Each day was a step forward even if it felt the opposite.

Carson was still stable. After the doctor visit, we had stopped by. No change was a good thing at this point. It been over twenty-four hours since life support had been removed. The doctors were optimistic that he would wake up any day now.

Gabe had asked if I wanted to come home while the doctors ran some additional tests on Carson. Seeing Carson was going have a busy day of tests, I said yes.

Plus, I needed to come home. Being there helped ground me.

I thought back to last night Trent came to the room after the discussion.

* * *

Trent opened the door and walked into the room. There was still some tension between the two men.

I took a seat at the table. "Gabe told me about your idea regarding Apple Blossom. I think it makes sense. What do we do next?"

Trent sat with me. "You should call to see if you can come as a guest teacher. Quite frequently they have guests as part of their curriculum. I've already had you and myself cleared with the standard school background checks. Under the premise of me being your assistant, I got the ball rolling. I've started the clearing process for Gabe, too. I expect to get the all clear any day."

"Wait. When did you start this?"

Scrubbing a hand down his face, Trent looked exhausted. "I started this as a contingency plan the day of your art show in case we needed to explore that option with Harley being a suspect. Apple Blossom was one of the few leads we had. I planned to discuss it, but with the accident I hadn't thought about it. I'm sorry. I should have told you sooner."

"I'm glad you had the foresight to be prepared for this possibility." Soon, I would be meeting Alex's son.

Gabe sat stiffly beside me as we turned right onto a road only five minutes from home. I placed my hand on his knee. "It's going to be okay."

"I haven't seen Mildred or Chris since before I was deployed. They spent the last six months thinking I was a terrible person."

I squeezed his knee and waited for him to look at me. Sometimes I forgot what Gabe was going through. To have someone usurp your life and turn it upside down had to be... I wasn't sure there were words to describe it. The one thing I loved about my adopted family is they loved without limits.

"They'll understand. All they want is for me to be happy."

"That's all I want." His gaze moved back to the road as we approached the turn to my house.

I leaned over and gave him a light kiss while placing my hand against his scruff. "I like it when you don't shave every day."

He smiled against my lips. "Thanks, sweetheart."

Since yesterday, I wanted to be near Gabe more than ever. Last night, he'd slept on the couch again. I had tossed and turned for hours on end, wanting him to be there with me.

"Did you sleep okay?"

I shrugged. "Off and on. Lots on my mind."

He pressed his lips to the top of my head. "We'll make it

an early night if that sounds good."

"It does." We weren't staying the night. There were still a few minor tweaks to security needed.

The familiar Tuscan-styled house in the Hamptons came into view with the expansive lawn. I still pictured Dad on the front porch waiting for me to come home. It was something I looked forward to—knowing how much he loved having me here. A small pang hit me, but it was lessened having Gabe with me. For the first time since Dad died, the loneliness wasn't trying to consume me.

I took a deep breath as I saw the ocean crashing onto the shore behind the house. It was magnificent. I was ready to paint again. The hotel wasn't a good place. I needed my space to create the images that loomed beneath the surface. The car parked at the front door.

Chris and Mildred came out, speaking over each other. "It's so good to have you home, Willow. We missed you so much."

My voice was bubbly. "It's good to be home."

Simultaneously, I was engulfed in a hug. It wasn't until Chris stepped back that Mildred released me. His eyes darted to Gabe but then came back to me. His smile only slipped for a second while his gray hair rustled in the light breeze.

From Chris's text earlier today, I knew Chris was techni-cally off today, but came to see me. It was touching beyond measure.

Mildred took me by the shoulders. "You look good." Her eyes glanced back to Gabe nervously. "Are you good?"

"I'm good. I have him back."

Tears formed in her eyes. Bennett had told Mildred and Chris about Gabe prior to visiting Carson in the hospital. In all the pandemonium, I hadn't thought about it. But now, I knew I should have been the one. They had been affected by Alex's hatefulness.

Mildred was turning when I caught her by the arm and made eye contact with Chris. "I'm sorry I wasn't the one to tell you guys about Gabe. You deserved to know."

She brushed some escaped red tendrils out of her face. "Oh nonsense, sweetheart. You've had enough to worry with. I was relieved we hadn't misjudged Gabe in the beginning." She looked to Gabe. "The resemblance is uncanny."

She reached out her hand and Gabe took it. "Take care of our Willow."

"I have every intention of doing that."

Smiling back at me, she said, "You did good with this one."

"I think so, too."

I glanced at Gabe. It was obvious he was relieved. Coming home felt more right than it had in a long time because of the man with me. So much had changed since I had been here last. Gabe was alive, I was pregnant with twins, and Alex was alive.

Inside I felt different in some way, but the house welcomed me regardless. When we had to leave, it would be too soon.

"I hope this young man has been feeding you good. I made lasagna for lunch."

Lasagna was my favorite. "It's so good to be home."

Chris gave me one last hug. "I hate to run, but my grand-daughter has a recital."

"Tell her I said congratulations. Hopefully she can come to the house and show me sometime."

Chris beamed. "I will. She'll love it." Hesitantly, he put his hand out for Gabe who took it firmly. "Take care of her.

She's like a daughter to me."

"I promise, sir. I hate what my brother did. I had no idea he was still alive."

"I know, son."

From the welcoming smiles on their faces everything would be okay.

———— ◆——————◆——————◆ ————

In the bedroom, down the hall from mine, I stood surveying the room. Currently, it was a guest room. Dad's paintings of the willow tree were leaning against the wall. They used to hang above my crib after I was born. The tree was colorful as the weeping willows incorporated all the colors. As a child, it was the first thing I saw in the morning when I woke up and the last thing before I fell asleep.

I checked the time. We were going to have to leave here shortly and I wasn't ready to go. Lunch had taken longer than expected as I filled Mildred in on Carson. For now, I wasn't telling her or Chris about the pregnancy. The fewer who knew, the better.

Mildred had left for the day to catch up with her sister, who was staying the night. Security was definitely tighter, but necessary. I had seen men circulating a few times while we ate lunch.

This morning on the way to the doctor I called Apple Blossom to inquire about volunteering art lessons for a day. The director had been hoping I would call to schedule something since she'd received the okay on my background checks. She loved my assistant "Joe."

Gabe came up behind me and kissed me on the neck, only teasing my already frustrated libido. I leaned back into him. "Is this where you want the babies' room?"

"It is."

I pointed to the corner. "I thought I could paint a mural over there for a play area. Something cute." Feeling a new wave of energy, I stepped from Gabe's arms and walked across the room. "And over here, I could paint something else that went along with reading. A rocking chair would be nice. Something comfortable." I walked across the room to the windows and waved my hands. "This would make a good place for the changing area. I know eventually the kids will want their own rooms. But I think it'll be easier to keep them in the same room for now." I pointed to the wall with the bed. "I figured two cribs could go over here. I wanted to put the paintings Dad did for me as a kid between their beds." I stopped when I realized Gabe hadn't said a word.

He was watching me with a huge grin on his face.

"What? Why are you staring at me?"

"Because right here. Right now. I have everything I ever wanted. You're going to be a wonderful mother. Thank you for having my babies."

My heart melted. "Our children are lucky to have a dad like you. They're going to be loved."

"Always." Gabe wrapped his arms around my middle and I leaned back. Things were good between us.

In a little less than eight months, this room would be filled with love and screaming babies. I wondered if Mom and Dad had planned my baby room similarly. I chuckled to myself. Dad probably had. Mom was more laid-back. Dad had always been the worrier. He had fretted for days, wondering if Mom would agree to marry him. Thinking of them reminded me of something he knew as I broke free of Gabe's embrace.

"How did you know about Dad and me going to the spot

every year where he proposed to Mom?"

When Gabe had been Tack, he had initially received my trust because he knew about my tradition with Dad. No one else knew. No one. Every year, we went to the spot behind our estate in Italy where Dad proposed to Mom. We laid flowers and stayed there for hours sharing memories. It was painful but healing at the same time. Since I lost Mom when I was younger, it helped cement those memories firmly in my mind.

"I came here before I left to go back to base."

He had? Dad never mentioned anything. My eyes darted back and forth.

Gabe walked to me. "I came here to declare my intentions to your dad. I wanted him to know how madly in love I was with you. It was important to me for him to know since I was leaving for an undetermined amount of time. I imagined how I would feel if it had been my daughter."

If there was ever a moment for me to fall more in love with Gabe, this was it. "Wh-when did you do this?"

"The day I took you to the park to carve our initials in the tree. I came by here first thing in the morning instead of going on my run while you slept. Your dad took me down to the ocean and we drank espresso. I was a nervous fucking wreck. Then he pumped more caffeine into me. It's amazing I kept it together."

I chuckled. Dad always started deep conversations with espresso. "That sounds like Dad."

"It was a tough conversation. Alfonso began by saying you had a pure love. There were no hidden agendas to your love. It was a gift to have a woman like that. He asked me why I thought I deserved you over anyone else."

Wow. What had he said?

Gabe moved me to a chair and knelt before me. My voice

caught in my throat. "I told your dad I didn't deserve you." I started to protest, but he held up his hand. "It's true, sweetheart. I don't deserve you. But, I told him I would never stop loving you and proving I did. I told him I would protect you until my dying breath."

Tears slipped free. "You do deserve me, Gabe. We deserve each other. Love isn't who is better. It makes us better and fuses us together."

"It does."

His hands grabbed mine. "I told your dad that I planned on making you my wife when you were ready and that I wasn't going to rush you. I swore to him I would protect you always."

That was the promise Tack spoke of when we talked. His words were beautiful. I was speechless. He caressed the side of my face.

"Alfonso then told me of your tradition. I asked him why he told me. All I got in response was a reference to the ocean. He said, 'the tide recedes and comes back again every day regardless of the weather. Love should be like the tide and always return even when things are difficult.'"

It was Dad's way of telling me he approved of Gabe. I threw my arms around him and knocked us to the floor. Gabe protected me so I was barely jostled. "I meant what I said earlier. My entire world is in this room. But it will be complete when you agree to be my wife."

I wanted nothing more than to be his. Forever. Fingers came to my lips. "I'm going to give you a proposal you deserve, but I don't want you to wonder what my intentions are."

"Gabe, I love you."

"You're my life, sweetheart."

Chapter Twelve

The cleaning smell was strong as I entered the waiting room. I had crossed paths with the janitor near the door. It was some sort of bleach with pine lemon smell. It was a welcome smell over burnt coffee.

Marissa and Rosie were talking to Marie in the waiting room. Only approved family were allowed in Carson's room. It seemed like Marie was filling in my friends.

For a moment I froze, wondering how I would explain everything. They knew I was married to Alex. Overall, the marriage had been kept low key due to Alex's supposed undercover cop job. He'd only met them once, maybe twice, in person. What a fool I had been. All lies.

At Martha's Vineyard I'd reconnected with my friends. They welcomed me back with open arms. In a little over five months, Marissa would marry her longtime boyfriend, Clay.

Rosie was in a league of her own. For years she had obsessed over Carson, or whoever was unattached in our circle of friends. I was still unable to get the image out of my head of

Rosie in teal feathered nightie when she wanted to seduce Carson at Martha's Vineyard. The horror of the visual lingered. But, that same weekend, Rosie had hooked up with Mitchell. Things were going strong between them.

Their eyes bugged out when they saw the man walking behind me.

"He's alive?" Marissa's eyes grew even wider. "I mean... I... I thought he was killed." She covered her mouth with her hand as she muttered, "Oh shit. I need to shut up now."

Rosie stood there frozen, too.

"Um..." *Great, Willow. Perfect answer.* I had no explanation. What was I allowed to say? They stared at me, waiting for a reason why my dead husband was alive.

Gabe gave my waist a squeeze just before he said, "Hey, Marissa. Hello, Rosie. It's been a while. Let's talk in a side room."

Robotically, they turned to me and I nodded. Gabe led us into a small office our security team had used to make phone calls. One of the security men left after Gabe gave him a nod. Honestly, I tried to keep track of their names, but it was difficult.

Marissa closed the door but kept a hand on the doorknob with Rosie holding her arm, ready to flee. The air was thick with discord.

Beside me, Gabe remained calm and at ease with a gentile smile. A hand went into his pocket and the girls relaxed minutely with his demeanor. "I'm not Alex, I'm Gabe. My twin brother impersonated me while I was deployed. He was an undercover cop and had used Willow without her knowledge to create a cover life."

I thought back to the conversations with them. I hadn't told them Alex had lied about being an undercover cop.

That was an interesting take on what happened and completely doable. Why not use the lie Alex had created to keep people in the dark about the black truth?

Marissa's chocolate eyes darted to me. I confirmed Gabe's statement. "It's true. This is the man I fell in love with. Not the man who tricked me into marrying him."

"Fuck a duck." Marissa's mouth still hung open on her last word.

"Yes, basically," Rosie concluded and patted her red sleek bob and straightened her spine. She cocked her head to the side. It was odd, but Rosie was like that. It was as if she were trying to work something out in her head but staring rather uncomfortably. Gabe had witnessed her ass-grabbing sessions with Carson once when we met at a club.

Stepping forward, Marissa switched into concern mode as her brows drew together. "Are you safe? Did they find the killer? Do they think the accident is connected?"

I was not prepared for all this. Mentally, I took a deep breath and then answered, "So far nothing else has been found. We're taking precautions just in case."

Rosie's look changed from skepticism to leery as she eyed Gabe. "You're not him?"

"No, I'm not. Because Alex was an undercover cop, I didn't share it with people. Willow and I had dated for such a short period of time, I hadn't disclosed it to her either."

Wow, Gabe had obviously thought ahead for this sort of scenario. Of course he had with him being some black ops man.

They relaxed a little. Marissa continued her inquisition. "Marie mentioned you were staying at the Whitmore. Do you think him being undercover is why someone is after you? Is that why you're staying at the hotel?"

Gabe leaned against the desk more at ease, which caused Marissa and Rosie to relax, too. It was amazing how he was able to control the atmosphere with body language.

"We're closer to Carson this way. With the accident, it's best if we keep travel to a minimum for her to keep healing." Gabe gave them part of the truth. If only they knew Alex lived.

"I hope to go home in the next day or so. With any luck, Carson will be awake by then. His vitals continue to improve," I added.

Rosie gave me a sweet smile. "We heard. That is wonderful news. Francesca must be ecstatic."

"She is. Extremely. She's waiting to hear the baby's heartbeat with Carson."

"That is special." Rosie glanced at her watch.

I was anxious to get out of this situation too.

Marissa gave me a hug. "I know you're probably ready to see Carson. Let us know if you need anything. Can we bring you dinner?"

"No, we'll order in. I'm going to take Francesca back with me for a bit so she can shower and maybe eat. Thank you, though." The hospital had accommodations, but she needed to take a break away from here.

"Of course. We're here for you. Everyone is thinking of you guys."

"Thanks, Marissa."

We exchanged good-byes, and they walked from the room.

I leaned against the wall. "I was not prepared for that. Thank goodness you were."

Gabe straightened and came to me. "It was on the list to go over our story to make sure you agreed. Looks like it's out now. I was hoping we would have time to change anything you didn't like."

"It's a good cover. Sticks to the truth they know." I closed my eyes. "I hate lying." Then something occurred to me. "Gabe, I don't want them to think our children are Alex's. I can't... I won't..."

He kissed me, instantly soothing my worry. "Don't worry. With twins we'll have the ability to manipulate the dates a little. We'll figure it out."

"You already thought of that."

"Willow, there is no chance I am going to allow there to be a question about whose children are growing inside you. They're mine. You're mine. No questions."

"No questions." I loved it when Gabe was possessive. He tried to let me have my freedoms, but he also made sure everyone knew I was his.

"Let's go see Carson." We walked out the door. The warmth of Gabe's hand pressed against my back. "I wanted to let you know that if he wakes up while we are here, I'm going to slip from the room until he's told."

That made sense since Carson had no idea about Gabe. If I had woken up to Gabe in my room, it wouldn't have been good. Gabe was thorough.

One hurdle down. Only a million to go.

Chapter Thirteen

This morning we had gone to the hospital to bring Francesca back. Last night she had decided to stay. Today, she needed a change of scenery if only for a few hours while Carson underwent testing. I understood it made her anxious to leave Carson for very long. No doubt I would feel the same way.

Currently, we were in her room and had ordered room service for lunch. Hopefully, a shower and meal rejuvenated her.

This morning there was no change in Carson's responsiveness, but the doctors were optimistic.

The room was similar to mine except a little larger. The shower went off as the door to the room opened. Gabe wheeled in our room service cart. "This arrived. I told Andre I would bring it down to you guys. How is she?"

My stomach growled as I smelled the food. "Tired and on edge though she's better now that Carson is off life support."

Gabe's phone buzzed. "It's Bennett. Let me take this."

"Okay."

I took the covers off the food. It was enough to feed an army. When we ordered, I think Francesca and I got carried away as we handed the phone to each other and talked to the waiter.

I was about to nab one of the nachos when Francesca called, "Hey, Willow, would you mind coming in here?"

"Sure." Food would have to wait. I walked into the room as Francesca wound her semi-wet brown hair into a French twist.

"I have something for you." There was a small present on the bed with a pink and blue bow. "Open it."

I touched the ribbon, moved by the gesture, and tore into it. It was a scrapbook that looked like a canvas with the words *How My Mom Came To Be* written in paint strokes. I brushed my hands across it. "This is amazing."

"Look inside."

There was an inscription on the cover page.

> *I wanted you to know how special your mom has always been. Francesca*

I turned the page. The picture was of Mom holding me the day I was born.

Tears pooled as my chest tightened. I flipped the page. In the top right corner was a picture of Carson and me in the tomato bath from when we had decided to wrangle skunks. Opposite was a picture of us looking dejected in the front of the exterminator truck after we decided to start an ant farm.

Mom finds out animals will not be the career for her.

The next page was a picture of me at my most recent art gallery event. I was laughing at something. It was candid. I ran my fingers over the picture; it was hard to believe that was me.

Mom bringing love and laughter to those around her.

The gift was breathtakingly beautiful. "Thank you. This is one of the most special things I have ever received. When did you do this?"

Francesca came to sit beside me. "I've had a lot of free time. Marie helped me. I made one for Carson, too. The bond you two share is so special." She blinked back the tears and mine puddled even more. "You have been there for me in a way I never expected. You love with your whole heart, Willow. It's unbelievable. You have had so much to deal with, but you've been my rock. When I wanted to give up, I saw your strength and perseverance. I wanted to capture those emotions in a book for your baby."

"Thank you. I will treasure this forever." We hugged.

Gabe called from the front. "Willow. Francesca. Get your things together. Bennett believes Carson is about to wake up. During testing he moved a little bit."

Excitement filled me as I put Francesca at arm's length. "He's coming back to you."

Francesca's face lit up like the day I saw her for the first time with Carson. "I can't wait to have him in my arms."

Me, either. Butterflies danced in my stomach as I watched Francesca race to put her shoes on. In less than a minute we were headed to the door when Trent walked into the suite. "Andre is waiting out front to drive you guys back."

There was all of this wasted food. "Trent, Francesca and I ordered this. Please see if your men want any of it."

"I will."

Not a moment to spare, we hurried down the hall at almost a jog. *Thank you, Carson. Thank you for fighting.* The ride down the elevator took forever.

Andre stood outside the driver's door. "Good afternoon, ladies."

"Afternoon, Andre."

Gabe sat in the front seat next to Andre wile Francesca sat next to me. She grabbed my hand. "I hope today is the day."

"Me, too."

It had been a long two weeks. I was on pins and needles waiting to have Carson back with us. At the hospital we were out of the car before Andre put it in park. At the door, a security team member greeted us to escort us upstairs. Gabe was close behind.

There were a couple of times this last week when I wondered if we would be having a moment like this. We were almost at a jog when we exited the elevator on Carson's floor. A nurse was checking Carson's vitals. When we stepped around her, I saw his beautiful blue irises staring back at me.

I gasped as I covered my mouth, choking an ecstatic sob. I had missed this face being full of life. Francesca was at his side in an instance as I stayed rooted in place giving them their moment. She was sobbing. Carson's hand came up and touched the back of her head. The movement weak and shaky. The tubes had been removed after the respiratory doctor and anesthesiologist gave the clear. He was stronger than I would have thought.

"Shh… it's okay, baby. It's okay," Carson said in a voice hoarse from being intubated for two weeks.

Reaching back for Gabe, he wasn't there. Frantically, I turned around and then saw him standing in the doorway. Carson. He had no idea.

Bennett came up to me. "He came to right after we called. We told him about Gabe. The cliff note's version at least. I figured when you two talk you could give him the full one. He knows you and the baby are okay."

"Thanks, Bennett." I hugged him. "We have him back."

"Yes we do, Willow. Yes we do."

I walked to the end of the bed and touched Carson's covered foot. He gave me his beautiful smile. Never again would I take that smile for granted.

"You gave us quite the scare." My voice was thick.

Carson looked me over. "You sure you're okay?" He sounded tired.

"Promise. We'll catch up in a bit."

His eyes squinted and I reached for the light switch dial on the side of the bed. "The light hurts the first day. You'll adjust."

For a second, Carson closed his eyes then reopened them to focus on me. "I kept hearing you tell me to fight and yelling at me like the time I competed in that triathlon."

"It's my job to be your pain in the ass." Carson had busted his leg and refused to quit the race. When we saw him from the distance, I screamed the entire way, telling him to fight.

"Yes it is." Carson looked around. "Is Gabe here?"

"He is. We weren't aware you knew, so he stayed in the hall. Gabe thought it would be a good idea for us to tell you first." I was rambling, a little worried what Carson might think.

Confidently, Gabe came to my side and slid his arm around my waist. "It's good to see you awake, Carson."

"Well, fuck me. It's uncanny."

Not sure how to take his words, I froze as Carson scrutinized Gabe, who remained silent.

"Welcome back, Gabe. I'm glad I wasn't wrong about you initially."

"Me, too."

Carson coughed and Francesca fussed over him.

Marie stepped in. "It's the tube he had in his throat. Doctor said it was normal."

Taking a sip from the sponge Francesca put in front of his mouth, Carson closed his eyes. "I'm going to rest for just a second."

Squeezing his foot again, I said, "Rest up. We'll be here when you wake up." I remembered how exhausting those first few days were when I came around, I slept more than anything.

Drifting off, Carson looked peaceful. I kept checking the monitors to make sure they were still tracking his heart rate.

"What did the doctor say?" I asked Bennett.

"Things look good. Responses are normal. Carson remembered it all. His first words were asking about the baby, Francesca, and you. Until you got here, we were going to leave the part about Gabe out. Somehow he knew we were holding back. So we told him. I'm sorry. I know it wasn't our place."

I held my hand up. "Bennett. It's fine. I'm glad he knows. Carson knows if you knew about Gabe then I was fine. The last thing he needs is additional stress."

Bennett grabbed my shoulders. "I have my boy back. We have him back!"

"Yes, we do!" The mood was lighter. With Carson back, things felt normal as if the dark looming ahead wasn't as formidable.

Gabe placed his hand on my shoulder. "I'm going to take Willow to the cafeteria to get some food. They were about to eat when we got the call. Do you want me to get Francesca anything?"

Bennett checked his watch. "No, I'll have something delivered. Thanks for telling me. I'll call you if he wakes up again."

Walking out of the hospital room, I let out a deep breath. "I'm so relieved."

"Me, too, sweetheart."

Needing to be in the moment, I threw my arms around

Gabe even as nurses walked around. "He's going to be okay. He's going to be here. He's going to see his baby grow up."

"Yes, he is."

Just hearing Gabe's confirmation made it all real. I held him and he kept me close until I was able to gather myself. My stomach growled.

"Let's get the three of you fed. My children are hungry."

A carefree laugh left me. "We are. Those nachos looked so good back at the hotel."

We entered the cafeteria and I scanned the board for what I wanted. *Nachos.* Score! I was in luck as I had craved those back at the hotel. The server fixed me a plate and handed it to me while Gabe paid. The cheesy goodness was like ambrosia. I had to refrain from licking the plate clean.

Gabe watched me with delight. "It's good to see you eating."

"I was so hungry. It's like a switch was flipped. I'm so full now." I made a mental note to eat something healthier for dinner.

I sat back in my chair. Now, I would be able to go home and not worry as much about Carson.

"What are you thinking about?"

I finished my water before I said, "Talking to Carson and heading home." Trent's men would have to be in two spots. "Wait. How will that work? Won't that spread Trent's men too thin?"

Gabe shook his head. "No. Some guys I knew from the force are joining the team at the house. Trent's vetting them to make sure he approves. They left the force within the last three years and haven't found the right job yet. If it works out, we'll have more people I know I can trust and Trent will have some damn fine men."

"Are people going to stay with the Whitmores?"

"Yes, but not as many. We'll have—"

The ringing of my phone cut off Gabe. It was from Apple Blossom. I connected the call after showing him the screen. "Hello?"

"Ms. Russo. It's Lisa Simpson at Apple Blossom."

"Hey, Lisa. It's good to hear from you. And please, call me Willow."

A delighted older woman gave a quasi-squeal of delight. "I'm glad you're feeling much better. I know it's short notice, but we wanted to see if you were available to come tomorrow. The teacher we had got sick. You and the two assistants have been cleared. I know it's soon, but I thought I would check just in case. Otherwise, it looks like we have an opening in about six weeks."

Six Weeks? No, I wanted to get this over.

Whew, Gabe's background check came back clear. That made the decision easier to go ahead with teaching. "That works great. Thanks for letting me come. I loved teaching while in college."

"Perfect, I'll see you tomorrow. If you could come an hour before class, that would be great. Andrea will be there."

"We'll be there. Thank you."

I ended the call and stowed the phone away.

Gabe raised an eyebrow. "Tomorrow?"

"Yes, you're cleared to go. I'm a guest teacher from eight to noon tomorrow."

Gabe sent off a text after we threw away our trash and walked out of the cafeteria. He received an immediate reply. "Trent's confirmed he can make tomorrow work."

Since coming back into my life, Gabe hadn't been far from me. "How are you going to deal with Alex Junior not recognizing you?"

I received a wink in response. "You'll see."

As we passed a closed door, Gabe yanked me in and closed the door. It was dark like it had been the first time I met Tack. His nose traced down across mine and I arched my chest into his.

"This is torment," I murmured.

"In five days, I think we need to add closet sex to a very long, list of places to fuck."

Oh, to feel him inside me was going to be the sweetest torture.

Only five more days.

Chapter Fourteen

I knocked on the doorjamb of Carson's room.

"Hey, angel." Carson had been awake for a bit. Earlier when he woke, he had spent time with Francesca. This time he had asked for me. They had moved him from ICU not too long ago. I was glad to be out of that part of the hospital.

"It's so good to have you back. You're looking better," I said, sitting in the chair beside the bed.

"It's good to be back. I feel better. Tired, but better."

I took it all in. Carson was here. Awake. I had prayed so many times for this to come to fruition.

"Thank you, Willow."

I wasn't sure why he was thanking me. Carson must have read the confusion on my face.

"You were there for Francesca when you had a shit storm to deal with. She told me all about it."

"Carson—"

He cut me off. "You were there for her and my baby. She said it was because of you she was able to make it."

I squeezed his hand. "Of course I would be."

Carson shifted. "They are going to get me walking tomorrow. I can't wait to get out of this damn bed. The doctors have scheduled some OT and PT to help with the muscle loss."

"I was worried. Really worried." My throat tightened. "I thought I'd lost my best friend. I—we—"

He laid his hand on mine. "It's okay, angel. I'm here. It's going to be okay."

With jerky movements, I nodded my head and willed the tears away. If I was upset, Carson would be stressed.

Carson took a sip of water before he cleared his throat. "I hated hearing you worried. I remember hearing your voice. You kept telling me to fight when all I wanted to do was sleep."

"I'm glad you fought. But we are talking about that clause in your Will. Carson, you'd better change it."

He coughed and took another sip. "I'm changing it. Francesca's already read me the riot act."

"Good." That had been easier than I expected.

"How are you, Willow? No bullshitting."

It was time. I filled Carson in on everything except being pregnant with twins. I wanted Gabe to be around when we told people and to experience this part of having a family since he had none. Reliving the highs and lows was exhausting. I laughed, cried, and felt joy. It was the spread.

Through the entire retelling of events, Carson lay there with rapt attention. I knew he was cataloguing all the events while making a list of questions. Squeezing the bridge of my nose, I leaned back in my chair. "I think that about sums it up."

"And you're okay with what Gabe did?"

Of course, Gabe was the first topic he wanted to discuss. I needed to share all my feelings. "I'm pissed he deceived me, but he thought he was protecting me. We all make mistakes. I know he loves me and I love him."

"Are you happy?"

The question had my lips turning up on their own accord. "Unequivocally." There was no denying the surety in my voice.

"That's all that matters, Willow. I want you to be happy." Carson still sounded a little unsure, which was to be expected. When the accident happened, everything had been different, and Alex had been my nightmare.

There was another knock. "Come in," I called.

Gabe stuck his head in. "Mind if I join you?"

Carson narrowed his eyes on Gabe, scrutinizing him like a big brother. His voice was friendly, but I knew Carson was not done making sure I was okay. "Come on in. I was making sure you were treating my best friend right."

The smile on Gabe's face lacked its normal luster. He had worry lines on his face. "What's wrong?" I asked. "Has something happened?"

Needing to feel Gabe, I stood and walked to him. He took my hand. "There's been a development. I've debated whether to tell Carson. But, if it was me, it wouldn't matter what hell I'd been through... I'd want to know."

This wasn't good. Carson shifted a little straighter in bed. "What happened? Tell me."

"David, one of Trent's men, was admitted to the hospital for severe stomach cramps this afternoon. It was serious. He had blue cohosh in his system. A lot of it. It's been traced back to the food that was delivered to Willow and Francesca this afternoon at the hotel. Cohosh induces labor. It would have killed the baby."

My hand clutched my stomach. The nachos. If I had taken

a bite. Or Francesca. I just... we would have... I shook my head. "Why? Hardly anyone knows I'm pregnant. How did they know?"

I almost... we about... it was hard to finish the thought. My lip trembled. Even though I hadn't met my babies, I loved them unconditionally.

Gabe brushed him thumb across my cheek. "It wasn't on what you ordered, sweetheart. It was in everything Francesca ordered, including the appetizers."

On the phone we had taken turns ordering our food. The blood drained from my face and I held on to Gabe.

"Motherfucker!" Carson's stare was hard as stone. "What else do you know?"

I was shaking as Gabe held up his hand to signal just a second. If I had taken a bite, I could have lost them.

Someone was after Carson and Francesca. Was Alex involved in all this? Or was it a separate issue all together? This was all too much, and I took deep breaths to calm down. I said another silent prayer of thanks.

Gabe gave me a bottle of water. "Small sips. Do you want to stay, sweetheart?"

"I almost took a bite of the nachos, I almost lost—"

Gabe knelt before me. "You're fine. Their fine."

I took another sip. The cool crisp water helped. I said, "What else do you know?"

Gabe stood, but kept my hand in his while rubbing soothing circles with his thumb on my wrist. "We're pulling hotel feeds. Someone messed with the ones in the kitchen. Trent had some extra cameras installed on a different circuit. We're checking those as well. Carson, I need to know if you have any enemies Trent isn't aware of? We're trying to see if we're dealing with three issues now—Alex, the accident, and now the poisoning."

Running his hands through his blond hair, Carson looked devastated. He watched me with apologetic eyes before focusing on Gabe. "Hell, I've brokered business deals where people were pissed. Some employees that were fired for not doing their job. But nothing so far as to warrant someone trying to kill my baby."

Someone had tried to poison Carson's baby. I almost ate the food. Regardless of all the precautions, we were still vulnerable. The safety we believed we had was a delusion.

Gabe gently squeezed my wrist. "Drink some more water."

Like a robot, I did as I was told.

Leaning forward, Carson looked formidable as he switched into protector mode. "Do my parents or Francesca know?"

"No. I don't think Francesca can handle it. She's been near her breaking point all week."

It was true, but I was shocked at how blunt Gabe was with Carson. Relief flooded Carson's face and I was glad she wasn't aware.

He nodded and said, "That was the right call. I want to keep it from them. I need to get out of this fucking hospital."

Carson's heart monitor spiked and the sister side of me came out in me. "You need to stay calm or they're going to sedate you. That won't do any of us any good. You've been on life support until two days ago."

Carson's vitals returned to normal and his monitors quieted.

Gabe continued, "The hotel isn't safe. I'm taking Willow back to her house tomorrow. I would suggest keeping Francesca here. It'll be easy for us to move forward without her knowledge. When you get out, we can move you to Willow's for a bit. After working with Trent, we have the place secured. We can start on your place next."

For a few seconds, Carson thought through his options. "I'll get her to stay here while I'm in the hospital. Are you okay with us invading your house, Willow?"

"Of course. Stay as long as you need to."

Tapping his fingers on the bedrail, Carson thought for another few seconds. "Let's make the plan to move to Willow's after I'm released. I'd rather us focus the resources on finding the fuckers after Willow and now Francesca. Do you think they're coming after me because of Alex?"

I hoped not. The last thing I ever wanted was to bring my friends in on this.

"I don't think so," Gabe said.

This was news to me as I whipped my head to Gabe.

"Why?" Carson and I asked at the same time.

Taking the empty blue chair next to Carson's bed, Gabe sat and motioned for me to pull my chair next to him. "You know about the two notes. I think the finger came from my brother and was meant for me as a way to draw me out into the open."

"Willow—" Carson coughed and I quickly handed him his water bottle. After taking a few sips, he continued, "Fuck, I hate this cough. Willow explained this earlier. You and Trent now think that the people who ran us off the road have a different vendetta against Alex."

Gabe's eyes cut to mine. "Until today, that was my theory. Now, I think whoever ran the two of you off the road was after you, Carson. I think Willow was the bystander. It makes no sense for them to hurt her if the suspects are after her money. If she dies, it all goes to different charities."

Gabe's words took root. Someone was after Carson. Why? I wasn't responsible for all this. But Alex still remained a piece of the puzzle. The same thought flitted through Carson's mind as his eyes widened. Unfortunately, it made sense.

With the grimace on his face, Carson said, "I'm so sorry, Willow. You know I would never put you or anyone in harm's way."

I stood and gave him a hug. "This is not your fault. Just like Alex wasn't mine. We will survive this. I don't blame you."

The nurse opened the door. "Visiting hours are coming to an end, Mr. Whitmore. The doctor has cleared Francesca and your mother to stay the night."

"Thanks, Nancy. Give us ten more minutes if that's okay."

The elderly woman gave us a sweet little nod. "That works. I'll be back with your meds."

The door closed and Carson looked to me. "What time will you be by tomorrow?"

Tomorrow. Oh, I had the teaching job that I hadn't filled Carson in on. "Um... after twelve." I was shit at misleading. I might as well as thrown up a huge neon sign that said I was doing something Carson wouldn't approve of.

"Willow, what are you doing?"

Straightening my spine, I gave a sweet little smile as I tried to play it off. "I'm teaching an art class at Apple Blossom."

His eyes shot straight to Gabe. "Why the fuck would you let her do that?

Carson knew Alex had taken my money to pay for his child's school with small automatic withdrawals sent to Apple Blossom. Alex Junior, who had autism, thrived at the school for special needs. After finding out the child was going to lose his place in school, I asked Trent to figure out a way for me pay the tuition through back channels as an anonymous contributor. There was no way I was going to punish a child for the sins of his father when I had the income to pay it.

I started to explain, but Gabe answered first, looking a little pissed at Carson's underlying meaning. "Listen, you and I still need to have a one-on-one talk about my choices and how they affected Willow. You're like a brother to her. I expect it. But, don't insinuate I am putting her in danger. Every action, and I mean every fucking action, is to keep her and my babies as safe as I possibly can. We believe Alex is still alive and Jack De Luca may have a vendetta. Or they may be working together. Now, we have another psychotic asshole who's trying to poison Francesca who could have gotten to Willow as well. I thoroughly reviewed this option before I gave it to her. This woman is my life—don't ever question that, especially in front of her, until we've had our chance to talk."

There was steel surrounding every word Gabe uttered. The two looked at each other while the tension mounted to an almost intolerable level. I was about to say something when Carson relented.

"You're right. It's been a hell of a day." His shoulders relaxed and he slumped back in the bed exhausted.

Gabe raised his hand. "I get it. Just as long as we're clear."

Carson looked to me. "Call me as soon as you leave tomorrow. I want to know you're safe."

"I will. Promise. I'll send Francesca in. Get some sleep."

Later at the hotel, I tossed and turned, trying to find a position to sleep in an uncomfortable bed. Nothing worked. I blew out a breath of air when I flipped onto my back. My eyes darted to the door. Gabe was in the living room. I was tired, exhausted actually. Even though I knew I was safe, I felt violated at the hotel. I had come so close to taking a bite of the poisoned food.

Flopping again, I swore there were lumps in the mattress. Maybe a glass of milk would help.

I walked into the main room and tiptoed around the corner. A faint glow from the under-cabinet lights spilled into the living room. As I rounded the table, I almost ran into Gabe who was sitting there.

"Oh gosh. I thought you were asleep on the couch."

"I was reviewing the files. Couldn't sleep." The bags under his eyes showed his lack of sleep. He closed the folder.

Inching closer, I suddenly felt shy. "What were you looking at?"

"Latest intel on Jack De Luca. There's nothing new."

Part of me was glad there wasn't anything else to contemplate for the day. I was on processing overload and scared.

"Come here, sweetheart."

Quickly I tucked myself into Gabe's lap.

"Having trouble sleeping?"

"Yes, I was going to get some milk, hoping it would help. I didn't want to wake you."

Gabe rubbed my back, which already had me relaxing. "Willow?"

"Hmmm…"

"Is there anything I can do?"

I looked up with tired eyes. "Will you sleep with me?"

Gabe stood, cradling me against his chest. "I'd love to.

Let me grab my book and I'll read to you while you fall asleep."

"Mmm..."

The vibrations from his chuckle moved through me. Taking me with him, Gabe flipped the lights off and I cuddled closer to him, feeling the drowsiness fall over me like a blanket.

The bed dipped and I found my pillow, sleep already encroaching. Clothes rustled and the heat of his body brought me close.

"Best fucking feeling in the world is having you in my arms."

Sleep had already won as I mumbled something incoherent.

Chapter Fifteen

I reached over and turned off the alarm. It was warm. Too warm. Gabe's arms slipped around me and held me tighter. Gabe. Momentarily I froze, wondering what happened. Then, I remembered going to the kitchen to get some milk and asking him to sleep with me.

He brought me to bed and held me all night long. For the first time since the accident, I slept well.

"Morning, sweetheart." The deep rumble of his scratchy voice exuded sex.

Four more days. Only four more days.

For now, I relished being in his arms. "Morning." I wrapped my arms tighter around him. "I don't want to get up."

"Me, either. I want to keep you in my arms and never let go."

"Then don't."

Gabe lifted me up a little to where I was able to look into the depths of his green eyes. "We're in this for the long haul."

Through it all, Gabe soothed my underlying fears. "I want

to go away somewhere and pretend none of this is going on."

"Soon, I'll take you somewhere."

The reminder alarm went off, breaking the magical spell we had woven to escape reality. "I better get up if we're going to leave on time."

In the next second, I found myself on my back. A squeal of delight left me as I clasped onto his biceps. "I think you forgot something, Willow."

I wiggled a little and felt his hardened length against my abdomen.

A deep guttural groan left his lips. "Behave. Only four more days."

I gave him a little pout and he nipped my lips. The warmth from his touch sent tingles through me. I needed more.

"Gabe..." I sighed his name before his mouth fully covered mine. Instinctively, I wrapped my legs around his hips to bring him closer.

The strong strokes of his tongue commanded mine, and his hand moved across my oversensitive breasts. And then he was gone. My eyes opened. Gabe was breathing hard while he knelt between my legs and tried to regain control. The molten fire that burned within told me he was as much a slave to our love as I was.

When we touched it was as if we became one, needing to join our bodies. "I think you should go take a shower, Willow."

All I wanted was Gabe. I blinked a few times to break the spell.

With ease, he unhooked my legs and scooted off the bed. "It is taking everything I have not to strip you bare and sink inside you."

"I want that, too."

Gabe's wrapped his fingers around my ankles and gentle pulled me to the edge of the bed, causing my nightgown to ride up my thighs and expose my panties.

"You are so fucking beautiful. I'm going to go get ready before I lose the last of my self-restraint." His deep gravelly voice was strained.

Without another word, he left the room and I felt the throb of my clit begging to be touched. I flexed my fingers to keep from touching myself. I blew out a frustrated breath. Now, I understood why someone would take a cold shower.

With one last look in the mirror, I made sure I looked presentable. The fog from my earlier desire was only now dissipating after a frigid shower.

My lavender gray eyes were wide and alert as I thought about what was ahead. In less than an hour, I would be teaching art at Apple Blossom. And inevitably, I would come face-to-face with Alex's child.

Glancing down, I touched my stomach. Alex Junior was going to have cousins he would never know about. With all that Alex was involved in, I wasn't willing to intertwine our worlds more than they were. An ache settled in my heart. Family was important to me, but they would never know Gabe's side.

I knew Gabe agreed with my thoughts on the matter though we hadn't discussed it at great length. Regardless of how he felt about his brother, I knew it cut deep not being involved in Alex Junior's life.

The clock showed it was time to leave.

"Gabe, are you ready?"

An older man with glasses walked in the door, similar to the man I saw at Precinct 54 the day I confronted Commander Taylor and learned Alex was not an undercover cop. I would recognize those green eyes anywhere. "I know why you wore glasses when you were pretending to be the older men."

"You would have figured it out."

I smirked at the Irish accent he adopted. If Alex sounded like Gabe in everyday life, his speech would have to be changed as well. Seeing the way his eyes lit up anytime we saw each other, I would have known.

I kept constant eye contact as I walked up to him. "Yes, I would have. The eyes are the perfect window to a person's soul."

"And yours is beautiful," he said.

"So is yours."

"Only because of you."

The words he spoke touched me as always. We were entranced with each other as we searched the depths of our love.

A distant beep alerted us to Trent opening the hotel suite door. "Willow? Gabe? Andre is ready in the car."

"In here. We're coming out!" I called.

Casually dressed, Trent walked toward my bedroom door as we exited. "I'll be riding with you guys. Security is starting to arrive on our strategic timetable. The supplies you requested are in the car." Trent gave a smirk. "Nice costume, old man. I think he might be too old for you, Willow."

I giggled.

"Fuck off, asshole," Gabe shot back.

Trent chuckled.

It was tempting to tease Gabe, but I needed to focus on the day ahead. "What are your names again?" I asked. They had told me yesterday at the hospital but I had been tired.

"Gabe is Ben Jones and I'm Joe Smith."

It was hard to keep a straight face as the man who didn't look like Gabe had his voice. "Those names are pretty boring."

"True, but that means there's a million of them and it made it easier to have a fake background uploaded for them to check against."

These two men had skills. They accomplished so much with so little time.

"Makes sense."

Yesterday, while in the waiting room at the hospital, I had come up with a lesson as well as the supplies needed. Due to time, I kept it easy and planned to use something Dad had taught me at an early age.

It was near time for Carson to be up, having always been an early riser. I checked my phone to see if I had missed a message, but there was nothing from Carson or his family.

"Have you heard from anyone at the hospital?"

Trent rechecked his phone. "My men made their rounds five minutes ago. Bennett is in the waiting room waiting for everyone to wake up. All is clear."

That was a relief. As we headed to the door, Trent motioned to the bar. "Fresh breakfast from a random bakery across town. We cleared out all the food yesterday from the suites and restocked Bennett and Marie's with new supplies. For security reasons, I advised Bennett we were no longer using room service to eliminate any potential risk due to the unforeseen video outage. Only my men, Carson, and you two know about the attempted poisoning."

It still made me sick thinking about what almost happened. An inconspicuous shudder moved through me. Last night, Nonno had said he would visit Carson today. "Is Nonno still going to the hospital?"

Trent checked something else on his phone. "Mr. Russo confirmed with security he would come to the hospital when you were there."

I hadn't seen Nonno since he left and missed him terribly. However, I wanted to thank him for having the foresight to understand what Gabe and I needed. Yesterday, I decided against telling Nonno about Apple Blossom. Until we had answers, it wasn't something he needed to worry about.

The muffins smelled delicious and I grabbed one and a banana. Gabe snatched two bottles of orange juice.

On our way to the elevator, I asked, "How is David doing this morning?"

Trent gave me a warm smile. "Good. He's pissed as hell and ready to be back on the job. The doctors expect a full recovery."

These security men were crazy half the time with how quickly they wanted to return to work. "Tell him to rest. I'm going to have something sent to him today if that's okay."

"That's very thoughtful of you."

I pulled out my phone, I placed an order for a get-well balloon arrangement on our way down. Balloons seemed manly enough. I wasn't sure David was the teddy bear type.

A knot formed in my stomach knowing Alex most likely would see us at some point today. We were about to potentially start down a path we would not return from. With us reaching out to Alex's child, we were about to poke an unhinged person. That alone had my nerves prickling with apprehension.

As we walked through the lobby, I looked at people wondering if they were somehow connected to all this. All of the people's faces were appropriately engaged. I looked for a sign, something, but saw nothing. With all the threats, our enemies had the potential to blend like Gabe. Even his gate was slower with a slightly slouched posture as he embraced every part of appearing to be fifty.

If Gabe had on sunglasses, I would not think he was the man I loved. It was unsettling to know the capabilities of people. Whoever wanted to take me could be in this room, watching as we walked across the lobby. The thought sobered me. But, I pushed forward.

We stepped outside. The city was awakening as the early morning light chased the night away. Every morning felt like a new beginning—a fresh start to correct the wrongs of yesterday. Hopefully, today would lead to answers instead of more questions.

Scooting to the far side of the black town car, Gabe got in a little slower. It was hard to take my eyes off him.

The car door closed and away we went as the sun crested over the horizon. Gabe handed me an orange juice. "Grabbed this for you. I thought this might be good for your stomach."

"Thanks." I settled in and ate my breakfast, hoping it wouldn't cause a bout of morning sickness. Inconsequential chatter filled in the interim—mainly sports talk. It helped ease the tension, but my mind flitted to what was ahead and beyond. Hopefully, this wasn't a mistake.

Poking the beast sometimes was worse than letting it sleep.

My phone vibrated with Carson's name, which brought a smile to my face.

Carson: Morning. Wanted to check on you. You okay?
Me: I'm good. A little nervous, but I'll be fine.
Carson: You'll do great. Text me when you're done and on your way back.
Me: I will.

Carson: I wanted you to know I support you. I shouldn't have said what I did yesterday.
Me: I know you do. It's a lot for us all to take in.
Carson: It is, but it's not an excuse. Do you forgive me?
Me: Of course, I do. I wasn't mad. I've missed you.
Carson: Miss you, too.

It was so good to have Carson back in my life. Every day I had him would forever be a blessing.

Trent turned around as he adjusted a small earpiece that was almost impossible to see unless you were looking for it. "Put this pendant on your shirt. It'll help us hear you just in case."

Taking the proffered piece of jewelry, I inspected it. The microphone was a little painter's palette with all the primary colors. I smirked. "Cute, fitting and practical. Just what the special forces ordered."

Andre disguised his laugh with a cough while Gabe and Trent shook their heads.

I pinned it to my shirt. "There."

There was a pause and then Trent said, "Good. It's working. We're reading you loud and clear."

Within a few minutes we pulled up to the school. It was an old church that had been renovated into a special needs education center. A widow had bought it and had it redone for her grandson almost two years ago. It was beautiful.

Andre pulled the car underneath a covered porch and things became real. I was here and about to meet Alex's son. At the hotel, I had similar thoughts but now the reality of the situation had increased in potency.

Deep breaths. I have this. It's the fastest way to draw Alex out. I want to be free of him.

I kept looking at the stone building, expecting it to reveal the answer to all the madness. Trent's words broke through my thoughts. "We'll be with you the whole time. If you feel uncomfortable, say you need some air. We'll get you out immediately."

"Okay." I swallowed, trying to remember the directions.

Glancing out the window, I looked over into a heavily treed area. Was Alex watching me? Was Jack De Luca? What about the person after Carson? Or were they misleading us? I closed my eyes. *I am perfectly safe. Gabe and Trent are with me.* My eyes swept over the area again, trying to see if I sensed anyone. There was no bone-chilling effect or raised hairs on my neck. But still... there was the possibility.

I can do this. This will hopefully be the beginning of the end to the madness.

Gabe touched my knee and I jerked toward him. "It's okay, sweetheart. You don't have to do this."

"I know." I placed my hand on his. "I want to do this. You'll be with me the entire time."

Behind Gabe a smartly dressed woman in her mid-thirties with wild brown curls piled in an updo exited the school. Probably Lisa.

"You okay, Willow?" I looked at Gabe whose was watching me.

Squaring my shoulders, I replied, "I'm good. Let's do this."

Trent got out and opened my door. "I'll grab the trunk of supplies."

"Thanks, Trent."

He stepped forward. "I'm, Joe for the day."

Oh, right. Shit. That was right. My face drained and his hand went to my elbow for a few brief seconds bringing me back into focus. He threw his voice low for only Gabe and me to hear. "You've got this, Willow."

I chanced a look at Gabe. Lisa was close enough that he wasn't able to touch me, but his eyes spoke what he wasn't able to do. "I'm Ben."

"Yes, yes. I've got it now."

"Ms. Russo, it's so wonderful to meet you. I'm Lisa."

Casually, I turned to face her.

She extended her delicate hand trimmed with a pearl bracelet.

We shook briefly as I responded, "Willow, please. It's a pleasure to be here. You have a beautiful school."

"Thank you. We're quite proud of it."

Politely, I gestured to Gabe and Trent. Both men who normally exuded intimidating had been transformed. Trent had on casual jeans and had slipped on a hat. Of course Gabe looked double his age. "This is Ben and Joe. They'll be assisting me today." Being deceitful made me feel grimy inside.

Lisa shook their hands and exchanged pleasantries. "Are you ready to get settled? Ms. Lane, the art teacher, is waiting for you in the classroom. Your first class is in about forty-five minutes. The students have already been prepared for a guest teacher today. I'm glad you were able to fill in so they weren't disappointed."

Autistic children relied on consistency in schedules. In the initial conversation with Lisa, she said they liked to have a guest teacher once a quarter.

"I can't wait to meet them." The words were surprisingly true. Art was something meant to be shared, and if I was able to give a little bit of that magic to a child, then it was truly worth it.

We entered through the large wooden doors. The stone

hallways were reverent. Our footsteps were muted as we walked down the carpeted hallway. Momentarily I paused at an archway to look at the stained glass window with a magnitude of colors. The sun shining through it cast a rainbow of colors around the room.

On the right were a few tables with children eating. A few watched me curiously as we passed. I waved but they just stared.

"I know this was in the e-mail I sent yesterday, but in case you hadn't seen it. You'll have four classes, each forty-five minutes long. Each class has five students with their own tables. Ms. Lane will be there the entire time to brief you on anything needed."

I had read it briefly to see how much supplies I would need. "Are there any children I should be aware of with extreme sensory issues?"

"There is one child. She'll be provided gloves."

In college, I had volunteered at a special needs school throughout my junior year. It had been part of the curriculum for my classes. Art came in all forms to all people and the teacher wanted us to understand that aspect. That class had been immeasurable to my experience though I hadn't decided to teach it myself.

We made one more turn and entered a large room. Seven art tables were set up. The comforting smell of paint filled the room as I walked in. A peace settled over the restlessness I had felt these last few days. I needed to get home to the canvas. At the hotel, I had doodled but the limitation in time proved difficult to set aside painting time. Tomorrow I would make sure I carved out some time for the studio.

I looked at the room more carefully. The art teacher had a well-equipped art room. Bright colors filled the room. Children's art hung on every available surface. From the loving way the pictures were hung, it was obvious she cared for these children.

"Ms. Russo, thank you for guest teaching in my class today." A young blonde-haired woman with a sweet demeanor stuck out her hand.

"Willow, please. Thank you for having me. This is Ben and Joe. They'll be assisting me." Trent came in with the roller trunk full of supplies. "I brought my own supplies for teaching. I hope you're okay with it. They're special canvases that only work with certain markers."

"Oh, that sounds lovely. The children will love it. Please call me Aubrey."

After the proper niceties were exchanged, Gabe and I quickly got to work distributing the supplies to each station. It was still odd seeing him move without his normal agility.

On the tables, we put the special markers next to the canvas and lined them up perfectly with the labels facing the same way.

The bell rang and I waited anxiously to meet Alex Junior.

Chapter Sixteen

Three classes down, one to go. I took a sip of water and blew out a breath. Alex Junior hadn't been in the first three classes. The process of elimination meant he was in this class. Aubrey had been concerned about three new faces in the classroom. I agreed. Trent stayed in the hallway just outside the door.

The school has a magnificent curriculum. Definitely impressed. It was obvious Alex cared for his child. There were many cheaper alternatives, but Alex had chosen one of the best. It only added to the enigma of his persona. Had he infiltrated my life to pay for it? I doubted it. The school payments were probably a bonus to whatever his endgame was.

To the core I thought he was evil, but this showed he had some good in him. But was it enough? I wasn't sure.

Gabe moseyed beside me, keeping a respectable distance between us. "How are you holding up?"

"I'm good. I needed this more than I realized. I'm anxious to get back to my studio."

He moved to touch my hand but then pulled back and balled his hand into a fist. Aubrey glanced our way before sending another e-mail. Lowly, Gabe said, "I hate that I can't touch you."

"I know. This is the last class."

Taking a few steps away, Gabe said, "I'll be in the back of the room."

"Okay."

Ding.

The bell rang and the children filed in. My eyes roamed over the first child. It wasn't him. The second. Nope. I felt the nerves shift into a higher gear. For a mere moment, I closed my eyes to project a calm exterior for the children.

I wasn't sure if the kids realized Gabe was there as they stayed in their individual bubbles. Curious students gazed at me before going to their desks. There was a little apprehension on some since I was out of their norm, which was understandable.

The third and fourth children weren't Alex Junior either. Between the first and second classes, I was given the Cliff's Notes version of the children. The child with extreme sensory issues requiring the gloves would be in this class.

The next child came in with his head down and I held my breath. Dark hair, strong build. He took his seat. I froze. He was almost a replica to his father and uncle. I glanced at Gabe who watched him with love. My heart broke in two with the look of sadness passing through his eyes. As it stood now, this was as close as he would get to his nephew.

Introductions from Aubrey began, reminding the students I was here today as a special teacher.

The room grew quiet and I realized they were waiting on me. Keeping my voice steady, calm, I started class. "I'm Willow. And I'm an artist. I heard you guys like to do art."

Some of the students stared at their canvases while others looked ready to get started. The student closest to me rocked back and forth as a coping mechanism to deal with an uncomfortable situation. I stepped farther back in steady motions and the rocking slowed.

"Today we are going to draw what we dream about while we are sleeping. The markers on your desk are magical. They only work on the canvas in front of you. No mess."

A few of the students picked up the markers as I continued, "Art is anything you want it to be. I paint my feelings all the time. It's also a way to communicate with your friends."

Autistic children at times had difficulty interacting with others. In a room, they play by themselves even if they are surrounded by a group of their peers. My teacher in college believed through art the social gaps could be bridged between people. I agreed.

One by one, the markers touched the canvas and different shades appeared depending on what color they picked. The kids' eyes grew in amazement as a couple accidentally dropped them on the desk and there were no marks.

Overall, it wasn't the most elaborate lesson in the world, but it would allow me a little time to talk to each child. Each student's ability to respond to directions showed that their teachers had worked diligently with them at this school.

One by one, I visited the tables quietly, asking what they were working on and teaching them a little about the stroke or style they were using. They were little sponges with not many questions. I gave praise. I met Gabe's eye as I made it to Alex's table.

"What is your painting of?"

The greenest eyes looked my way. I was stunned for a

moment and my heart broke when I had to refrain from touching him on the shoulder. I wanted to shower this child with love like I would Carson's.

A lump formed in my throat.

Alex Junior simply replied, "My dad."

Alex? Again, I froze.

The man who had done so much damage had created this special child. Unbelievable. I glanced at the painting and saw the outline of the man. This little boy had artistic talent. "What is your dad doing?"

"Visiting me." He moved the marker and drew a smaller figure next to Alex. He was in his bed. "That's a sweet dream."

"Not a dream. He visited me last night."

Alex was alive.

I flexed my fingers as the reality hit me. The thought clawed at the inside and I struggled to remain calm. I glanced at Gabe who appeared to be physically restraining himself from coming over.

Remain calm. I have to remain calm. Dryness consumed my mouth. We thought... I knew... but to have the truth was a different story. Though it was from a child, I knew there were no falsities to his statement. Alex was alive. And he wanted to wreak havoc on our lives.

Tremors radiated through my fingers. I squeezed my hand into a fist.

Alex was alive. The man who schemed against Gabe, attempted to steal Dad's Botticelli, and then married me in a last ditch effort to get easy money while Gabe was deployed. The thoughts circled faster through my head.

Again, I peered over at Gabe. He moved as if almost to rise. I shook my head minutely to keep him in place.

"Dad misses me and says he's going to take me from here soon. He tells me he loves me."

Words from the little boy brought me back. Imagining Alex capable of love was hard. I needed more information. Finding an inner strength I forced my voice to remain calm. "Where are you going?"

"Somewhere with lots of trees with my daddy."

Aubrey tapped me on the back and I stood not wanting to end my conversation with Alex Junior. Before I faced her, I released a breath and then plastered on a neutral expression. "Alex's parents have not shown up for the last six weeks on visitation day. We've heard from the mother, but nothing specific. It's heartbreaking. He's been projecting his emotions this way."

Cocking my head to the side, I mentally wanted to shake this woman. Autistic children were brutally blunt. At times it was even awkwardly social though the child was unaware. Alex made it in here somehow to see his child. Gabe had been right.

"Thank you for telling me."

Why wasn't Candy showing?

I squatted next to Alex. "You're doing wonderful, Alex. When your Dad visits you tell him Willow taught you about art and you drew him."

"Okay."

The answer was simple and I knew that was all I was getting as he focused on drawing this little figure. I assumed Alex's dad would ask about his day. This message would undoubtedly make it to him if he was asked.

I moved on so as not to bring unwanted attention to me.

The class ended and the children filed out. At a loss, I stared at the back of Alex Junior's head before the vice principal followed him out blocking him from my view. Aubrey came up. "I'm going to escort the class to lunch. Thank you again for coming, Willow. I would love to have you back."

"I would love to come back."

The principal came back in. "Thank you again for coming, Willow. I peeked in from the window a few times, and from what I saw, I think the children loved it."

"It was a pleasure. Thank you."

Lisa turned and then stopped before raising her hand in thought. "By chance are you related to Alfonso Russo?"

My father? How was this woman acquainted with Dad? "Um... he was my dad."

Her eyes grew with delight as she faced me again while waving her hands and rapidly talking. "Then it truly was fate that brought you here. I had no idea. Before Mr. Russo's death, he came here and donated to our art department. All of the equipment was upgraded thanks to him."

I stared at this woman who looked elated to see me confused. "He... when... why did he come here?"

Desperation filled my voice. I needed to calm down and focus my thoughts to get what I needed. This simply might be a coincidence. But... doubt lingered at the edges of my thought.

"Um... let me think." She tapped her chin. "Oh yes. He called us to set up an appointment as he had heard wonderful things about our program. A week or so later, he toured the facility and met some of the staff and children."

Cotton filled my throat as I struggled with what to do with this new information. I managed to respond somehow. "That's wonderful. You have a great program."

Her hands waved again. "Your dad thought so, too. In fact, he drew with the little boy, Alex, who was in your last class."

Wait. Dad had seen Alex Junior?

The room was spinning as I grabbed on to the desk.

"Willow, are you okay?"

It was Gabe. I sat in the chair. His accent only slipped a little. My eyes were wide.

Lisa was in my face. "Is she okay?"

"She's hypoglycemic." The answer was automatic from Gabe.

I almost protested, but figured Gabe was covering for me.

Movement to the right brought my attention away from Gabe. "Oh dear, let me get her something. I'll be right back." Lisa left in a flurry as I tried to right my world.

Hands came up to my face and my eyes went back to Gabe's after noticing Trent at the door. "Willow, focus on me."

The world kept spinning. "Willow, look at me." My eyes connected with Gabe's with his stern command. "We need to get out of here. Lisa is going to come back with something to eat. You can't eat it. We don't know if it's safe. We need to start moving toward the door."

I nodded. With a proffered arm, I took it as we walked from the room. The hallway felt as if it were closing in on me. Dad had been here… with Alex. Why had he not said anything?

Lisa stood in front of us with a candy bar. "Here you go. How are you doing?"

Get it together, Willow.

I smiled. "Thank you. I had something in my purse. I'm doing much better. I got immersed in class and forgot to eat something."

That seemed to appease Lisa as her shoulders dropped in

relief. "Oh good. I'm glad. Can I get you anything else?"

Our time was coming to an end. If I wanted any more answers now was the time. "I think I'm good. Thanks for sharing your memory of Dad with me. It's always wonderful to hear something I didn't know about him."

Maybe the opened ended statement would encourage her to say something else. I cleared my throat as the thickness increased from the emotional realizations. *Keep it together, Willow. Only a few more minutes.*

"Yes, I would imagine so. I wish I had more to tell you. I'm glad I put the two together."

At the entrance of the school, I realized there was no more information. Andre pulled up in the car. I felt ill and the acid in my stomach churned. How was this happening? Saying one last good-bye, I got in the car, glad to be away from the situation.

Trees and shrubbery blurred as Andre drove us away from the boarding school. I gathered my thoughts, hoping there was another explanation. Trent was on the phone. He mentioned a donation as well as the school name to my accountant, I assumed. Tears welled in my eyes as I faced Gabe.

In a flash he ripped off his mask leaving little bits of plastic on his face. My lip trembled not able to say the words yet. "I know, sweetheart. I know."

A tear escaped and I tried to ask the question swimming to the surface. "Do you think... is it possible... did Alex..." The thought hurt too much to finish.

Warmth radiated from his thumb when he brushed away an errant lock of hair. "We're checking. I don't know, sweetheart."

Finally, the thought broke through into my consciousness. *Had Dad been killed?*

Chapter Seventeen

In Carson's room, we were surrounded by friends and family. Carson looked better and had switched his hospital gown for gray lounge pants and a blue T-shirt. At least he looked and felt better.

I tried to be part of the conversations and laugh when appropriate, but I wasn't able to focus. At least Gabe helped keep up the pretense. What I needed were answers to why Dad had visited Apple Blossom. A weariness enveloped me. I was ready to go home and get my thoughts righted.

Home. The mental word brought me comfort. At least I was going to sleep in my own bed tonight.

Nonno stood and stretched his arms before he walked toward the door, bringing me back from my troubling thoughts. I met him at the door.

"This old man is going home, baby girl."

"Bye, Nonno. It was good to see you. I missed you."

"Missed you, too. I'll be by to check on you in a few days. You look tired today." Underlying his statement, Nonno was asking if there was anything else wrong. For those close to me, it would be easy to see through the façade.

Leaning into him, I hugged him fiercely. "The first trimester is exhausting. I'm tired and ready to go home."

Not a lie. Making two kids was work.

He looked at me for a bit longer, and I mustered up a halfhearted smile. Satisfied, he kissed me good-bye, and we made plans to see each other again soon. Nonno disappeared behind the corner and I leaned against the frame. I hoped we could leave soon, too.

"Do you guys mind if I spend some time with Willow?" Carson asked.

The mention of my name caught my attention. Carson watched me. Oh shit. He knew something was up. The room stirred as Marie and Bennett stood.

Francesca kissed his cheek. "Of course. I'm going to get something to eat with your parents. Do you need anything?"

"I'm fine, baby. Thanks."

One by one they left. It wasn't uncommon for Carson and me to talk alone like this. But, by the way his brow wrinkled, this would be more a probing session than a friendly chitchat.

Gabe kissed my cheek and murmured, "Do you want me to stay?"

"No, I'm good. Promise." I pecked his lips.

Gabe was the last one to leave and made sure to look me over one last time. The way his eyes held mine told me he wouldn't be far in case I needed him.

Before he left, Gabe gave Carson a warning. "She's had a rough day."

A nod from Carson was the only response he received. The door closed and almost on cue Carson opened his mouth to speak. I held up my hand. "Let me sit before we talk. I'll tell you everything."

After taking the seat Francesca had used, I looked up at the ceiling for a second, to gather my thoughts.

Where do I begin?

I took another deep breath and allowed the clean smell of the room clear my thoughts. It felt as if my emotions wanted to swallow me whole. I had to remain strong. Later, I would allow myself time to break down.

The words I needed to say were locked away. Since we learned about Dad, I hadn't verbally said my thoughts. Telling Carson would make this nightmare real. And this was a nightmare I wished would end.

I blinked a few times rapidly to rid my eyes of the tears threatening to spill over. "I... uh... let me see where to start." My fingers massaged my temples. *I can do this. This is Carson. Start from the beginning. Keep it simple and to the point.* "I... taught at the school today. Met Alex Junior. He confirmed our suspicions that Alex is alive. Alex visits his son at night somehow. Trent's monitoring it."

"Son of a bitch." Carson's biting tone expressed the sentiments I felt.

Placing my hands in my lap, I met Carson's stare. "It gets worse. Much worse."

Carson shifted and his mouth was firmly set while bracing himself for the news. "When we were leaving, the woman who runs the school, Lisa, asked if I was Alfonso's daughter. Long story short, I found out Dad had visited Apple Blossom right before he died."

"When?"

I shook my head. "Don't know. Trent's getting that information from my accountant. We'll be able to tell by the date of the check. We'll know shortly." I looked at my knotted hands, feeling utterly defeated. "Dad saw Alex Junior. Lisa said he spent time drawing with him. There is no way Dad would not have noticed the resemblance. Alex Junior is a younger version of Gabe and Alex."

"Oh fuck." Carson threw back the covers and sat in another chair next to me. His movements were wobbly and not fluid, but the warmth of his hands chased away the chill.

"Pretty much." My lip quivered. "What if I was the reason? What if?"

I had to stop my train of thought. The possibility cut too deep.

The pressure from Carson squeezing my hand brought my attention back to him and away from the fears that had plagued my thoughts since learning the black truth. "This is not because of you. If your dad's death is connected. This is on Alex. Only Alex."

"But I brought Alex into our family."

Carson's stern voice spoke with conviction. "No, you brought Gabe into our family. Not Alex. Don't carry that burden. It's not something your dad would want or agree with. Don't let this taint your life more than it has."

The guilt still churned inside. "But... he might still be here."

"You don't know that. You can't know what the future would have been. The past is the past and that's where it belongs. All you can change is the future."

His words were undoubtedly true. Later, I would process his wisdom.

Thankfully Carson changed the focus of the conversation. "What are Gabe and Trent doing?"

I cleared my throat. "Um... Trent is looking at the coroner's report again. We'll compare it against the check date to see how close it was to his death. I'm sure Gabe and Trent will want to chat with Gabe's mother at some point."

The sound of Carson scrubbing his hand over his face caused me to glance at him. His blue eyes looked saddened as he shouldered this knowledge with me. "Are you going with Gabe to meet his mother?"

"I want to, but we haven't discussed it yet." I leaned my head on his shoulder. "It's like I can't escape this nightmare. Will it ever get better?"

Wrapping his arm around my shoulder, Carson said, "It will. We're going to get our happy ending. We've been through too much not to."

"But at what price?" That was the ultimate question. Sometimes the price was too heavy for the things we wanted.

The question hung out there. I continued to drive the point home. "I met my children's cousin today. He was a sweet boy. Talented. But, because of Alex and who he is connected with, I can't put them in harm's way. That little boy is an innocent bystander. It guts me, Carson."

"I know it does, angel. I know." Silence ensued for a few reflective minutes. Carson leaned away from me and narrowed his eyes. "Wait. Children? Yesterday, Gabe said babies."

Oh shit. I had slipped. So had Gabe. "Um…"

"Willow… are you?"

"Um…" There was a flash of hurt in Carson's eyes and I decided to tell him. We rarely kept anything from each other. "Gabe and I found out we're having twins. We haven't told anyone yet."

Carson's smile grew. "We are so fucked. We're going to have three teaming up against the four of us. We stood a chance at two, but now we're screwed."

The first genuine smile appeared on my face since this

morning. "We are. I feel bad for Francesca and Gabe. They're paying for our sins through all this."

He chuckled before becoming serious. "Are you happy, angel?"

This feeling had been missing for so long while he was unconscious. And now I had Carson back. Through all of the trials we faced, there were blessings. He tucked his blond hair behind his ear like I had seen him do so many times. "I am happy. Gabe completes a part of me I never knew was missing until we met. It's why I fought so long to try to save my fake marriage to Alex. You know that song Dad loved, "O Sole Mio' by Luciano Pavarotti?"

"Yes, he played it a lot while he painted. It was your parents' song."

They loved that song and danced to it often.

"It was. I get what the lyrics mean now. I mean I really get them. Since finding out I was pregnant and having Gabe back, I finally feel in my heart what Dad was trying to explain all those years about love being more beautiful than the sun."

Carson squeezed me to him and I relished the touch. "I'm happy for you. It looks like you have truly forgiven Gabe."

"I have. I want to be his forever."

Chapter Eighteen

We were home.

Finally.

Today had been one of the longest days of my life. After arriving home, I ate some soup and went down to the beach. The waves reflecting the approaching sunset were a cacophony of colors. Even though Andre was on my left and Michael was on my right, they gave me enough space that I felt as if I were in my own private bubble while I sorted through the chaos.

Gabe had taken a phone call shortly before I walked to the beach. I asked Mildred to let him know where I was when he finished.

The waves crashed and inched closer to me on the shoreline.

Why hadn't Dad told Trent about seeing Alex's child? Or me? Alex must have known and stopped Dad from telling anyone. *Otherwise, wouldn't he have moved Alex from Apple Blossom?* Why hadn't Candy gone to see her son? I wasn't sure. All this led to was more questions.

Of course, it hadn't been confirmed that Dad had been murdered by Alex. But, the timing was beyond suspicious. Why had Alex gone to such extremes? If all of this had been for the money, I would have gladly given him my fortune in exchange for Dad's life.

The water came up to my toes and I curled them in the sand. I loved the feeling as the sand disappeared beneath my feet. I have an old family movie of me as a child with Dad on the beach. He held my hands, and when the waves hit my feet, I would scream in excitement. At least I had the memories to pass on to my children.

I sensed him before he wrapped his arms around my waist.

"We'll get through this." Warmth radiated from him, chasing away the dark shadows invading my thoughts.

"Was that Trent on the phone?"

"Yes, he got a copy of the donation check. It was dated the day your dad died." Closing my eyes, I felt the anguish wash over me. "There's more, sweetheart. Do you want to know right now or do you want to process this first? You've had a lot thrown at you today."

More so, how could there be more? At some point there had to be an end to all this.

My words were barely above a whisper. "Yes, I want to know."

"Trent pulled the coroner's report. Three days ago, the coroner was found dead. He'd been burned."

That was three people related to this who had been burned to death—Commander Taylor, the unknown accomplice in the Botticelli theft, and now the coroner.

The fist clinched tighter around my already aching heart.

Commander Taylor was a dirty cop involved in selling the lie of Alex being an undercover cop.

"Alex is cleaning things up and tying up his loose ends. De Luca burns bodies. Do you think he's trying to frame him?"

Gabe's chest rose and fell with a deep sigh. "That's my theory. Whatever he has planned, he's about to act. If there's no one to left who was part of the crimes, he'll be untraceable."

Untraceable.

The words left an empty feeling inside me. Would he try to hurt Gabe, someone else I loved, or me? We had to catch him before he hurt anyone else.

The sun dipped below the horizon. "Do you know where Candy's been?"

"She hooked up with Harley and sold the house she shared with Alex. It looks like the money went into a joint account she has with Harley."

Being abandoned by your mother was incomprehensible to me.

Gabe hugged me and said, "Let's head inside. The wind is picking up."

In silence we walked back. The slight change in temperature felt as if there was a storm brewing in the distance. We entered the house. Besides the security team, we had the place to ourselves. Mildred had retired for the evening and Chris had gone home to his family. The house had a comforting ambience to it as we ascended the stairs though I knew security was all around.

We walked into the bedroom and I saw Gabe's luggage next to mine.

"I hope that wasn't too presumptuous."

"No, I want you in here."

"Good. This is the only place I want to be. I have something for you."

My brow quirked as I followed Gabe into the bathroom. The bath was filled with a bubble bath and the scent of lavender wafted through the air. "I thought you might relax. I checked and you can have warm baths."

I kissed his lips. "Thank you."

"Anytime, sweetheart."

Refreshed after the bath, I lay on Gabe's chest in bed. Halfway through, Gabe had returned and washed my hair. I felt cherished as he lathered me with love and affection. Gabe closed the book after he finished reading the chapter.

"You with me, sweetheart?"

As he'd read this evening, my mind had wandered. "I am now. I can't stop thinking about it. I try, and I feel better, but my mind won't stop going there."

His fingers trailed up my back before making their way back down. "I know. Me, either."

I wrapped my arms around his middle. "What do we do next?"

"I thought we would stay here tomorrow. Spend some time together before Carson and Francesca arrive. Then, I need to go see my mom."

I raised my head.

"I know you want to go, but I can hardly stand the thought of her being near you or my babies. Willow..."

I moved up his chest and pressed my lips to his. "Let's talk about it tomorrow. I'm too tired to make an important decision. I won't go if you feel that strongly about it, but I still want to. Your brother potentially killed my father and so much more. I feel like I need to meet her, to understand and be there for you. I know it doesn't make sense."

"I don't think you'll get the answers you need."

"Maybe not, but we'll be doing this together." How would I feel to only end up with more questions? The scenario completely plausible, but the need overshadowed the worry.

Searching my face, Gabe brought his hand to my cheek. "You are the most precious person in my life."

"I feel the same way about you." Pressing my lips to his, I kissed him. Hard. The twins and I were Gabe's everything just as he was mine. *The twins.* I sat up, remembering my earlier conversation with Carson. "Oh, Gabe, I let it slip. Well you let it slip first by saying babies. And then I said children."

Gabe quirked an eyebrow in confusion.

"Carson knows we're having twins. I hope you're not upset."

He laughed heartily. "No, sweetheart. I can't wait for people to know." I opened my mouth to speak, but Gabe cut me off. "When you're ready. I don't care when, but I think I have a girl's name picked out."

Since our time under the tree, I hadn't thought about names. I loved our plan to name them. "Do I get any hints?"

He shook his head, the light of joy seeping into his eyes. "In a little less than eight months, I'll tell you."

A giggle escaped. "I can't wait to meet them."

Laying on my back, I touched my stomach. Gabe scooted down the bed and rested his mouth near my abdomen. "I can't wait to meet you both. You're going to have the best mom."

"And dad. They're going to have a terrific father."

His lips pressed to my navel. "I will love you both equally."

The vow broke my heart. To question the love of your parent was incomprehensible. I ran my fingers through his hair. "They will never doubt that, Gabe."

"What if I'm a horrible father?"

The worry tore through me. "Gabe," I whispered.

His saddened eyes met mine, but he didn't say a word.

"When your actions are filled with love, it's impossible. Think about how you are with me. You are the most caring and loving boyfriend. The way you are completes me."

Pressing his lips against my navel again, he whispered something unintelligible to our children before scooting up the bed.

I snuggled into his side. "Loving you is as easy as breathing."

His muscles relaxed under my touch.

"And so will loving our children."

Chapter Nineteen

All morning long, I had been in my studio painting up a storm. My thoughts calmed as I moved the paint across the canvas. I finished the last stroke on the smaller canvas and grabbed a Twizzler, my after-painting treat.

A man and woman's hands reached across the canvas, their fingertips touching as their hold on each other became surer. Like Gabe and me.

Three rapid taps at the door brought me out of my reverie. "Come in," I called.

Gabe entered, carrying a lunch tray. "Mildred thought you might be hungry. How's it going?"

"I just finished." I took a step away from the canvas. "What do you think?"

Laying down our sandwich tray, Gabe walked to the painting and studied it. His eyes roamed the canvas, but his face remained blank. I loved watching someone take in a piece of art for the first time as they connected emotionally with the painting. What was he thinking?

"I'm never letting you go, Willow. Our hold on each other will only strengthen."

He got the meaning. A smile crept over my face. "I hope so."

Seriousness took over his face as he turned to me. "I will never let you go. You are it for me."

"You're it for me, too."

He grabbed my hands and led me away from the painting toward the door. "I have a present for you. It came this morning."

A giddiness took over as I bounced on my toes. "What is it?"

"Go look outside."

Quickly, I jogged outside and found a wrapped package about the shape and size of a canvas leaned against the wall. I picked it up. The feel of it confirmed it was. Whose art would he have bought me as a gift? Excitement bubbled through me as I took it inside and grabbed the card under the huge white bow on the front.

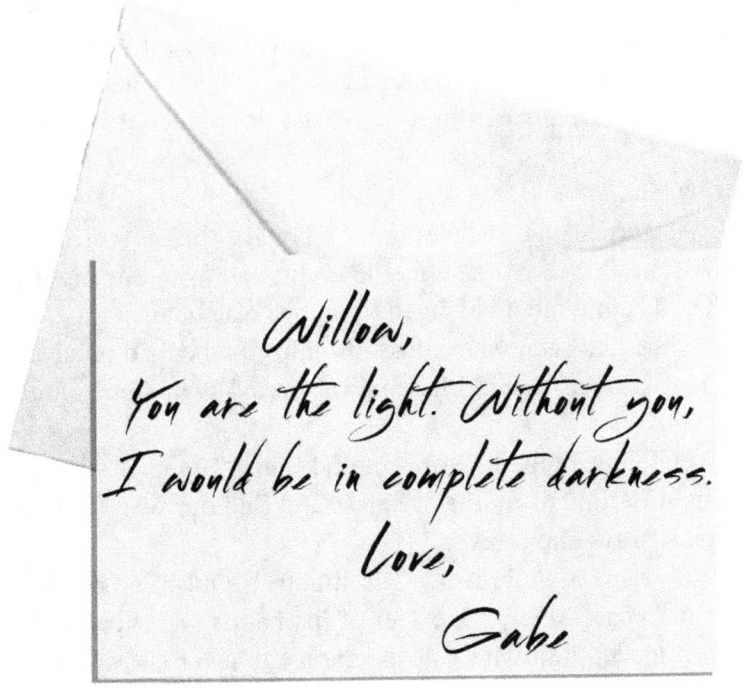

Willow,
You are the light. Without you,
I would be in complete darkness.
Love,
Gabe

Gabe's expression gave nothing away as I glanced at him. "Those words were beautiful."

"Open the gift."

The silver paisley wrapping paper tore easily and the image revealed itself. A gasp left me in a whoosh as I stared at the image. The image of a man walked through the forest toward a light at the end of the road. The hues became warmer as the light drew near. Darkness beckoned him from the other side. Though his hand reached toward the light, he was still only halfway to his destination.

This had been the painting I completed the morning after I made love to Gabe at the hotel. The night we conceived our twins. Now, it took on another meaning. A meaning Gabe knew at the art gallery at my show. I had thought it was Alex finding his way back from the clutches of PTSD when I initially painted this canvas. But it was Gabe finding his way back to me.

"Gabe..."

He turned me to face him. "I bought this before the art show started. When I saw it, I knew it was from our night together. That moment belonged to no one else but us."

Gabe had seen what I hadn't realized when I'd painted it. If I had known, I would have never parted with something so special.

Elated, I threw my arms around him. "Together we create the light to fight away the darkness and find our way with each other. Always and forever."

"Always and forever." His mouth found mine while he held me possessively. The feel of his hands were like molten lava. I needed him with a desperation I'd never known before. With a touch, I was a slave to the passion. Just as he had all the times before, Gabe pulled back. "Soon, sweetheart. Soon."

The rapid heaves of his chest synced to my own. We were going to combust with desire.

After a quick peck on the lips, Gabe led me to the table. "Let's eat before I lose all self-control."

"You seem pretty controlled."

The raised eyebrow challenged me. "Trust me, it's taking everything I have not to strip you bare and claim you. I want nothing more than to feel your heat surrounding me."

My nipples hardened and I took a step forward. His hands on my shoulders stopped my advance.

"Don't ever doubt my need for you."

I was grateful for this day of reprieve. Sometimes the importance of simply being with each other in all the madness was cast aside. "I feel like the most important person when I'm near you."

"That's because you are."

My stomach growled and Gabe grinned. "I think our babies are hungry."

Another growl answered and we laughed. "The kids have spoken."

We sat on the couch and ate. The pear and brie sandwich with caramelized onions melted in my mouth. "Mildred thought you would like this. I told her you weren't in the mood for sandwich meat."

At some point, I needed to tell her and Chris about the pregnancy. For now, I wanted to keep it quiet with Alex still blowing in the wind. "Thanks. Does it bother you? I don't want to tell anyone yet besides those who already know."

Gabe swallowed his bite. "No, I prefer it until we catch my brother. I don't want him to know. He'd use it against me."

My pregnancy created a vulnerability. And Alex knew no bounds. An unpleasant shiver ran through me at the thought.

I needed a change in subject. "I talked to Carson this morning. They're releasing him tomorrow. He has to keep his actions limited, but he sounded relieved to get out of the hospital. I thought they could setup across the house in the large bedroom on that wing. It's not Carson's normal room, but..." I wagged my eyebrows.

Gabe laughed as he said, "It'll give us all privacy."

The mental imagery of Carson doing the deed did not sit well with me. "Gross, he's like a brother. He can worry about that on his own. It's purely selfish based on my own lack of orgasm state."

Plus, if he was cleared, which I didn't want to know,

hearing them would scar me for life and require immense therapy.

Gabe leaned over. His tongue traced the shell of my ear, effectively obliterating the unwanted imagery. A needy whimper escaped my throat, igniting the earlier need. "I think it's a perfect idea. We'll get the confirmation from Dr. Jamiston this afternoon that we're cleared in three days."

We were able to move our appointment up unexpectedly this morning at the request of the doctor's office. Soon the ache would be soothed. "If he doesn't clear us, I don't know what I'll do."

"You haven't exhibited any signs they warned us about, so I don't think you'll have a problem getting cleared."

A true blessing. With spotting being normal with twins and something to look for, I had been nervous and checked regularly. So far I hadn't bled at all. "I haven't, thank goodness."

Gabe had been worried every time I checked—a silent burden we both carried. Once we got the official clear, the stress would lessen. "What's on the agenda tomorrow?"

Setting his sandwich down, Gabe cleared his throat. "Nothing. I hope we can have another relaxing day."

"What about the day after that?"

"I've discussed it with Trent. I think we should go talk to my mom."

"We?"

He brushed his hand through his hair, making it wild and sexy, but the movement was nervous. "Yes, we. I thought about what you said and we are stronger together than apart. But, fuck, I don't want her to mess with you."

I set the tray aside and scooted onto Gabe's lap. "She won't. I promise. You'll be there."

Mentally, I added, *and I'll be there for you.* Whether Gabe knew it or not, facing someone who was supposed to love him unconditionally would be harder than he imagined. Children were born to love their parents regardless of how shitty they treated their children.

The front pocket of Gabe's jeans vibrated underneath me. With a little jostling, he fished out his phone. "Hello. You did? Yes. Okay, we're on our way." Gabe hung up the phone. "That was Trent. They think they have the person behind the blue cohosh on tape. He's meeting us in the office right now if you want to come."

"Yes." Finally, we might get the answers to eliminate one of the threats.

At a clipped pace, we left the studio and made it across the yard. At the kitchen counter, Mildred expertly guided the flour dough into the pasta maker for homemade ravioli, Carson's favorite. Nothing beat homemade pasta.

Carson was going to be in heaven with this surprise. Absentmindedly, I wondered when he would officially propose to Francesca. Nothing had been said.

We made it to the study where we found Trent dressed in a black polo shirt and jeans, standing in the middle of the room while he read something on his phone. He glanced up when the door creaked open as we entered and grinned.

"How's it feel to be back home, Willow?"

"Wonderful. Thank you for all you and your team did to make it happen."

He gave me a quick hug. After this mess, Trent would forever be part of our family. "I think being here has lifted your spirits."

"It has. I painted all morning, which you probably already knew from your security reports." A wink confirmed Trent had received the reports. "Do you have the tape?"

"I do." He pulled a laptop from the satchel on a nearby chair. As he opened the computer and started a program, Trent explained, "This person used an employee's badge. We've been cross-referencing badges that were reported missing. Emily Tapperson reported hers yesterday when she came back to work after being gone for a week on vacation. Sure enough, her badge was used the day of the incident a few minutes before you and Francesca arrived at the hotel."

The program finished loading and a freeze frame of the outside of the hotel appeared. "Do we know who it is yet?"

"We're running it through facial recognition. Her face is obscured from the hat. All we have is a woman with a petite build. The suspect matches none of the people on our list. Employees have been questioned but don't remember anything."

Of course, the kitchen feeds were knocked out. The suspect could have changed and disguised herself as an employee.

Trent's fingers moved the mouse to hover over the Play button. Once pressed, the black and white feed moved. There wasn't any sound. The footage was empty until a woman in a hat walked up to the keycard scanner where she easily gained access with the stolen hotel badge.

"This is who we believe the perpetrator is."

The hat rode low on her head, obscuring her face. The one time her face angled even remotely to the side, large sunglasses covered any prominent identifiable features.

A weariness filled me as I remembered what it felt like to learn someone had tried to abort Carson and Francesca's baby. Knowing if Francesca hadn't called me into her room, I might have lost the two miracles inside me. Bile rose. Gabe laid his hand on my lower back. When I glanced his way, he looked murderous.

The screen went black. "Is that it?"

The image had been grainy and it had been hard to discern much detail. How would they run something through a facial recognition program? The most we had was part of a chin and a neck. Why had I thought this would be easy?

Another image queued on the screen after a few clicks. "This is the last of the footage we have. We haven't been able to determine how the suspect left the premises unless she changed disguises, which is a possibility. We've been pulling anyone of the same height and build who left that day. So far we've come up empty handed, but we will find her. Watch this next segment."

Again the screen flickered to life. The woman entered the hallway. Long sleeves covered her arms and keys dangled from her left hand. Trent pointed to the screen. "We're working on enlarging the image to see if we can determine a make and model of the car from the keys she's carrying."

I nodded as I intently watching the woman. Who was she? My mind flitted through anyone I knew Carson associated with in business. No one came to mind. As she passed in front of the camera, something dropped from her other hand. It looked like a pill bottle. "Is that?"

"Yes, we think that was the processed cohosh."

Hatred filled my veins as I stared at this person. The pressure against my teeth intensified as I ground them together. I stared at the woman as she kneeled to pick up the bottle. She stood up and walked out of camera range.

Then something registered at the back of my mind and I jumped. "Rewind it! Go back to where the woman was kneeling."

Without a word, Trent complied. I felt Gabe's gaze on me as I fought through the memories of someone with a birthmark on the back of her neck. Where had I seen that clover-shaped mark? I knew this person.

The image reversed and then played. "Freeze it!" The screen stopped.

I leaned in closer, my heart rate escalating. "Can you zoom in?"

More clicks on the screen. Then Trent responded. "A little, but the distortion will increase some."

"That's fine."

Gabe touched the small of my back. "What are you seeing?"

"I'm not sure. But... I think I've met this person before."

Gabe balled his hand into a fist on my back before he released the tension. I felt the same way. Focusing on the woman, I looked at her hair, which was pulled back in a ponytail. If her hair was down, the birthmark would not be seen.

Clover-shaped birthmark. That was the key. Think, Willow, think. I closed my eyes and an image from Martha's Vineyard came to my mind.

"Oh shit." My eyes shot open. "Oh shit. NO! How could she? Why would she?"

Gabe came around and stood between me and the monitor. "Who is it?"

I shook my head, not wanting to believe it. "It's Rosie. Our friend, Rosie." Taking a few steps back, I sat in the chair. "It's her. I know it's her."

"Why do you think it's Rosie, sweetheart?" Gabe knelt in front of me.

Trent typed something on his phone.

Swallowing hard, I organized my thoughts. "You know the trip I took with Carson to Martha's Vineyard?" Both men nodded their heads. I had met Trent for the first time on that trip. Gabe had been there when I had drank too much to make sure I was safe. That seemed like a lifetime ago. "At the beginning, Rosie had been all over Carson. It was normal Rosie behavior. While Carson was sleeping, we were in the kitchen eating. She wanted to know if Carson would like this teal and feather nightie. While she was asking, she kept playing with her hair and I saw the birthmark. I distinctly remembered it being clover shaped like it is in this video. I hadn't ever seen it before, and Rosie fits the build of that woman."

Fire burned within Gabe's eyes. "We need to tell Carson and get this taken care of." There was a deadly venom in his voice. "He's got twenty-four hours or I'm handling it."

Chapter Twenty

My nerves were shot as I sat in my studio, watching the second hand tick down. Minutes seemed like hours. The pressure from Gabe's hand on our interlocked fingers reminded me he was here.

Alex hadn't been involved with the poisoning. In some ways this felt worse, having a friend do something so vile.

Our eyes were glued to the computer screen that had the camera feed of my front door. After much debate Gabe, Trent, and Carson agreed I could safely remain on the premises as long as I agreed to come to the studio. Two of Gabe's military friends were outside. I had met them briefly when they arrived this afternoon. The introduction had been short, but I sensed a deep loyalty between the men. So far, Trent was impressed with their work.

After the discovery of Rosie yesterday, Trent drove to the hospital to talk to Carson about Rosie and give him Gabe's time limit. With the Alex situation, we also had a limited window of time to see his mother. Rosie was something that needed to be dealt with swiftly. Since the cops were involved with this, the last thing we wanted were the two intertwining at the same time. Otherwise, Alex might be disappear like he had when Gabe was a child. Thinking of him interfering with us down the road when our children were older was not an option.

After re-examining all the evidence, Gabe and Trent believed Rosie was the person driving the Hummer also. Someone fitting the same description of the person in the hotel video had rented one three counties away a couple of days before the incident.

I turned my attention back to the screen. Last night I barely slept, knowing a good friend of ours had done such a thing. The realization made me doubt most things in my life, but I refused to let Rosie have that power over me. Part of me hoped I was wrong. It would have been easier to understand if it had been someone with an ax to grind. Sick, I know.

But, Rosie.

All those years we thought her to be crazy yet lovable. What else had she done? Or had the knowledge of Francesca's pregnancy sent her over the edge?

The concern she had for me in the hospital was evident, but ultimately an act. Through the night, I tried to remember all we talked about. The conversations were normal, but exactly what we talked about evaded me.

Shortly after Trent gave him the news, Carson called me on a secure line. Livid was an understatement. He asked for permission to have Rosie over to the house today.

I leaned my head on Gabe's shoulder needing the support. "I know, sweetheart. It's hard."

Carson had arrived about three hours ago. Francesca had fussed over getting him settled. After two hours, Carson asked her to get some things from his house with Marie. Of course she jumped at the chance. Everything was going according to plan as the doorbell chimed elaborately.

Andre came to the door. Rosie stood there with a huge Cheshire grin on her face when the door opened. Dressed like a slut, her shirt was low and her skirt high.

I saw her in a completely different light and my stomach roiled.

Gabe turned up the volume on the monitor.

"I'm here to see Carson Whitmore. He's expecting me."

This morning Carson called Rosie and asked if she could visit him this afternoon. He asked she come alone so they could talk "privately."

"Yes."

Rosie entered the house and looked toward the living room. The view on the monitor changed as they walked down the hall and into the office. Gabe hit another button to display the feed from office. Rosie stopped at the door. "Carson. You're looking better. Thank goodness you're okay. I tried to see you, but they wouldn't let me."

Motioning to Andre, Carson "dismissed" him. The door clicked shut giving the illusion of privacy. Carson wore lounge pants and a T-shirt. To the normal observer he appeared to be relaxing on the couch. The ticking in his jaw told a different story. "Thanks, it's been tough. Doctors expect me to make a full recovery."

Tentatively, Rosie took a few steps closer. "Oh good. You have no idea how relived I am."

Yeah, right, considering you put us in the hospital.

"Come, have a seat." Carson patted the space next to him. "I wanted to talk to you while I have the chance. Since waking up, I haven't had a moment to myself. Sorry I didn't call sooner." He delivered the line smoothly as he gave her his patented smile that won over most of the female population. He had to be tired, but he pushed through.

For a brief second, Rosie looked around to see if they truly were alone. As she walked toward him, she asked, "Where's Willow, Gabe, and Francesca?"

There was a hint of disdain as she said Francesca's name. Had Rosie's erratic behavior masked the clues to a more serious problem that had been there all along? Apparently, it had. I thought she was happy dating Mitchell.

Carson raised his arm behind his head, showing off his abs. The way Rosie gravitated toward him while staring at the exposed skin lured her into the illusion.

"Willow and Gabe went to eat. I sent Francesca on a fake errand."

Slowly, Rosie lowered herself on the couch. Breathily, she jutted out her chest while asking, "Why?"

Gross. Disgusting. Sick. All those words described this unfamiliar friend.

Leaning forward, Carson placed his hand on hers and the image revolted me.

Gabe squeezed my hand. "Willow, he's acting."

"I know." My voice was tense as I focused on the scene. Gabe rubbed soothing circles on my hand with his thumb.

"Rosie, I needed to see you alone. There was something I realized the night of the accident that I need to tell you."

She leaned in. "What is it?"

My skin crawled. *This is only pretend.*

Carson remained relaxed. "I have feelings for you. And I want to explore those feelings and see where they go."

"Really? Are you serious?" She was sickening as she bounced on the couch.

Certifiably insane.

"Yes. I've wanted to talk to you ever since the night of the art gallery when I realized there was something more between us."

Her breath was needy as she leaned forward only inches from his face. "You did?"

"There's something about you, Rosie. But, it's complicated because of Mitchell and Francesca." He shook his head as if utterly defeated and stood. "I think Francesca is playing me for my money."

In a drama-filled gesture, Rosie's hand went to her chest as if the thought caused her physical pain. What a sick psycho. "Oh, that's terrible, Carson. I can't imagine. Why would she do that to you?"

"And now with the accident, I think someone's after me. Until I get that cleared, I'm going to have to keep up the charade with Francesca." Carson's shoulders drooped while he paced a few feet away. With his back to Rosie, the disdain leaked through as his mask slipped. Carson scrubbed a hand over his face. He swayed but righted himself and leaned a nearby table.

All of this hinged on Rosie confessing to what she'd done. The more things she confessed the more offenses could be added to her prosecution.

Rosie's voice made him pause mid-stride. "Do you want to explore things between us?"

Bingo.

Carson turned and knelt in front of her. "Yes, I do. But I won't cheat. I couldn't start something with you based on a lie. First, I need to figure out who ran us off the road before I end things with Francesca."

She leaned forward with an ever-so-sweet expression like the world had just handed her a prize. "You're safe. I promise."

He cocked his head to the side and asked, "How do you know?"

"Oh, Carson, I can't tell you. You'll hate me." Tears fell on her cheeks.

Here we go. The confession was on the verge of breaking free. Beside me, Gabe's nerves looked as though they were strung tighter than mine as he watched every move.

Carson's hand went to her face in a loving manner and Rosie closed her eyes.

I wanted to gag at the sight.

"I could never hate you, Rosie. I've fallen in love with you. I think I can stomach anything if I know you'll give me a chance. I've been an ass all these years ignoring what could have been. But, I may have to go through with the marriage proposal until I can figure it out. Francesca is pressuring me."

"No, you can't!" she screamed, startling me and Carson, who tried to lean back but Rosie clutched his hand to her cheek. "You can't, Carson!"

"Why?"

Here we go. Sweat formed on my brow as the anticipation grew. The answers we sought hopefully were about to come out.

She stood and so did Carson. In a loving gesture, her hand went to his chest. "Darling, you are safe. I thought Francesca was in the car with you. But, it was Willow. I never meant to hurt her. I love Willow. I never meant to hurt you. I found out Francesca was pregnant and it sent me into a blind rage. I couldn't let another woman have your baby... at any cost."

Liar.

She had rented the Hummer beforehand. This was all planned.

"Why?" Carson's voice was on the verge of becoming terse.

In the heat of her rant, Rosie paced the room. "Because I want to have your baby. I had planned to make my move at Martha's Vineyard, but Willow needed you that weekend. I understood. You guys are so close. I don't mind you two being that close. I used Mitchell to pass the time. But then, that bitch got pregnant. I had to do something before she trapped you. I had planned to do something all along but she needed to be eliminated."

Oh hell, we had it. I wanted to jump in celebration. The confession had been easier than expected with how meticulously she planned things. Having Carson within her grasp must have obliterated her guard.

Carson's eyes widened for only a brief second. With his jaw locked, he *attempted* to calmly ask, "You ran us off the road?"

Running across the room, she threw her hands around Carson's waist. "Oh, Carson, I'm so sorry. I had no idea how the car would flip. All I could think about was not letting that cow have you. I've been so patient while you've slept with other women."

There was a minor tremor in Carson's hands as he placed them on her back. "I'll have to deal with the baby." The words sounded forced. This must have been hard for him as he loved his unborn child unconditionally.

Rosie pushed away and use her hands animatedly as she said, "You can't have that on your conscious, my love. I have extra blue cohosh. All we need to do is give some to her and the problem will be solved. You can do it tonight at dinner."

I closed my eyes for a brief second wondering how someone could end someone's life without a second thought.

"Why do you have that?" The storm behind Carson's calm façade was slowly breaking free. We were almost out of time.

"Because I tried to do it myself, but somehow I must have done something wrong. Or Francesca's not pregnant like you suspected."

My hand went to my mouth. "Gabe."

"I know, sweetheart. That fucking bitch." The tendons on his free hand popped out in rage as he spit the words.

Carson's jaw flexed and his shoulders tensed. "How'd you do it?"

Lost in her own world, Rosie walked around the room as she bragged. "I have a friend who works at the hotel. I knew she was on vacation so I took her key card. Willow told me she was taking Francesca back to the hotel to eat, and I followed them back. I posed as one of the kitchen staff. It was quite simple to blend. I love you, Carson. I would do anything to have you."

Carson muttered something indiscernible.

Rosie stopped and walked to him. "What did you say, my love?" He truly was her world. Crazily so.

"You fucking bitch. You tried to kill my baby." Domineering, Carson's mood and voice transformed.

Rosie scrambled away at the change. "Carson, you want me. You love me."

He shook his head. "I could never love you. You almost killed Willow, me, and my unborn child."

"Carson... please. I love you!"

With a wave of his hand, the closet door opened. Trent and two police officers walked into the room.

While one of the officers moved behind her, the other stepped forward and began reading Rosie her rights from his notepad. "Rosie McCormick, you are under arrest for the attempted murder of Carson Whitmore, Willow Russo, David Greggers, and Francesca Morino."

"What?" Rosie's eyes grew wild. "You can't do this. I'll fucking kill her and the baby. She can't have you. She can't have you!"

I flinched at her hate-filled words.

The officer behind her wrestled her into handcuffs as she screamed.

Carson walked up to her. "You will never get near Francesca, my child, or Willow ever again."

"I don't want Willow dead. She's my best friend. She's going to be my maid of honor at our wedding."

This woman was more than unhinged, and I remained motionless as I watched the scene unfold.

Carson spoke to the officer. "Take her away. My lawyer will meet you at the station. He's at your disposal to ensure she doesn't receive bail."

"Yes, Mr. Whitmore."

Rosie kept thrashing. "Where's Willow? Willow! Willow! They're hurting me! Carson's gone crazy! Willow! Save me!"

They left the room, and Carson swayed and fell back on the couch.

"Carson!" I yelled but realized he wasn't able to hear me. Not thinking, I left the studio and sprinted to the house. I was almost to the back door when Gabe captured me by the waist and gently scooped me up.

"Wait, sweetheart. I need to confirm Rosie is out of the house. Trent is with Carson. He's fine."

Two guards stood at the right ready to intercept me, too if Gabe hadn't.

The phone was out of his pocket before I responded as he set me down. "Andre. Is it clear? Okay. Thanks." He hung up. "You can go."

Not wasting any time, I threw the door open and ran to the office. Carson was on the couch leaning back with his eyes closed. "Carson, are you okay? Do I need to call a doctor? Carson?"

He slowly opened his eyes. "I'm okay. That took a lot out of me. I hate the recovery process."

"I'll be right back. Stay put." My instincts took over as I left the room. Gabe was right behind me. I grabbed the blood pressure cuff and pulse/ox monitor from the closet in the hallway. Dad insisted we had it on hand for Nonno in case something happened. Back in the room, I put the cuff on his arm and pressed the button. "Put your hand over your heart."

"Willow, I'm—"

I glared. One look at my face and he stopped in his tracks. He offered his finger for the pulse oximeter.

The readings came back clear. "I need you to take it easy and *not* end up in the hospital again."

He leaned back. "I promise. I'll be good as new shortly. We got her, Willow. She can't hurt you or Francesca ever again."

Chapter Twenty-One

After Rosie had been hauled off with the detectives, her parents called Carson and me. On advice from the attorneys, we sent the phone calls to voicemail. At this point, the judge confirmed no bail would be granted due to the heinous nature of the crimes and the instability Rosie exhibited when she arrived.

The scene I watched from the studio replayed in my head.

Soon the news would spread to our friends. I was surprised they hadn't called given how desperate Rosie's parents sounded on the voicemail. They begged us to drop the charges and promised to get her help. None of us could take that chance. The depth of Rosie's deception warranted our weariness. But still… she had been our friend.

The sting of betrayal would spread and our group of friends would be forever altered. The innocence of past scenarios with Rosie were tainted. What other damage had she caused? Only time would tell if other wrongdoings would come to light.

There had been times I'd felt uneasy around her. But who wouldn't when their friend chased boys and slapped their ass for the hell of it. Everyone had explained this with a simple "That's Rosie for you."

The car accident and the poisoning were now explained—two problems solved. And Alex had not been involved. Now we were back to the original dilemma. Alex was behind the remaining dilemmas, but in what capacity.

In hindsight, Alex had remained quiet since the finger. We knew he'd visited Alex Junior the night before I taught the class at Apple Blossom. What plans Alex had for us scared me. Sometimes I felt like a puppet while he pulled the strings, making us dance.

Laughter brought my attention back to the group. Nonno retold a story from his childhood when he tried to make his own wine. In the end, his mother ended up with a messy kitchen and smashed grapes everywhere. I'd heard the story many times, as I was sure Marie and Bennett had, too. Nonno once told me that a good story should be told often.

I agreed.

After dinner, we retired to the living room to visit. The ravioli had been a smash hit with Carson and earned Mildred a bear hug. She loved every second of our praises. The aroma of oregano and cheese from the homemade Italian dish lingered. Utter perfection. Aside from Mom and Dad's absence, having everyone here felt like old times.

Carson shifted in his seat, and I looked him over to make sure he was okay. Overall he'd recovered quickly from the exertion of this afternoon. Francesca was radiant as she sat beside him. Such a drastic difference from a few days ago. Now she thrived versus barely surviving.

Carson decided when we had more definitive answers on

Rosie's sentence he would share it with Francesca. I trusted he knew best for her. We never used the TV and overall were unplugged from social media. It would be easy to keep her in the dark for a bit. When Francesca found out the truth about what had happened with Rosie, I wondered how she would take it. Trials were long and cumbersome. Hopefully, we were able to expedite the process.

I told Carson marriage should be transparent. If Gabe kept that from me, I would be livid. But... we were two different people and I knew Francesca preferred to remain in the dark from our talks. At some point he planned to tell her. Their relationship worked and that was all that mattered.

I snuggled into Gabe's side as we shared the large overstuffed leather chair. It wasn't until Francesca told everyone about her doctor's appointment that I remembered the one I had today. It had left my mind in all the chaos. We were cleared for sex in two days.

Only two more days.

I had nearly jumped off the table in glee, but somehow managed to keep my cool. Or at least I pretended the doctor didn't notice my obvious jubilation.

Life was complete in this moment.

"Baby, would you mind getting me a little water?" Carson asked Francesca as they cuddled on the love seat. Francesca watched closely over Carson. It was obvious how much she truly loved him. Hopefully we had time to hang out together again soon.

She kissed his cheek. "Yes, be right back. Does anyone else need anything?"

No thank yous were murmured by everyone. As she left the room, Carson grinned, gave me a wink, and stood near the fireplace. After a long nap, he appeared more rested. Marie gave me a curious look in my peripheral vision, but I remained focused elsewhere. This was Carson's moment. Only I knew the secret after our talk this afternoon.

Before anyone had a chance to ask, Francesca bustled back into the room. "Here you go." She noticed he'd moved. "Did you need to stretch your legs? Are you feeling okay?"

Carson tucked his hair behind his ears and blew out a quick breath. "I need to ask something else of you."

"Of course. What is it? Are you okay?"

He took her hands after setting down the drink. "You are the one for me. The only one. And you're giving me the greatest gift in the world... a child." She looked down with a smile on her face, embarrassed.

Gabe dug his hand a little deeper into my hip. I wasn't sure he was aware of it, and I wondered if the words struck home with him.

Carson brought her gaze to meet his with his fingers. It was an intimate moment passing between the two as they stared into each other's eyes. "As you know, the night of the accident I had planned to ask you to marry me."

"I know." The answer was somber, bringing back the awful memories and the hard fourteen days that had transpired since.

Bringing her right hand up, Carson rubbed the engagement ring she received from Bennett at the beach house. "Dad gave you the ring as a symbol of our love while I fought my way back to you."

The women in the room started to sniffle, including me. We were lucky to have all of us here to experience this moment.

"I love you, Francesca, with my entire being. You are the other half I was meant to be with. Will you do me the honor of becoming my wife and building a life with me?"

Her head nodded before she quietly responded, "Yes! Yes! Yes!"

Cheers erupted as she threw her arms around him. Carson spun her around she squealed in delight.

"Dad told me what you said. And now I'm here to move it to the proper hand." Before everyone descended on them, Carson moved her engagement ring from her right hand to her left.

With her hand extended, she looked at the ring. "It's perfect."

Seeing them bound together gave me wistful thoughts of wearing Gabe's ring and being his in every way possible. A beautiful dream. When would we be ready? I turned to see Gabe watching me. I mouthed, *I love you.*

He mouthed back, *I love you forever.*

A girlish giggle bubbled inside of me. It was my turn to hug Francesca after Marie.

As we embraced, I said, "I always wanted a sister."

"Me, too. I couldn't ask for a better one."

"Me, either."

Since Carson woke up, Francesca hadn't mentioned the engagement once. She had Carson and that was all that mattered. I respected her confidence in their love and for not pressuring him ever even after becoming pregnant.

Next was Carson. "I'm so happy for you."

"Me, too, Willow. Me, too. I'm happy for us." He brought me closer to him. "Never forget you deserve this, too."

———•———————•———————•———

In bed, I read reviews and ratings of baby items Francesca and I had found. She had gone to bed a while ago. Two of almost everything would be needed. The expense of having a baby blew my mind. Since we weren't finding out what we were having, I would need to stick to gender-neutral colors.

The pros and cons blended together along with the warnings. My word, I needed a manual for all this baby stuff. Earlier I'd placed the paint order for the colors I decided on for the baby room. Next week, I'd start outlining the drawings on the wall. I wanted the walls finished before I got too large.

Carson, Gabe, and Trent were in the office. While they talked, I'd hung out with Francesca, not wanting her to be left out while they went over security measures. I figured there was more on the agenda, but Gabe would tell me when they were done. Not once this evening had Francesca mentioned wanting to be there for the security discussion. Truly she seemed happy remaining in a bubble.

When my eyesight became blurry from staring the screen too long, I set my tablet aside and picked up the memory book Francesca had given me. In the rush to get to Carson, I had left it in her hotel room. When we retired to my room to drink hot chocolate, she brought it to me. It truly was a beautiful gift— one I would always treasure.

A yawn escaped as I scooted farther down in the bed and flipped to the last page. Sleep would be upon me soon. *I should text Gabe and check on him.* I stared at the picture.

The door opened slowly and Gabe crept in. "I'm glad you're still awake. Sorry that took so long. What are you doing?"

"Looking at the scrapbook Francesca gave me."

I turned it around for us both to see. The picture of Gabe and me from the studio was set at an angle on the last page. It was my favorite one of us. We had taken it right before he left. We were happy. In love. His arms were wrapped around my shoulders while my lavender gray eyes stared at the camera. I read the caption read.

When love found your mom and refused to let go.

"I remember this picture. Your eyes always take my breath away. They're so expressive."

"So are yours." I ran my fingers over the picture. "She nailed the caption."

Gabe's smile widened as he commented, "She did. I used to think I didn't deserve love."

Putting the book aside, I reached up, asking for a kiss. "Everyone deserves love. It's the one thing that can save a person."

"I couldn't agree more." Gabe gave me a quick peck.

On cue I yawned again.

"I'm glad I have that effect on you."

"I'd rather you be in me." I slapped a hand over my mouth. "Oh my gosh! Why?"

Gabe chuckled. "I like that effect a lot more."

"At least I kept it together today at the doctor's office. No slips." Glancing at the clock, I realized almost three hours had passed. It was almost eleven. "Wow, I hadn't realized how late it was. No wonder I'm tired."

Gabe shucked off his shirt revealing his tan chiseled chest and dominant black sword tattoo. Instinctively, I licked my lips. My earlier statement was true about wanting him inside me. His strong arms went to the button of his jeans and he jerkily yanked them off. For the first time, I saw his anxiousness. The façade slipped momentarily. Gabe scooted in beside me and I molded to him and felt his escalated heart rate.

"Are you okay? Did something happen?" I asked.

"Not like you're thinking. We finalized some details."

By the tone of his voice, I wasn't going to like the details.

"And?" Sitting up, I waited for him to respond, my earlier sleepiness forgotten.

"This will hopefully give us some answers and end this mess sooner rather than later."

My voice was hesitant. But the idea appealed me. "How is that?"

"Turn it around on Alex. Focus the heat on him."

"And how are you going to do that?"

"Visit De Luca."

"Gabe... what if?" I cradled my head in my hands. The repercussions spinning wild.

He brought his hand up to my face. "Sweetheart, we've been trying to figure out who our enemies are and how to take care of them. I've requested a meeting with De Luca. I think Alex is framing him. If that's true, then De Luca will want him taken care of."

"Gabe, what if he doesn't believe you? What if he doesn't care? What if one brother is as good as the next?" All of the scenarios of things going bad played through my head, ending with Gabe hurt or even worse.

I knew what it was like to not have Gabe in my life. And now I was pregnant with his twins. Being a single mother was not something I wanted to experience... ever. My children needed their father. I needed Gabe.

"Willow."

My hands sliced through the air. "Gabe, I don't like this. At all."

"Willow."

I got off the bed and paced. "Why in the world did the three of you think this was a good idea?" My voice rose. "I mean, this could leave me alone. Our children fatherless."

"Willow."

Another five steps and I turned back to face Gabe. "This is a bad idea. A really bad idea. Why in the world would you think I would be okay with this? De Luca is dangerous. He may not be after me, but the fact remains he is still a criminal."

"Willow." Gabe's commanding voice got my attention as he rose from the bed.

I snapped. "What?"

In his black boxers, he took a few steps toward me—strong and powerful. "He isn't going to hurt me. I'm going to have back up."

"But—" Closer now, I looked up to his towering figure.

"Willow, I'll be fine."

I swallowed, not wanting to argue but apprehensive.

"Sweetheart, if needed I can be a dangerous motherfucker myself." The certainty in his voice quelled my nerves a little.

I remained silent as I searched his eyes for any doubt.

"Willow, I will be here for you and our babies. I've got this. I know it's the right move. I've known for a while but needed to wait to act on it."

Meaning he needed the doctor to clear me because he knew this would stress me out. I took a deep cleansing breath. The least I should do was hear him out. And then determine if I wanted to argue about this further. "What's the plan?"

"You'll stay behind." I went to rebuke his comment, but he held up his hand. "I need to make sure you are safe so I can do what's needed."

Meaning Gabe may need to turn into a dangerous person. A person I had yet to see. Someone he hoped I would never see. "Where am I going to stay while you're there?"

"Here at the house. Trent and a few men will come with me. Andre and some men I served with will stay here with you, Carson, and Francesca. I trust these men, Willow. You will be safe."

I kept searching his eyes. In that moment when his vivid green eyes met mine with certainty, I decided to trust Gabe's instincts. "Okay."

"Okay?" A raised eyebrow told me he thought I would put up a stronger fight. It pleased me to surprise him. Normally he read me so well.

Taking his hands in mine, I squeezed them. "I trust you. Do what you have to."

His lips descended on me and I giggled.

"Good grief, I love you so damn much," he murmured against my mouth.

Apprehension still lingered, but I wanted these problems behind us. "When are you doing this?"

"I don't know when the meeting with De Luca will happen. We probably won't have much time to get there. I'll only have one shot with him. I still plan to visit Mom tomorrow. I need Alex off his game."

Alex probably thought he knew Gabe. However, Gabe was doing the unexpected. Or at least that was my theory. If Alex fiercely protected his child and mother like we thought... this would send him off kilter.

There was one thing I had to have from Gabe. "I need you to promise me something."

He knew exactly what I was going to ask by the loving

look he gave me. "I promise I will come back to you, Willow. I will *always* come back to you. I swear to it."

"That's all I ask."

Chapter Twenty-Two

Early morning light trickled into my room. I reached across the bed and found it empty. Cold. *What time is it? Had I slept late?* The clock read just after six. Too early. A feeling a déjà vu came over me as I remembered the morning he left me in the hotel room to confront Alex. That morning I felt abandoned and utterly alone. I shook my head to clear the thoughts away. Gabe loved me and wouldn't leave me.

"I'm over here, sweetheart."

Relieved, I turned, "Why are you out of bed?" I squinted. Gabe was dressed in black cargo pants and long sleeve matching shirt. "Why are you dressed? Like that?"

His appearance gave him a military vibe. He looked dangerous and my sex pulsed at the thought.

He came over and sat by my side. "I left in the middle of the night."

The fog of sleep abated. "What? Why?"

"I left a note in case you woke up," he said, nodding to a

piece of paper on the nightstand. "You needed your sleep and I figured I'd be back before you woke."

I grabbed the piece of paper and read it.

Willow,

I had to step out.

Go talk to Carson.

I will keep my promise.

Love,

Gabe

The note hadn't revealed anything. "Where did you go?"

"I met with De Luca."

I shot up and screeched, "You what! When? How did that happen? So fast?" That was not what I expected him to say.

He touched the side of my face and then traced along my

jaw. "Willow, calm down. I'm safe. You're safe." Some of the tension eased when his words registered. "In the middle of the night, we got word De Luca wanted to meet. We only had a thirty-minute window to get there. No time to think it through. You were sleeping. I almost woke you, but decided against it. I didn't want you to worry."

"Oh, Gabe." That was all I had to say not knowing if I was relieved or irritated I slept through the whole ordeal. Irritation won at the moment. "You should never leave without telling me. Seriously? What were you thinking?"

Pushing the covers away, I tried to move away but Gabe blocked me by forming a cage on either side of my body with his arms. With all my might I pushed but to no avail.

"Move," I bit out.

"No." The one-word answer and the finality it held pissed me off more.

Incredulously, I glared. "Move, Gabe."

"No, we are going to talk this through. I get you're pissed. I knew you would be, but I'm asking you to hear me out."

Like a child, I crossed my arms over my chest and stared him down. It was the most effective way to show my irritation since pacing was no longer an option.

"Would you have been worried the entire time I was gone?"

I dropped my arms. "You know I would have been. This whole situation worries me."

"Would there have been anything for you to do?"

Going had been out and listening would have been out, too. Maybe he had a point, but I wasn't ready to let go of my feelings... yet.

"Go on." I locked my jaw.

He relaxed his arms beside me.

Damn it, he knew the worst of my aggravation had left.

"We met in an abandoned warehouse. When I got there, I was searched for wires. Once we got through the pleasantries I had to prove I was a twin. To begin with they were less than open to my claim of not being Alex."

I searched Gabe. "Are you okay? Did they hurt you?" I ran my hands over him to make sure he didn't flinch anywhere. He appeared unharmed.

"Sweetheart, I am fine. It was easy to prove. Apparently, he gave Alex a scar on his lower abdomen not long ago. A nasty jagged scar about four inches long."

Lifting his shirt, Gabe showed me his smooth stomach, which only had one scar to the right on his lower rib cage.

"What's this from?"

"A little scuffle in the Middle East," he said effortlessly.

It took me a minute to process. "What?"

"Willow, what I did in the military was dangerous, really dangerous at times. When we met, I was in town, deciding if I wanted to reenlist or not. The military was the only real family I'd ever had, but there was something missing. The job became less fulfilling. I didn't realize it, but I'd been searching for you."

I added to the story. "The day we met you planned to send in the reenlistment paperwork, but held off when I bumped into you on the sidewalk."

If I had kept my planned massage, Gabe and I would have missed each other. Fate knew what she was doing down to the second.

Gabe's hand came to my stomach. "Yes. Bumping into you was life changing. I felt something and put off sending the papers. After our first night together, I tore up the papers and gave my notice. But, I had to see this last mission through, and even though something went wrong during that mission, I got out."

I closed my eyes. "I'm glad you're out."

"Me, too, sweetheart."

We were off topic and I wanted to know what happened. "What did De Luca say when he saw your stomach?"

"Apparently the scar was bad enough that plastic surgery couldn't have fixed it. Also, it had happened within the last few months, around the time De Luca was arrested by Commander Taylor. We're now using it to identify myself with the men along with a code word and hand gesture."

This became more and more complicated. "What gesture and code word did you guys decide on?"

"The word green and a scratch under my left ear."

"That's it?"

"The simpler the word and gesture the harder it will be for anyone watching to decipher."

Minutely, I shifted to be a little more comfortable. "Do you think De Luca is connected to any of the burnings?"

"No. I don't. He told me he was being framed. Alex worked for him and has carried out orders for De Luca in the past. In the meeting nothing concrete was said, but I got the drift."

"What else did you tell him?" Ignorance sometimes truly felt like the better course. Knowing too much sucked us into the fold and we wanted to leave it behind us.

Gabe put a hand to the back of his neck. "I told him about the DNA test we conducted on the finger. I gave him a copy of the test results. I left Alex Junior out of it all. I gave him a copy of the only picture I have of Alex and me together, and De Luca seemed satisfied. I'm sure his team is checking the authenticity of it but I'm not concerned."

Alex's web of lies became thicker with all the intricacies. "What happened next?"

"I asked him point blank if he was the one who sent the note to you in Italy. I was prepared to pay off Alex's debt to keep him away from you."

I held my breath, waiting to hear the answer.

"De Luca thought you were Alex's mistress. You were simply someone who had poor judgement. He assured me that you and Alex Junior were safe. He didn't comment on the debt."

So De Luca knew about Alex's son. Of course he knew. De Luca had to be vigilant to avoid the law if the rumors were true about the burnings. If Alex had turned him in to Commander Taylor in some sort of power struggle, De Luca wanted his life, no doubt. The pieces were falling into place.

Gabe added, "De Luca asked me if I knew who took care of Commander Taylor. I let him know I suspected Alex was behind the three recent burnings. Trent's team has been monitoring Commander Taylor's family and nothing has been done to them. No threats. Nothing."

A disbelieving noise left me. "A crook with a conscious?"

Gabe lay down beside me and wrapped his arms around me. "I wouldn't go that far. A cautious crook. We're going to keep watching him from a distance. De Luca wants revenge on the man himself and asked me to contact him if I found Alex. He informed me he would ensure Alex never bothered us again."

A shiver raced down my spine. Alex had made his bed and now he had to lie in it. As terrible as it sounded, Alex Junior would have a chance at life without his terrible father. "What's next?"

"We'll see my mother today. De Luca asked me for any

leads and I told him my plan. From a distance he'll be tracking me, too. It's best if I'm forthcoming with him for the time being. The sooner this is behind us, the better."

Gabe's phone beeped and he read a message. "Just the security checks. All is clear."

"What if De Luca goes to see your mom?"

"He will for sure. Alex has another monkey on his back searching for him. The pressure will increase. He's going to become careless when he panics about his world falling apart. I think he'll also visit Harley."

Thinking of a killer visiting my parents would have me in a tailspin, but I had to remember Gabe's was a different story. For all we knew his mother had been conspiring with Alex this whole time.

Another piece of the puzzle was in place. I pulled the covers on top of us. There were still too many things that could go wrong. "What if De Luca decides you could turn on him?"

"He knows I have nothing on him. He said nothing incriminating. Our meeting was clean."

My head hurt with all the possibilities. "Are you tired?"

He kissed the top of my head. "Exhausted."

I snuggled closer, listening to the sound of his breathing slow as Gabe fell asleep in my arms. We planned to leave midmorning. At least he would get a few hours of sleep.

Chapter Twenty-Three

A t breakfast, I placed the last crepe onto the plate after adding the strawberry mixture and cream. I had stayed in bed until the last possible minute to let Gabe sleep as long as possible. The moment I shifted he woke— always completely aware of my actions.

After the morning of revelations, I needed comfort food and decided to make Mom's recipe. Carson and Francesca walked in, dressed for the day.

Dramatically, Carson walked up and sniffed the air. "Morning. I thought I smelled crepes."

"Morning. I promised Francesca I'd make these when we were at the hotel."

Carson had known Gabe left in the middle of the night. He'd been asked to tell me if I'd woken up and asked.

I raised my eyebrow letting him know I knew. "Grab a plate while they're still warm. Gabe's finishing up in the shower."

Carson gave me a quick hug and whispered, "He made

the right decision, angel. Don't be too mad."

Truth was, I had forgiven Gabe and Carson. At least it was over. "I know he did."

"Good, I'm glad I'm forgiven." He patted my head and I swatted it away, laughing.

"These smell delicious. You'll have to give me the recipe if it's not a family secret," Francesca said while taking a plate.

I turned. "Even if it were, you're now family, Francesca."

She stopped and smiled big. "I am. It's hard to believe." As she walked to the table, she pointed to Carson. "You did good picking your best friend. Now, I'm going to steal her."

"I'll share. That's the best offer you're getting."

I grabbed plates for Gabe and me and sat down. "There's plenty of me to go around. Or..." I held my hand out to the side, palms up. "We could get into a bribing war. I do like those." In the hospital, I had told Francesca about the cologne story.

Both she and Carson said at the same time, "I'll share."

We broke out in laughter, and I savored the moment. For the last five months, my house had felt like a tomb. Now it brimmed with life like it was meant to. Looking down, I knew Dad and Mom would be pleased.

The flavors from the crepe spread across my tongue. "These never get old. Best comfort food around," I mumbled around the deliciousness.

Gabe walked in freshly showered. "Morning. How'd everyone sleep?"

"Wonderful. I think we were glad to be out of the hospital and able to sleep in the same bed," Francesca said before she took a bite.

Raising his voice in a cheer, Carson added, "Here. Here. And getting crepes for breakfast. I think we may give up our beach house and live here."

"Not a chance, buddy. In two days I have the all clear," I quipped.

Everyone's forks froze halfway to their mouths.

"Oh shit. I can't stop thinking about sex." I dropped my fork. "I mean, yes, sex is good, but I'm not counting down. No sex for me."

Gabe's shoulders silently shook with laughter.

I threw my napkin at him. "You're not helping. It's your fault I'm addicted to you. And all your teasing hasn't helped."

Carson dropped his fork and he looked like he was going to be sick.

"I'm stopping now." I put my fingers to my mouth, locked it with an imaginary key, and threw it away. The heat rose to my cheeks. Never in my life had I been this bad.

Carson shook his head. "Pregnancy has lessened your filter."

"I know. Trust me, I know."

I chanced a glance at Gabe, who winked at me. "Stop it. I blame you because of my current state."

Fingers snapped to my side. I looked at Carson. "What?"

"Let's change the subject before we get more details on a part of your life I don't need to know about."

Mashing my lips together, I nodded. I had almost slipped, again. I checked the time. The plan was to leave for Gabe's mother's in about thirty minutes.

"What are you guys doing today?" There, that was a safe subject.

"We're going to take Carson to the doctor for a checkup and maybe get some baby furniture from that store we looked at last night."

With Rosie being locked away, the threat to Francesca

had been eliminated. "That'll be nice. I need to start laying out the murals in the room to paint next week. I picked out my color scheme finally."

Francesca nervously pushed a piece of crepe around her plate. "I was wondering... well, we were wondering if you would be willing to paint a mural in our baby's room. I loved the idea of what you're doing and it would be so special to have a piece of Aunt Willow with the baby."

I loved the thought. Ideas swirled around almost immediately. "Are you serious? I would be so honored. Once we have your colors and theme picked out, I'll start drafting."

Francesca and Garson grinned, and Francesca got up and gave me a hug. "Thank you. It's going to be perfect."

"Anything for my little niece or nephew."

Francesca gave Carson an imploring look and his smile grew. Something else was up. "Francesca and I have something else to ask."

They looked back and forth between Gabe and me.

"What's that?" I asked.

Carson set down his fork, nearly done. "Would the two of you be the godparents to our child?"

"Yes! Yes! Yes! I would be honored. So honored." I stood, my chair scrapping back in protest. Being asked to be a godparent was one of the highest honors to bestow on someone.

"I don't know what to say. I'm... this..." Gabe seemed a little taken aback. For the first time, he was at a loss for words.

I squeezed his hand as I said, "I'm not the only one who sees how wonderful you are."

Francesca leaned forward and laid her hand on Gabe's. "I've watched how you've taken care of Willow and watched over me while Carson wasn't able to. The love and dedication you've showed and still do is incredible. To have someone like you pledge to watch over our child with Willow would be a blessing."

Though Francesca seemed to be out of the loop most of the time, she was actually more perceptive than I gave her credit for. "I would be honored to be your child's godfather."

Hugs were given. I grabbed Gabe's hand and he chuckled when I nodded.

I looked at Carson and pointed my finger. "Just so you know... you stole my thunder."

Gabe cleared his throat before Carson could fire back. "Willow and I talked some time ago after we first found out we were having twins."

Francesca's eyes widened. She held out her hand. "Wait... you're having twins?"

The shock registered on Gabe's face and he muttered a curse only I could hear. We were terrible about slipping.

I answered for him. "We are. We haven't told anyone yet. You guys are the first to know." Well, Carson already knew because of our earlier slips. I elbowed Gabe. "I'm not the only one with word vomit."

He shook his head and deadpanned, "You're contagious."

"Twins! We're going to have so much fun with three babies! Twins! Oh, how wonderful!" Francesca's burst of excitement stopped our playful banter.

It felt good having her know until we told the world, and it would be nice having a female to talk to. I touched my stomach.

"You saw the trouble Willow and I got into from the scrapbooks you made. And there were only two of us. Payback's going to be a bitch," Carson added.

More laughter. Gabe and Francesca had no idea what they

were in for.

Gabe squeezed my hand and got me back on track. "While Carson was in a coma, Gabe took me to the tree we'd carved our initials into. We talked and decided to ask you two to be the godparents to our children."

In a fluid movement, Carson picked me up and hugged me. "Thank you, angel."

Happiness flowed as I called, "I'm getting the ice cream to celebrate!"

Chapter Twenty-Four

In the car, we were about thirty to forty-five minutes from Gabe's mother's house. Two SUV's followed us with our security team. The air conditioner was on high to combat the mugginess that had settled over the area. The weather felt like Gabe's mood. For most of the ride, he had been relatively quiet.

I laid my head against his shoulder. "What are you thinking about?"

"I'm worried about you meeting my mom." The tension in his voice was tight and his muscles contracted at the thought.

I rubbed my hand over his chest to connect. "What is her name?" All this time, I hadn't asked.

"Chasity." The word was filled with hate.

The name was less intimidating than I imagined. I put my hand on his knee. "It's going to be okay, Gabe. We'll get through this. Don't let her cloud that beautiful heart of yours. She can't touch you now. And you have me."

A few minutes passed. "Are you nervous?"

Was I nervous? The thought of meeting Chasity unnerved me more than anything. "I'm worried about you."

He took a deep breath and looked out the window. All life left his eyes and I hated the power this woman seemed to have over him.

"Sweetheart, I'll be fine."

Andre slowed the car as we turned on a dirt road. Clouds of dust surrounded us. "Gabe, you're about to come face-to-face with your mother who mind fucked you through your childhood."

"Yes, I am." His voice was steel, but I sensed the trepidation. After all I had heard about this woman, she had to be the definition of a nightmare.

"We'll get through this." I hoped facing her allowed Gabe to deal with it so he could truly move on.

He smirked, some of the sparkle returning to his depths. "I think that's my line."

"We're a team. And when one needs support the other one is there."

Leaning farther back in the seat, he raised the partition for privacy. Trent and Andre had been discreet, appearing to pay no attention to our conversation. We had been talking low, but I should have been more aware. "We haven't discussed much about Alex Junior since we found out about your dad."

"No, we haven't." I wasn't sure where this was going.

This morning Gabe seemed all over the place mentally.

He closed his eyes before he reopened them, burning with an intensity. "Willow, I saw my nephew and he seems like a good kid. And now that De Luca is somewhat sorted, Harley will be sorted, and Candy is not plugged in. There is a chance we can get to know him someday once Alex is taken care of."

I hadn't thought about it, but it made sense that his nephew was on his mind. If I had a nephew or niece, I would want a relationship with them. Alex wasn't officially my nephew, and my heart ached at the thought of never being part of his life.

"If there comes a time we think it's safe, I want to know Alex Junior, too."

"I want that more than I realized." He blew out a ragged breath. "When Carson asked us to be godparents, my thoughts went to Alex Junior. I want to give him a family."

Not having a family gave Gabe a need to have one. I got it. And he never wanted someone he loved to go through that. "We're on the same page, Gabe. I understand the need you have. I have it, too. Has Candy had any contact with him?"

"No. I don't understand how a mother can do that to a child." Gabe let out a frustrated breath. Seems like Alex had found an uncaring mother like his own. "Willow, I... fuck... I don't want to see my mother." And we came full circle to the crux of Gabe's problems.

"I know." *And this is why I fought to come,* I thought. "You love your children unconditionally without seeing them. It's going to be hard seeing your mother, knowing how she treated you and the lack of love you received from her."

"It is."

I took Gabe's face in my hands. "But... that doesn't define you or what you're capable of. Your mother has no power over you." My hand moved to his ear. "I've seen the love you're capable of and it's pure, Gabe."

He touched his lips to mine. "I need you."

"I'm right here."

Kissing me again, he pulled me to him in a silent thank you. Nothing else was said as we rode. I became the strength

Gabe needed.

Trent's voice came over the intercom came on. "We're pulling down the last road."

Gabe hit a button. "Thanks, Trent. I'm ready. Is everything set?"

"Yes, everything is in order."

We straightened up as the partition rolled down and Trent looked back. Gabe's vulnerability diminished and left hard edges forming an impenetrable exterior.

"I need you to listen to everything I say when we get there," Gabe said.

"I promise."

The lane was desolate. Tall weeds covered the vacant lots. An abandoned house trailer added to the already eerie feeling. A dog ate from a carcass on the side of the rode. Blindly I reached for Gabe's hand. He was there to hold mine as I imagined a little boy running down the road. "Were these the conditions you grew up in?"

"This looks much worse. It had been bad, but cleaned enough to keep social services away. Fuck, this is worse than I imagined."

My heart ached. The man next to me was born to love, and yet he had been deprived of it most of his life. Never again. With me his life would always be filled with joy, love, and happiness.

Andre turned the car down the gravel driveway where a shell of a house sat at the end. A rundown car on cinder blocks was abandoned in the driveway with a few stray cats sunbathing on the hood.

"Stay in the car until we create a perimeter." Trent's voice left no room for argument as he exited the car. The paint on the house peeled away as if repulsed by what resided inside. The woman who had done terrible things lived behind those walls. I fidgeted with a loose piece of blonde hair as I watched the men surround the property.

Gabe responded to his earpiece. "Understood."

"Willow, I'm going to get out. Andre is still in the front seat. When it's safe for you to come in, he'll get the all clear. Listen to him. No hesitating."

Nerves set in. "I promise." I looked out the window at the men who were almost in position. It was like ants descending on a place.

"I'm going now. Are you okay?"

Too quickly, I nodded. "I'm fine."

He kissed me and then vanished out the door. The heat nearly swallowed me up as it fought its way inside the vehicle before he closed the door with the whirl of the air conditioner.

Alex might be in the house... waiting. The thought gave me pause as Gabe walked up to the door. I wanted to run to him and pull him back to the safety of the car. Part of me was glad I slept through the De Luca meeting as the sound of my heartbeat speeding up filled my ears.

Please keep Gabe safe. Please keep them all safe.

Gabe's posture was alert and he moved his head to scan the area. He walked up the rickety steps and knocked three times on the door.

A reflection on the window kept me from seeing if anyone had appeared.

"It's Gabe! Open up!" Gabe boomed.

I jumped at the complete coldness in his voice.

The door creaked opened. Gabe and four men disappeared inside.

I held my breath as I waited for someone to tell me everything was okay.

The seconds ticked by. The minutes never seemed to pass.

From the front seat, Andre said in a calm voice, "Walter is coming to get you. He's taking you straight in the house."

Walter was someone Gabe served with overseas at some point.

A long breath left my body. "I'm ready." My voice came out calmer than I felt.

Heat hit me as I opened the door. On steady legs, I emerged from the car into the heat of the day. The stench of garbage hit me full force. *Please don't make me sick. Let me get through this, little babies.* Breathing through my mouth helped as I walked, flanked by two additional men.

At the bottom of the steps, Gabe emerged from the door. His eyes scanned me with a worried look. Something was on his mind. "You okay?"

"Yes. Was Alex here?"

He wrapped his arm around me as we climbed the steps. "No, but he has been. I think we missed him. Listen, it's bad inside. Looks like she's started doing drugs at some point. Are you sure you want to come in? This woman is a worse version than the one I knew."

"Yes, I want to do this."

Oh shit. How was that possible?

Garbage littered the floor and the strength of the smell nearly overwhelmed me. *Shallow breaths. Breathe out my mouth.* I pressed my fingernails into the palms of my hands.

"Who the fuck is this?" The scratchy voice sounded like someone who'd smoked habitually for years.

My eyes adjusted to the dimness of the yellow dingy lamp. A bone-thin woman sat in a tattered chair, the color indiscernible. Greasy hair matted on top of her head—dark like Gabe's. "I'm, Willow. Gabe's girlfriend."

A squeeze on my hand reminded me Gabe was here.

"You sent that cocksucker to talk to me this morning. And now you think by bringing me your whore I'll talk."

De Luca came to visit already. Of course he had.

The firmness of Gabe's tone left no room for argument. "I had nothing to do with that man. He's after Alex."

She went to stand, but Peter placed his hand on her shoulder as Gabe said, "Don't move, Chasity, or I will have to restrain you."

"You fucking bastard. You brought this on your brother, didn't you?" The hate from this woman was unimaginable.

A deadliness not to be trifled with came from Gabe. "No, Alex fucked with the wrong people. He double-crossed him. I'd say he learned that from you. Where is he?"

Cackling, she threw her head back, revealing only a handful of teeth. "He played you so well. I thought our little games were over until he told me about the rich girl you landed. I never thought I'd get to meet her." Dragging a hand across her face, she eyed me. "So, looks like my little Gabriel has fallen in love. Do you actually love him back?"

"I do." I met her stare head on.

She scoffed. "Impossible. Are you sure you didn't fall in love with Alexander?"

Her power diminished every time she talked. I felt her lose any hold she had over Gabe, too. "I'm certain I fell in love with the right man. I pity you." This woman was vile. I had nothing else to say.

"I don't want your pity."

The way her gaze moved over me unnerved me, but I kept my spine ramrod straight. How had this woman stayed alive? I never imagined people willingly lived like this.

"We're leaving, but tell Alex the gig is up. People know

about him being a twin. And I've visited his son."

There it was… all out on the line.

"You were always a fool." She spit on the floor. "Alexander doesn't have a son."

Gabe paused. Alex had kept part of his life secret after all. But why? "Alex does have a son and a wife. How did you not know this?"

The woman visibly flinched, showing weakness for the first time. "You lie. I have tried to get him to have a child. We needed someone to continue our game with."

The thought made me ill and I had to swallow the bile that rose in my throat. If she knew I was pregnant…

"Think what you want. We're leaving now. Give my message to Alex if you see him."

"You always were a disappointment, Gabriel." She stared at him with dead blue eyes, making me wonder if he favored his father's looks more than his mother's.

"So were you, Mother. And now you're a junkie who has no one." The title came off Gabe's tongue with complete distaste.

"I have my son! I have Alex!" she screamed. Trying to stand, Gabe's men held her down without much effort. "FUCK YOU! Leave! Leave my house! Alex will get her!"

Oh my gosh. My eyes widened at her words. It was time to leave. Gabe sensed it too as he led us from the house at a clipped pace to the car. Gabe remained silent as we sped off in the car, leaving a trail of dust behind us.

Chapter Twenty-Five

The tension in the car grew. Beside me, Gabe sat silently as he looked out the window. Trent and Andre were on the phone nonstop. The veins in Gabe's neck bulged as he reined in his rage. Right now, he needed to gather himself. When he was ready for comfort, I would be there.

His mother... that woman... how had he survived such conditions with no love?

I couldn't have imagined in my wildest dreams a scene so dismally full of hate. The deadness in his mother's eyes haunted my thoughts. He said the home he grew up in wasn't as bad, but anything remotely in the same arena would be unacceptable.

Imagining Gabe in such conditions when he was young and defenseless broke my heart all over again. My hand reached for him but retracted on a second thought. The muscles on Gabe's arms tightened.

He still needed time.

I kept to myself as we sped forward. The exit approached.

Unexpectedly, the car kept moving forward. Maybe they were taking the next exit. Sometimes when traffic backed up, the other highway had less traffic though it was longer.

The silence between us became overbearing. The next exit came and we passed it without a thought. Was something wrong? I glanced out the back. Only one of the two of the SUV's was behind us.

"Where are we going?" My voice penetrated the edgy environment.

No one answered for a few seconds, but Andre looked back in the rearview at Gabe while still on the phone. I almost said something when finally Gabe responded without looking my way. "We're headed out of town. To Italy. On Carson's plane."

Italy? Carson' plane? What the hell was going on? I waited for an explanation, but all I received was the view of Gabe's back. *Stay calm, Willow. It's been a stressful afternoon.* I shifted in my seat to face Gabe and counted to ten before probing.

"Why are we going to Italy?"

Again silence from Gabe. The irritation bloomed.

One. Two. Three. Four. Five. Six. Seven. Eight. Nine. Ten.

Keeping my voice calm, I became sterner. "Gabe, please tell me what is going on."

He looked at me with a set jaw, face devoid of emotion. "Not now, Willow."

Not now? Not NOW! NOT NOW! This involved me as much as him. I tried again, hoping he made the choice to elaborate. "Carson's plane?"

"Yes, damn it. Not now." There was the use of those two words again. *Not now.* The cold tone sank bone deep and sent me back to the days I lived with Alex. I clinched my fist, furious I from dismissed so easily.

Any calmness I had evaporated. My lips pressed together as I stared daggers at the unresponsive man I didn't know in this moment.

Carson knew.

I bristled at the thought of being left in the dark. Irritation flared to an all-time high. Taking out my phone, I thought about texting Carson for a brief second before I put it away. I refused to undermine our relationship by bringing Carson in the middle of it. We would have to work this out together or... that wasn't a thought I wanted to entertain.

Gabe glanced at me and then resumed his intense stare out the window.

With every ounce of venom I was able to muster, I said, "I'm glad we got that all cleared up."

No response.

I took a deep breath and mirrored his pose while looking out my own window. Utterly ridiculous. Wait, what if Alex changed places with Gabe? This cold distant act was unlike him.

"Show me your stomach where the scar is supposed to be."

My words sent an electric jolt through Gabe as his detached gaze met mine. Without a word, he lifted his shirt to reveal a smooth hard abdomen. I breathed a sigh of relief. *This is Gabe.*

I whispered, "Why are you acting like him?"

No response.

Part of me wanted to demand Trent take me home. But, I trusted his decision. He went against Gabe before regarding Apple Blossom. Something was wrong. First, I needed to be safe before I had it out with anyone.

Before long we pulled up to the tarmac. The gates slid open and we pulled into the private hanger of Whitmore Hotels. The men exited the vehicles. Six boarded the plane in front of me.

The car door opened and the heat of the day fueled my temper. At a clipped pace I boarded the plane, staying away from Gabe. Trent gave some hand signals and the men moved about.

Upon entering the cabin, the flight attendant, Vanessa, greeted me with a cheery expression. "Good afternoon, Ms. Russo."

Gabe stepped to the side to talk to the pilot at the cockpit door. Men came on board from our little convoy. "I'm going to takeoff from the bedroom if that's okay. I need some time to myself."

I should have been more pleasant, but I needed to be alone. Later I would apologize for my behavior.

"Of course. There are seat belts on the couch."

"Thanks."

Without glancing at anyone, I walked past them but Trent caught my eye. He took the phone away from his ear. "You okay, Willow?"

"What do you think?" I snapped, then held up my hand. "I get it. Something is up. But, we'll be talking later."

He nodded. "I'll come back and explain if Gabe doesn't. There was a lot of shit happening at once. Your safety is my number one concern. It's too much to go over until we're safely in the air. I have to finish making some arrangements first."

At least my suspicion was right. This pressure was not good for the babies and needed to calm down. "I want you to keep anyone from coming back and disturbing me. And I mean anyone."

"I understand. Let me know if you want me or Gabe to come back to talk when you're ready."

I felt the hard stare of Gabe behind me, but I refused to turn around. Instead, I marched forward and shut the door with more force than needed.

Voices, particularly Gabe's and Trent's, were faint in the cabin. It sounded like an argument about coming to see me.

Click.

The voices stopped as I locked the door. I leaned against the wall and blew out a breath. How had things flipped upside down? Understandably, Gabe was upset from the visit. What I had a hard time understanding was the tone and attitude he'd used with me.

Unacceptable.

I had to calm down for the sake of the babies and me. The flight attendant came over the intercom to advise everyone to buckle up. On the beige leather couch, I fastened my seatbelt.

Now, I could calm down.

Knock. Knock. Knock.

Fuck.

"Willow, can I come in?" Gabe's voice had lost its nasty edginess.

Now, he wanted to talk. Well, too bad. I wasn't in the mood anymore.

"Willow."

"Not now, Gabe." I said, throwing his words back to him with all the irritation I felt. *Take those terrible words and shove them where the sun doesn't shine!*

"Willow?"

I refused to answer. And if he walked in here, I would call Carson and get off this plane. He was lucky I'd let this stunt go as far as it had.

The reasons I had stayed were one, I trusted Gabe, two, Carson knew and trusted Gabe, and three, Trent knew and trusted Gabe.

However... I still had the right to be furious for the time being. Maybe after we took off and I'd had something to eat and a nap, we might try talking. For now, Gabe needed a reality check. I was not the enemy.

The plane moved forward and I stared out the window at the concrete, watching it move faster. The wheels lifted off the ground giving that sense of brief weightlessness. I hated the feeling. Flying always made me a little nervous.

My phone vibrated with Gabe's name.

Gabe: You okay? I know you hate flying.

Things were not going to be fixed via a text. I thought about not responding, but I decided against that action. Without an answer, he might bust the door down, thinking something was wrong.

Me: I'm fine.
Gabe: Can I come back there to talk?
Me: No.

Vanessa's voice came over the intercom, announcing we were able to move about the cabin. Another text came.

Gabe: I'm sorry. I love you.

The damn broke as I crawled into bed and silently cried into the pillow, unable to answer him. I loved him more than anything. But for the first time with Gabe... I felt lost.

Chapter Twenty-Six

Groggy, I opened my eyes and rolled over. Where was I? The plane. Carson's plane. Headed to Italy. I threw my hand over my face, wishing I could go back to sleep and ignore it all.

The white noise of the engines purred on. They had put me to sleep shortly after all the tears were expelled. I wiped my cheeks feeling a little of the moisture from my wet pillow.

The fight with Gabe. His tone. The coldness. It had been horrendous. I hated feeling out of sorts.

"I'm sorry, sweetheart. So fucking sorry."

I startled and turned.

Changed from earlier, Gabe sat on the couch pensively watching me. "You've been crying."

Instinctively, I touched my tear-stained cheeks. "What are you doing in here? I want to be left alone." My voice was scratchy.

"Salvaging what I wrecked."

His fingers were pressed together under his chin as he

watched me closely. He looked as wrecked as what I imagined I did.

After sleeping, I felt calmer. Instead of anger, sadness and loneliness filled its place.

"Can I come sit beside you?"

I shook my head and he closed his eyes.

"I deserve that. I lost my cool back there. And the worst part of all, I reminded you of Alex."

Remaining silent, I sensed Gabe wanted me to take the lead in the conversation. Well, this was his show to right the wrong.

When he figured I was not going talk, he continued, "I am so sorry about what I did. Hell, being at my mother's and finding Alex's back room did a number on me. I felt like I'd been thrown back into my childhood, and I coped with things wrong. It wasn't right."

Drawing my knees up to my chest, I watched him.

Gabe ran his fingers through his hair. "Alex had been living with Mom for who knows how long. We found a hidden room… more like a closet behind a tattered rug on the wall." He closed his eyes. "There were pictures of you and me leaving the doctor's office. A schedule of when your next doctor visit is, guard rotations at the house."

I drew in an audible breath.

"The security schedules weren't accurate, but they were close enough. He planned to kidnap you. The warehouse I found from his encrypted papers was the location he planned to take you. I don't know what his plan is. There wasn't time to explain everything and I wanted to talk in private. Carson and Trent threatened to call if I didn't tell you soon after take-off."

Fear grabbed me. Chasity's warning about Alex getting

me hadn't been a junkie's nonsensical thoughts. I needed to feel grounded in Gabe's arms. When I reached him, there was no hesitation when he brought me into his arms.

He let out a sigh. "Thank you. I needed to feel you, sweetheart." He kissed the top of my head. "When I saw all that, I had to get you away from your environment. Do something unpredictable. We have you covered, but I just poked the bear. No doubt he's going to strike back and try to hurt what matters most."

"Me and the babies." The thought left a sickening feeling inside of me. I'd never forgive myself if something happened to them.

"Yes. The men gathered it all and took it out the back door while we talked to my mother. Trent has a team looking into it. And hearing her confirm they targeted you from the beginning in order to continue their sick game. A game? A fucking game? You and I are not a game." He took a calming breath.

I touched his cheek. "Gabe..."

"There are photos of Alex watching me for years when I was stateside. He saw the moment I fell in love with you. Willow, he has pictures of me wrapping my arms around you on the balcony the first night we made love."

"Why now? Why did he wait all that time? Why try to ruin us?"

"Because I finally had something worth taking. I had someone I couldn't live without. He knew it."

The thought sobered me. The vulnerability I heard sent me on edge. All those years of watching Gabe and he never had anything worth losing... until me.

The depth of Alex's deception went deeper than either of us imagined. Our lives were merely pieces to manipulate. But, we had each other. Through all the lies, we found our way back to the truth, the light. The darkness had no hold over us.

"I am trained to pick up on this stuff. I missed it. I fucking missed it. How the fuck was I so stupid?"

Earlier, Gabe's state made more sense. Fear drove people to act and protect their loved ones at any cost. The anger stemmed from not being able to protect me. "Gabe." I waited for him to look at me. "If I had to go through all this heartache to have you... I would. You are worth it."

Surprise flickered in his eyes as they warmed, leaving the cool icy feel behind. I had him back. Completely.

"I never wanted this for you. You are my world... my life. Having all that threatened knocked me off kilter and I didn't handle it well. You are my light, Willow. Please forgive me."

I leaned up and kissed his mouth. "I do forgive you. We make the light together."

"I would never forgive myself if something happened to you." His hand moved to my stomach. "Or them."

It seemed like we were passed the rapids and moving into tranquil water. "When did Carson find out about the trip?"

"When I found the pictures and schedules in the back room, I called Carson. He arranged for the plane. We've been in constant contact. He messengered your passport to the plane. Francesca packed you a bag. I know it seems like I betrayed my vow to you, but I needed to make sure you were safe first. Giving you only a piece of what was going would have been worse than withholding."

I agreed. Every situation had extenuating circumstances. All of this was moving at an exponential rate. "Wow..."

Gabe added, "I'm not slipping into old behaviors and keeping things from you. I know it seems like it, but I've had to make some tough judgment calls."

In the same situation, I would have made the same decision.

"I'm sorry, Willow. So fucking sorry."

I heard the anguish in his voice. I squeezed him tighter to me. "I think you get a pass."

"No, I don't. When you have something as precious as the love I have from you, I don't get a pass. I don't ever get a pass. But, I had to get you safe first."

We needed to be closer together. "Come, let's lay down."

Before I could put my feet on the floor, Gabe carried me to the bed. He toed off his shoes and slid us under the covers in one fluid movement. He pushed up my shirt and placed his hand on my stomach. "We're going to get this behind us. I pray I haven't made a mistake."

"You know what you're doing. I trust you. Why did you choose Italy?"

Maybe talking about his decision would ease some of the apprehension. "Trent has a team there already because of Carson's hotel. I doubt Alex knows about the team. Trent assembled it under a different name for his global division while you and Carson were here last time."

Dad would be proud knowing Trent had taken his company global. "Where are we going once we get there?"

"We have a couple of choices. We can go to your estate or Trent has located a cabin to use not far from your place."

A lump formed in my throat. I hadn't been back there since Dad died.

"It's your choice, Willow. We need Alex to chase me without thinking. We need him to want to strike back at me. He's a methodical bastard and will wait years to do anything. This has to end now. I can't have him fucking with our children's lives. I can't."

I understood the urgency. I felt it, too.

The longer it took Alex to find us, the longer the unease would drift around us. The chaos Gabe created might settle, giving Alex time to rethink things and eventually get to me or our children.

"I want to go to the estate. How long are we staying there?"

"Until we catch the asshole. There is no redemption for Alex. He won't get another chance." Gabe's words implicated death as the final solution.

"Can't we turn him over to someone?"

"No."

"Do you think he'll know where we are?"

"Yes."

"How do you know?"

"Because I left him a note that said 'Italy.'"

I sat up. "You what?" Why put a beacon right on top of us? Alex knew about my estate in Italy. In one of our arguments, he'd asked me to sell the place. Of course the answer had been no. "He's going to come straight for you."

"We had to take control of the situation. I know it seems rash, it isn't. Trent and Carson both agreed to the plan. We create the fake chaos. Alex thinks I'm fleeing because I'm scared he's too close. He's going to think I'm reacting instead of planning. But, in reality we have the upper hand. And since we came to his turf, took his things... I've pissed him off. Trent is increasing the watch on the school for Alex Junior just in case."

The memory of his mom sitting in the chair in filthy tattered clothes was still vivid. "And you told Chasity about his son."

"Yes. I was so fucking pissed. I wanted to send Alex over the edge. I want him as irrational as I feel. I want him gone. Alex will come for me."

Mentally, I added, *And me.*

Chapter Twenty-Seven

This time the car ride felt more at ease with Gabe holding me close. We landed about thirty minutes ago, Carson's plane was to be left at the airport indefinitely in case we needed to leave.

The men had outlined contingency upon contingency, estimating Alex would be in route within the next couple of days. At this point, he hadn't surfaced. Men had been placed at his mother's house to monitor when he came home and left. From there the plan was to track him. They wanted him to get to the airport and come here. It was all part of the plan. De Luca had also been informed.

All of this kept me nearly scared to death, but I kept a cool front. It was unfathomable how soldiers prepared for war. I made a mental note to contribute to a veteran's facility. The respect I had for our armed forces was immeasurable with what they went through.

As the afternoon sun sank behind the trees in the distance, it cast a purple orange hue in the sky. Sunsets here were always magnificent. The stone fence approach signaled the beginning of our land.

Gabe squeezed my hand. "You doing okay?"

I gave him a watery smile. "I'm home. And I'm here with you. I'm better than okay."

"Oh, sweetheart." He leaned over to give me a kiss. "We're going to spend a lifetime making memories here."

"Promise me."

"I promise."

Those two words brought an immense amount of comfort to me. The road wound back and forth as we drove through the hills. The house was located away from civilization. Compared to our place in the Hamptons, this house had a more intimate feel—almost cottage like in a sense, though bigger. The house was nestled into one of the vast hills of the estate with a barn off to the side that had been converted into a studio. The appeal to use as a base of operations was evident.

My phone rang. It was Carson. "Hello."

"Hey, how you holding up?" He was worried.

Gabe stroked soothing circles on my hand.

"I'm managing. Thanks for all you did this afternoon. How are you feeling?"

"I'm good. Don't worry about me." Francesca inquired how I was doing from somewhere in the room with Carson. "Trent and Gabe asked for us to stay here. You good with that?"

From the front seat, Andre and Trent confirmed Gabe's decision. "Yes, you should stay. Gabe and Trent know what they're doing."

"I don't like this."

"Me, either, but hopefully it will be over soon."

Carson answered another one of Francesca's questions

about coming over. It was apparent she liked the idea of me being away less than Carson. On the plane, Gabe told me Carson told Francesca all that had gone on. "How'd Francesca do with the news?"

"She was shocked. Then pissed. And now she wants to make sure Rosie is convicted."

In the face of trials, people were stronger than we anticipated. "Did you hear from your attorney about Rosie?"

He let out a frustrated noise. "I'd rather talk about this when you get back, but I know you won't let it drop."

A small chortle escaped. "You know me so well."

"She's officially been denied bail. They've sent over a plea bargain."

There was a message from Marissa I hadn't listened to yet. I'd sent her a text saying Gabe and I were headed to Italy for a quick getaway and I'd call her on my return. One problem at a time. "What did they offer for the plea bargain?"

"Reduced sentence... it's all bullshit. It's a way for them to open up negotiations."

People believing they had the ability to manipulate my life and control my decisions appalled me. In this case they should be punished to the fullest extent of the law. Like Alex, Rosie had crossed an unforgivable line. "My vote is for Rosie to get the maximum sentence the prosecutors can get with no chance of parole."

"Then we're all on the same page. I'll let the lawyers know."

Andre made the last turn. In less than two minutes I would be home. "Thanks again, for everything you did. We're almost there. I'm going to let you go."

"Okay, angel. Call me if you need anything. As soon as we're cleared to come, we'll be on our way."

"Sounds perfect."

I hung up as I looked at the stone walls of our Italian two-story home as it came into view. The place was timeless. The bottom floor consisted of the master bedroom, kitchen, office, dining room, and two living rooms. Upstairs were the rest of the bedrooms.

After the car stopped, I disembarked. I walked to the water fountain in front of the house and ran my fingers through the cool water. Lilly pads circled about. On numerous mornings Dad and I brought our canvases out to the front yard to paint the rolling hills that spilled toward the never-ending horizon.

"It's breathtaking." Gabe's obvious awe brought a smile to my face as he walked up behind me.

"It's magical." The trees swayed in the light breeze like a lullaby.

"I see why your dad proposed to your mom here. This was your great *Nonno's* house?"

"Yes, he gave it to Dad when he passed."

Our hands intertwined. Bringing my wrist up, he kissed my knuckles delicately. With Gabe by my side any apprehension vanished. It was unbelievably good to be home despite the terrible situation we faced.

"I'm glad you're here with me."

"Me, too, sweetheart."

The Italian security team came from the house to greet Trent and the men he'd brought. The Italian accents were thick. If the caretakers were here, they'd have been beside themselves with worry. Carson had informed them I'd be arriving and given them a paid trip to the coast of Spain for the week as a thank you for all they had done. For now, they were out of the way.

I let the sun's rays absorb into my skin as if part of the beauty of the countryside would be forever imprinted on me. I was home. The missing part of my heart felt a little less empty.

The pea gravel path crunched under our footsteps. The large wooden door with the iron trimmings greeted me like an old friend. I pushed them open easily to reveal the Tuscan style of the interior.

Trent motioned us to the living room where the computers had been set up. The dark set of his brow caught my attention. Something was up.

He turned to Gabe. "Men at the perimeter of the property heard a gunshot from your mother's house. They investigated and found your mother had been shot point-blank in the head."

Oh shit. "Alex?" I whispered. Chasity had been killed.

Gabe went stock-still. Another vibration from Trent's phone temporarily broke his focus.

"We believe so. As we planned, the men kept a lose perimeter. Alex entered the house, they heard the gunshot and then he left. They've tracked him to the airport and he's on a plane."

"He's coming here?" A darkness crept over Gabe. But this time, he held me close instead of pushing me away.

"Yes." Trent turned his phone so we could see a picture of a note scribbled in blood on the wall.

"Oh my…" I took a few steps back away from the image. "H-he's…" This image would stay with me forever. The angry slashes on the wall showed that Gabe had been successful in his attempt to unhinge Alex. In fact, the plan had been too successful.

Gabe roared, "For fuck's sake, Trent."

My eyes shot to Gabe. "He's coming." It all sank in. The danger more vivid. For some reason, it seemed less volatile with Gabe at my side. I heard Trent say something, but the world swayed a little. My feet left the ground and I was carried to the kitchen.

"Get me something to drink," Gabe barked. The darkness crept in. "Hang with me, sweetheart. Don't pass out."

I fought it and a glass touched my lips.

"Drink," Gabe commanded. A few gulps of juice trickled down my throat. "Slow slips."

Light found its way back as it pushed the darkness aside. "I'm with you."

"Thank goodness." He pressed his forehead to mine while his fingers pressed against my wrist. "Keep taking slow breaths."

I took another sip. Trent started to say something, but Gabe raised his hand silencing him.

"You better?"

"He's—"

"I won't let him get you. I swear you'll be safe."

The proclamation quelled the fear inside me marginally. "Why do you think he killed his own mother?"

"Because of his son."

Of course, the one thing he'd held from his mother tore them apart. He denied her the one thing she wanted… to continue the game. Were we responsible for her death? The woman was evil to the core, but—

"Willow, don't go down that path. My mother chose her path. As did Alex. This is not our fault."

Somehow it still felt like it.

Trent walked back into the room. "Sorry, Willow."

"It's okay."

"Let me get Willow settled," Gabe said Trent.

I clutched Gabe's arm. "No, I'm staying with you!"

He stared intently into my eyes. "Willow, I don't want—"

"This is not an option, Gabe. I can't be away from you." My pleading overruled any reservations he may have had.

Trent laid a map of the area on the white marble countertop beside me and pointed to where men were stationed.

Gabe looked at it intently. "Like we talked about on the plane, we're going to create a sense of vulnerability. Alex needs to have the illusion he's slipping through like he did at Mom's house. It's the only way he'll come after me. Alex is pissed. And now that our mother is dead, he's going to want to finish what we started all those years ago."

"Do you think it'll work?" I asked.

Gabe scrubbed his hand down his face. "Yes. He's going to be one pissed off cocky son of a bitch. Alex has no idea we have a team here. Six people to cover this type of estate is inadequate. We create the holes to funnel him where we want him to go."

"Won't he see it?" This sounded crazy. We were the target, which meant Alex would head straight for us.

"Not if we keep it subtle. Make him work for it." Taking a marker, Gabe put X's on the map and showed the funnel effect. "We left the U.S. unexpectedly. We'll turn it around on him. The faster he strikes, the easier it'll be. If he has time to do much reconnaissance he'll see what we're up to."

"And I'll be with you."

"Alex will know something is up if we aren't together. This is what I used to do. Trust me."

"I do… with my life."

Chapter Twenty-Eight

The sun had set some time ago. We were in the master bedroom. The second hand ticked by on the mantle clock.

Tick. Tick. Tick. The sound maddening—never-ending. The time was nearly eleven. Though I was beyond exhausted, my nerves had me wired. Gabe leaned against the headboard, alert. The glow from the lamp gave off the only light in the otherwise dark room.

"I'm going to turn out the light now." Though low and quiet, Gabe's words pierced the silent room.

"Got it."

Since retiring to here at ten, we'd left the light on for a bit. The house was visible from a distance and it had to appear as normal as possible.

The floor creaked beneath the weight of Gabe's feet. The room was blanketed in darkness. Within seconds the mattress dipped as Gabe crawled into the bed. "I'm here. You're safe."

"I wish we could have a nightlight tonight."

"I know. I wish I could do that for you."

Shifting, I brought myself a little closer. I had on high-tech Kevlar pants and a shirt. Overall, it was lightweight but not what I was used to wearing to bed, and a little uncomfortable. It added to the element of danger we faced. The sooner this was over, the better.

Throughout the afternoon, Gabe took my pulse. He even used a baby monitor at one point to listen to the babies' heartbeats. Everything was fine with all three of us. Knowing I needed to stay as calm as possible for the health of my babies kept me from completely freaking out.

Alex's plane had landed almost two hours ago. An hour ago the security confirmed he was on the property waiting… with Harley.

Alex was on my property. He remained on the edge, waiting to make his move as the men did their patrols knowing where he was the entire time. At some point I'd asked why not just take him down when we knew where he was. Gabe and Trent took turns explaining that Alex was cunning and they wanted to reduce the risk of him escaping. The farther he came onto the property, the harder it would be for him to escape.

The thought kept me checking every shadow while pretending to sleep next to Gabe.

My senses were hyperaware as I focused on every sound. At some point, Alex would have forced this scenario. All afternoon Gabe and Trent ironed out the details. I hoped I never faced something like this again. The thought of the unknown while someone stalked me brought out a fear I had never known.

Creak.

My breath stuttered and I held my pillow tighter. "It's only the house settling, sweetheart. Try to get some sleep. Alex hasn't moved from where he is. Harley is on the other side of the property."

"Okay."

"After tonight, this will all be behind us."

I hoped so. Oh, I hoped so. To go through this for days would be maddening.

Gabe massaged tiny little circles on the back of my neck. "That feels good."

Methodically, he kept going and I relaxed into the mattress, letting my mind drift as sleep finally found me.

I felt the blanket whip on top of me. It was a special Kevlar blanket. A hand landed on my shoulder.

"He's in the yard. Be still. Don't move. You're safe. I'm going to intercept him before he gets in this room," Gabe whispered.

Adrenaline coursed through me. The man who wanted to hurt me was close. If given the chance, he would take the babies and me from Gabe forever. "Keep your promise to me."

"I will."

The pressure on my shoulder was gone. Gabe piled pillows against me to create the impression of his body.

Alex was here.

In the yard.

Coming for us.

More specifically—me.

It took all my strength to keep my breathing under control as I listened to the silence. The quietness was never-ending. I strained to hear something, but there was nothing. I was on the verge of throwing rational thought out the window. What worried me most was that Alex wanted to do more than kidnap me. He wanted to take me away from Gabe forever—the ultimate punishment. Death.

Tick. Tick. Tick.

I nearly jumped off the bed with the sound of the clock. My pulse jumped at the base of my neck and my muscles tensed for the arrival of the predator. *Stay calm. Gabe is near. He knows what he's doing.*

Creak.

My breath caught. Was that the house settling? Was it Alex? Where was Gabe? *Focus on my breathing. Breathe in... one, two, three. Breathe out... one, two, three.* The mental technique helped.

Tick. Tick. Tick.

After this, that clock was leaving this room. I gripped the pillow tighter, willing this to be over. Was Alex near the room on the outside of the house? Having someone unwanted on the premises made me feel violated.

Creak.

Oh shit. Was that the house settling? I wasn't sure. Had that been the same sound as before? I strained harder, but didn't hear anything. I squinted to see if he was here in the room.

Where was Gabe?

Aside from the clock, the room grew eerily silent. I wanted to scream in terror but choked the noise back.

Crash!

The noise came from the patio outside the room. The muffled sounds of struggling and grunting filtered in. I pulled myself into a tighter ball. Was Gabe okay?

More footsteps outside the door. Gabe cursed. Or was that Alex? I had to fight my instincts to push the blankets off and check to make sure he was okay.

"Get him out of here. Take him to the barn. I'll be there shortly. No one talks to him until I get there." That had to be Gabe.

More footsteps.

In the darkness a voice screamed into the night, "I will kill her! I will take away everything you've taken away from me!"

Alex wanted me dead and his words caused a chill to run through me.

More talking and cursing faded away. Lights flicked on and filtered in but only shadows passed in front of the blanket.

The blanket peeled back and light blinded me. I needed to be in Gabe's arms so I scrambled to an upright position. He caught me and brought me to him. Tremors shook me to the core.

"Shh... it's over. It's over. You're safe."

I wrapped my legs around Gabe's waist. I leaned back, searching him with my hands to make sure he remained un-harmed. "Are you okay? Did he hurt you?"

"I'm good. It's over. That's all that matters."

I wasn't sure as I kept searching. "You're bleeding." There was a cut on his lip.

"It's nothing." He started to set me down, but my I wound my legs tighter around him. "Okay, sweetheart. Let's sit to-gether."

After all the time alone under the blanket, I wanted to feel connected to him. Gabe moved to the edge of the bed and handed me a glass of orange juice. "Drink this. It'll help."

Slowly I let the juice trickle down my throat. "Are you sure you're okay?"

"Yes. The men got Harley also. They're both in the barn

until I give more direction."

"It's over?" Gabe was okay and I clutched him harder to me. There was a slight tremor in my hands as I touched his cheek.

"Yes."

It was done. We were free. My shoulders sagged in response. "I never want to do this again. You swear it's over?"

He held me closer to him. "I swear."

Putting a little distance between us, Gabe pulled up his shirt to show me his scar less stomach. "I don't want there to be any doubt." I hadn't doubted his identity simply from the way he cared for me. Alex had never been able to show this amount of emotion.

I trailed my fingers over the flatness—thankful he was unharmed. "It's really over?"

"Yes."

Timidly, I asked, "What happens now?"

"I'm giving De Luca the option to take them. We'll know within the hour if he wants them."

Searching Gabe's face, I wanted to make sure he was okay with this decision. "How do you feel about that?" Basically, handing over his brother was a death sentence.

"I don't have a choice. Alex pissed off a lot of people, which connected our world with his. He sure as hell can't go free and I'm not putting our future on the line for the bastard. We may share the same DNA, but that's it. A brother would have never done the things he did to you and me. If De Luca doesn't take him, we'll have to deal with him."

When he put that way, I hoped De Luca took him. From what he's insinuated, Gabe had killed before while working for the government, but I wouldn't want him to the bear the death of his brother. Regardless of how much Gabe hated Alex, kill-ing him took it to the next level.

I nuzzled him. "I hope De Luca takes him."

"He will. He wants revenge." His confidence held no doubts. "Let's check you out. I hated how much stress this put you under." With efficiency Gabe checked the babies' heart rates. Everything was fine regardless of how rattled I still felt. Gabe rubbed my back, and I held onto him.

A thought suddenly occurred to me. One I hadn't imagined I'd want if given the chance. "Can I see him?"

Gabe's eyes bugged out. "Yo-you want to see him? No. Absolutely not." He vehemently shook his head to emphasize the point.

I understood Gabe's reservations. I had them also, but this was something I needed to do. "Gabe, I need to do this for closure of Dad's death."

Through all of this, Alex had left us with were more questions than answers. I wanted this part of our life closed. And with De Luca more than likely taking him, this was my only shot.

"Let me ask him. I'll tell you everything." His voice was frantic and pleading.

Gently, I kissed his lips. "This is something I have to do or I'll regret it for the rest of my life."

Understanding dawned and he said, "The Kevlar stays on. You keep your distance. If I get the least bit concerned, you're leaving."

"That's fine." The Kevlar was an irritant, but it kept me safe ... well safer.

We stood and Gabe radioed directions to prepare the men for us to come to the barn. After I put on some shoes, we left the premises hand in hand. Andre and two other men surrounded us with their guns still drawn.

Had I made the right decision?

Everyone was still on high alert. Rightly so, but the stress of the situation penetrated me to my core. Yes, I needed answers or I would forever wonder.

The warmth from the lights inside the barn glowed in stark contrast to the evil lurking inside.

Night dew from the grass gathered on the soles of my shoes. The stars twinkled in the sky as the cool breeze blew.

Ironic such disaster lay behind the barn doors when such peace resided out here.

When we made it to the door, Trent stepped out. "You sure you want to do this, Willow?"

"I need to know if he murdered Dad."

Trent glanced to Gabe who nodded. "I won't deny Willow closure. I've offered to talk to him instead, but she wants to do this."

With how close Trent had been to Dad, I thought he'd understand. Trent blocked the door, the turmoil evident on his face.

I touched his arm. "I need to do this. If it was about your sister, wouldn't you want the same thing if there was a chance to get answers?"

Trent's jaw locked as he held his emotions at bay. With his sister committing suicide, he had a lot of unanswered questions.

After another moment, he stepped aside, not saying a word.

The door swung open. Five men with guns drawn surrounded Alex and Harley who sat in chairs, bound and gagged.

"Remove Alex's gag." The command from Gabe was followed swiftly.

As soon as the gag was removed, he spit and wiped his

chin on his shirt. Our eyes met and I saw nothing but hatred in Alex's. The cold glare I grew accustomed to when we lived together met mine.

"Well, if it isn't my brother's whore. You were a terrible wife. Always bitching and complaining."

Surprisingly, the words had no effect. "Your mother called me something similar." Alex flinched at the word *mother*. "I heard you killed her."

His lips thinned. "No, you two killed her. She demanded I bring Alex Junior to her."

The thought of the innocent little boy I'd met flashed through my mind. Chasity would have ruined another innocent soul.

Alex's mouth hardened. The broken man showed through the cracks. The years of mental abuse taking its toll. He was beyond repair. Alex tested his restraints and Gabe took a step forward while I went the opposite way, waiting to see if I needed to leave. The movement stopped.

Beside him, Harley watched us. I asked, "Why did you do it?"

"Do what?" Alex practically spit the words.

"Seek me out. Make Gabe's life hell. Kill my dad."

His head shook. Again the shattered man appeared before he masked it with hatred. A calculating look passed over his face. I wasn't sure he would tell me. For a couple of minutes Alex stared at me deciding. Finally, he spoke, "It's all part of the game. And I always win the game. Your dad got in the way. He knew. Somehow he knew after he questioned me about proposing to you."

I swallowed. Dad must have asked him about the secret he told Gabe about us going to the spot where he proposed to Mom. It was hard to keep my lips from trembling. Dad had been murdered. Taken before his time.

I pressed forward. "Did you know he met Alex Junior?"

No response.

I tried again. "How did he die?"

"Poison. Strychnine." The words were spoken with true satisfaction.

I gasped and tears welled in my eyes. Pure evil stared back at me with a look of complete enjoyment. Harley watched him with an unreadable expression. Reliving anything would give Alex more power than he deserved. He wanted to lay all the details out so I would forever remember them.

"I'd followed him the entire way home from the school, jamming his cell phone signal. He was probably trying to call Trent. I walked into the studio where he was sending an e-mail. I held him down while I forced him to ingest the poison. I assured him I'd take *real* good care of you."

The tears fell and Gabe put his arms around me.

"His dying word was your name."

The satisfaction on his face made me sick. I needed to leave. "I-I-I want to go back to the house." No more. This was part of Alex's sick game to break me.

I turned to see Trent's glower at Alex. Dad's death had been worse than I expected. So much worse. It was the black truth emerging from all the white lies.

Gabe's arm around my waist barely registered as he propelled me from the barn. He ordered, "Don't knock him out. I need to question him first."

Behind me, my father's killer screamed, "Come back, bitch! We're not done! I want to tell you how he begged!"

As we exited the barn, he continued to call after me. I covered my ears with my hands. The tears fell faster than ever, causing my vision to blur. I stumbled, but Gabe was there to pick me up as I sobbed into his chest. Alex's screams continued to penetrate the air until we closed the door to the house.

Gabe turned to one of the guards. "If De Luca calls, tell him he can get Alex and Harley in two hours."

I cried harder as Gabe stroked my back. "I know, sweetheart. I know. I'm so sorry."

"He's a monster." How had Gabe survived all those years like that?

He held me tighter. "I know. I wish you hadn't gone out there."

"I needed to know." It was hard to regret a decision that gave me answers so I wouldn't always wonder, but I hadn't expected the brutality of the situation. As the sobs erupted from me, Gabe comforted me. Soon nothing was left and I felt empty.

"I need to go finish sorting things out, sweetheart."

Numbly, I nodded.

"Andre is going to stay with you. I'll be back."

Gabe pressed his lips against my forehead. He said something to Andre I hadn't the energy to process and left me on the couch. He walked out the door while I worked to right myself mentally.

Chapter Twenty-Nine

At some point, I laid my head down on the arm of the couch. Mercifully, sleep found me. A light jostling stirred me.

"Gabe?"

"It's me. I'm taking us to bed."

Early morning light splattered through the windows. Other than our footsteps, the house was quiet. "Where is everyone?"

"Rotating their posts. We're safe."

A lump formed in my throat and I swallowed past it. "Where's Alex?"

"Gone. De Luca took him and Harley."

Sleep subsided as I remembered what Alex had said. He'd watched Dad die. A few tears slid down my cheek. We entered the bedroom and Gabe locked the door. He placed me on the bed before he removed the Kevlar. In all the sadness, I'd forgotten to take it off.

As soon as Gabe crawled into bed, I nestled beside him.

"Did you find out anything else?"

He cleared his throat. "We did. Do you want to know?"

"Is it as bad as what he's already told me?"

"More of the same, but not about your dad."

Did I want to know? Yes, I needed to know. Tonight I would find out everything there was. Tomorrow I would start the healing process. "Yes, tell me."

Gabe's fingers rhythmically stroked my back. "The man they found burned was a third accomplice named Brian Holder. He tried to steal the Botticelli with Alex and Harley."

I lifted my head. "Wait, Alex was there at the theft?"

"Yes. Harley was supposed to kill Brian once the painting was taken. Trent found them too fast. Somewhere through all that, Alex decided to become me. He told Harley. In exchange for Harley's help, Alex promised to give him Candy."

My brows scrunched together. "He bartered his wife?"

"Yes. Alex found out Candy had cheated on him. He planned to kill her, but Harley stepped in. In exchange for Harley's help, he got Alex Junior. They were going to disappear with the money from the trust."

A headache loomed in the back of my head. "How did Alex get the partial dental identification?"

"He had his lower left teeth pulled and placed in Brian's before he died. Before, he had a cast of them made for a bridge to replace them. As suspected, he killed Commander Taylor, the coroner and Brian. They were all being blackmailed to do Alex's bidding and manipulated the reports to hide any inconsistencies. After I came back, Alex started cleaning up his mess. He decided to finish what he started. Alex sent the note to you in Italy and at the art gallery with the finger."

"Why?"

"I finally had something worth losing. It was all a fucked

up game to make me suffer. I know it seems like there should be more of an explanation. If there is, Alex is taking it to his grave."

A shiver ran through me, which caused Gabe to pull me closer. I placed my head on his chest. Alex truly was a terrible being. Everything felt icky when it involved him.

"What happens now?"

"De Luca took Alex and Harley. He promised we would know they'd been dealt with permanently."

There was so much to process and understand. He held me close and I knew he would never let me go.

It was over.

The game Chasity cultivated was finished.

Chapter Thirty

It was late afternoon as I walked along the back of the property with Gabe. A stillness settled over the place and I felt contentment.

Events from the night before played over in my head. True to my word, I worked on healing from all the hate. It would take time, but with Gabe by my side, we would find our happy ending. The only outstanding issue was whether De Luca would keep his word and stay away. Though he knew we lacked incriminating evidence to turn him in, we still wanted to be watchful. The men stayed in place for now. Security would be needed for the foreseeable future.

I glanced to the barn. It was empty now when only a few hours ago, a man I despised had been there. How things changed. It was as if the incident had never occurred.

Had Alex loved his son? I believed he had. It had to be the only human piece left in him. Maybe I wanted to believe he loved him. At the core of all people there was good.

My thoughts might have been naïve, but it made the

world a little less scary.

"What are you thinking about?"

"Alex. He'd lived with me for nearly six months yet he was a stranger. Last night, I saw all the hate spew from a battered and broken man. It's a tragedy what your mother did to you boys."

"It is."

Thank goodness Gabe had been strong enough to survive.

We took a turn down the path I walked millions of times through the years. The trees created a magical feeling canopy.

The time had come for us to move on. Sun filtered through the trees, giving them a luminary feel. At the end of the path was the gazebo. Letting go of Gabe's hand, I walked to the center where a fountain bubbled with water. This had been Dad and Mom's special spot. The place he proposed to her.

"This is the place—" I turned to see Gabe on one knee. My hand went to my mouth as a jubilant laugh left me.

"Willow Loren Russo, I have spent my entire life looking for you. You are the sun that chases away my darkness. I have loved you from the moment I laid eyes on you. Will you do me the honor of not only being the mother of my children, but my wife?"

I threw my arms around him, knocking him off balance. Gabe braced me against falling and took the brunt of it. Another giggle left me.

"Is that a yes?" he asked.

Oh no, I had forgotten to answer. "Yes! Yes! Yes!" Kissing him with all my might, I bound myself to him. Then, I remembered. "We can have sex! I can have sex now."

"As my fiancée."

My smile grew. "I like the sound of that."

"Me, too. Would you like to see your ring?"

"Yes! I have a ring!" I nearly squealed with delight as he opened up the ring box. The sapphire diamond I thought was lost forever sparkled back at me. My throat tightened. Barely above a whisper, I asked, "Where did you find my mother's ring?"

Delicately, Gabe took it from the box and slipped it on my left index finger. "I left something out about the day your dad told me about your tradition to come here to remember your mom."

I gazed at the diamond with reverence.

"Before your dad told me the story, I'd asked for your hand in marriage."

My eyes connected with his. "You did?"

"Yes. And he gave me the ring for safekeeping. It was his approval."

"This is perfect. Thank you for giving me the world."

He stood with me in his arms like I weighed nothing. "Now, on to your next surprise."

Chapter Thirty-One

Our car pulled up to the Whitmore Hotel. The bellman hurriedly got our luggage from the trunk and took it inside.

"Evening, *Signorina* Russo, *Signor* Thompson," Tomas greeted us. His familiar face reminded me of my last trip when I'd been here with Carson.

"Hello, Tomas. How's your daughter?"

"Very good, *Signorina* Russo. That is sweet of you to remember. I received the art supplies you sent her. *Gratzi*. She loves it and made you a card. I'll bring it tomorrow."

I gave him a brief hug. "I'm so glad. I can't wait to see what your little artist made."

"It's wonderful to have you back." With an outstretched hand, he welcomed us into the hotel. "We have everything arranged as you asked, *Signor* Thompson."

I glanced at Gabe who gave nothing away.

"*Gratzi*, Tomas."

The grandeur of the hotel remained the same. Low classical music filled the atmosphere. The white marble floors had distressed gray marks through them. In the center of the room, the giant crystal chandelier hung massively over a ginormous flower arrangement wider than I was tall. The fragrant flowers of white lilies and violets permeated the air—both symbolic flowers of Italy. Everywhere you looked, another treasure waited to be discovered like the sculptures in the corner of the room.

Smooth polished marble met my hands as we climbed the three stories of the grand staircase. As we rounded the corner, I felt the heat of Gabe's stare and stopped. My stomach clinched with anticipation of things to come.

We were about to have each other... finally.

I wasn't able to take my eyes off the way Gabe's muscles moved. For so long I had worked on squelching the desires to make the need for him a little more bearable. But now, nothing stood in our way.

Money exchanged hands before Tomas left the room. In a haze, I waved good-bye but nothing deterred me from the man I loved. We had survived against so many odds.

Click.

The lock moving into place heightened the sexual tension as heat radiated off my skin begging to be touched.

Gabe faced the other direction with his back to me, the anticipation building for when he took what was his. Me.

"Undress, sweetheart. When I turn around I want to see you."

A little smile formed because of what I had on underneath my lavender sundress. Francesca packed some lingerie with a note that told me to use it wisely. Oh, I planned to.

The energy between us grew and I quietly slipped my sundress over my head.

Holding the fabric out to the side, I let it drop. Gabe turned with a deliberate control and his eyes heated with an intensity I remembered from the last time we made love. With measured steps he strolled to me. The heels of his shoes sounding against the marble.

The heat from his body met mine, creating an almost combustible inferno. My breathing sped up, but still he kept a millimeter of space between us. I itched to reach out and feel his body against mine, but I waited.

An agony to have him built slow and steady as he walked around me. The heat of his skin licked mine as my nipples puckered, waiting to be stroked and begging for attention. As he passed behind me, his fingertip touched the upper part of my shoulder, and with deliberate slowness he trailed it across my back. The minuscule touch became the worse kind of torture.

"You are fucking gorgeous and mine to have."

"Yes." My breathy reply gave him the answer he needed.

His fingertips skimmed the tops of my panties as he came around to my front. "Are you wet?"

"Very. I need you inside of me."

"It's taking every ounce of control to savor this." His finger dipped below my panty line, causing my stomach to tingle.

I wanted Gabe to lose control, but the reward when he did would be that much greater. A needy whimper escaped as his hands reached the sides of my panties where they tied together. The sound of fabric swooshing filled the silence. The air kissed my now bare skin as my panties dropped to the floor.

He took a step back.

He looked at me as if he wouldn't survive without me. I felt wanton. His hand came out and unsnapped the front snap of my bra releasing my breasts, heavy with desire. The bra slid down my arms and landed on the floor. I was completely naked except for my ring signifying I was his.

Another step closer brought us back together. Our breaths mingled as he lowered his head, but kept enough distance to drive me mad. "Do you feel it, Willow?"

"Always."

His thumb and index finger rolled my nipple, creating the most delicious friction. I jerked at the increased sensation. "You're sensitive and I can see your breasts are changing."

"Everything is more intense. Please, Gabe. Please." At this point, the begging in my voice was a necessity and what decorum I had left went out the window. "I'm ready."

"You're almost ready, but not quite." The scruff of his face brushed against my jawline while strategically placed kisses peppered down my neck.

I closed my eyes, trying to regain some of my senses before I lost control. The feeling of Gabe vanished and I opened my eyes.

He stood two steps back and removed his shirt. The pulse in his neck beat wildly. The reins of control were slipping. Next, he toed off his shoes and unbuttoned his jeans. Going commando allowed him to spring free as he released the zipper. It throbbed with as much desire as I felt.

In the hotel room, sun trickling in from the balcony while we basked in each other only heightened the sensual desire.

As he removed his jeans, my pulse beckoned to be touched and I slid my hand down my abdomen. Almost to my goal, a little gasp left my lips and the last of Gabe's control diminished. The hunger in his eyes came alive as he scooped me up.

I wrapped my legs around his waist and felt the tip of his cock seeking entrance as our mouths collided. Teeth clashed against each other as our tongues intertwined. We moved in a zigzag pattern trying to get to the bed. I pressed down and moaned when I felt him barely enter me.

"Oh fuck, Willow. You feel so good. Fuck. Fuck. Fuck."

I arched my back and his mouth came to my nipple. The biting sensation caused another louder moan to break free from me as our bodies found the bed. His dick pressed a little further in and I grabbed onto his arms, urging him to take me. Claim me. Make me one with him.

"I should prime you more."

The thought of him withdrawing gave me physical pain. "No, no you shouldn't. I'm ready. Oh, Gabe, I can't wait any longer."

He pushed in a little further and we both gasped. The veins in his neck popped out.

I urged, "More! Please, Gabe!"

My feet dug into his ass, and in one solid movement he thrust inside me, filling me, and deliciously stretched me.

"Best fucking feeling in the world. You okay?"

"Yes, oh yes. Don't stop. We'll go slower next time."

Pulling out, Gabe paused only briefly before surging back inside.

"Yes!"

Our mouths found each other as our bodies synced and became one. Our fevered movements brought a sheen of sweat to coat our bodies as we climbed higher. The world faded away. More thrusting and we were calling out incoherently.

With one twist of his hips, I fell apart as euphoria capsized over me. Gabe stilled as the look of pure bliss covered his face as he found his release in me.

He rolled onto his back and brought me with him and, leaving us still connected while he remained almost hard inside me. "Hell, that was worth the wait, but I never want to go that long without you again, sweetheart."

"Me, either."

—————•——————•——————•——————

Lying in bed, our legs intertwined, I basked in the glow of our lovemaking still reeling from the intensity of my earlier orgasm. I looked at my ring glimmering on my finger.

"Why didn't Dad say anything when I wasn't wearing mom's ring?"

"Alex told him it was getting sized and he wanted to surprise you. That was when I think your dad started investigating on his own. I couldn't tell you this last night or it would ruin my proposal. But there's nothing else I'm hiding from you."

There were still unanswered questions that concerned Dad. "I wonder why he never told Trent."

Gabe shifted beside me. "I don't know. Neither does Trent. I think he's taking that part pretty hard."

I made a mental note to talk to Trent at some point. More peace settled over the room before I said, "I want to get married soon."

The hand trailing up my back stopped. "How soon?"

Did he want to wait? I doubted it. If I said today, Gabe probably would have someone here within the hour. I thought about our wedding and what I wanted. The bells and whistles of something fancy disinterested me. All I wanted was to move forward from the past and start our bright future together.

"Before we go home. I want to get married where you proposed to me." I settled my chin on his chest. Gabe's smile turned radiant and my suspicion was confirmed. He wanted this as much as I did.

"I'd love that. We'll start planning it tomorrow. Today, is about you and me and nothing else."

Our bodies shifted as Gabe entered me with an exquisite torture. "There's no place I'd rather be than inside you."

My back arched off the bed as he pushed all the way in. "I feel complete when you're mine."

And for the second time, Gabe and I found that place we only had with each other.

Chapter Thirty-Two

Three days later

Soon the whole family would descend upon us. Francesca and Marie wanted to help plan the wedding. They had been ecstatic when I handed over everything but the venue—the place Dad proposed to Mom and Gabe proposed to me. But when I told them they had only one week, things kicked into high gear. I hardly heard from them. Even my dress was a surprise, but I trusted them and knew it would be perfect.

Gabe was in the bedroom, finishing his shower. I stepped onto the back porch and found Trent staring out over the hills. For the last few days he'd been unusually quiet. I sensed he was avoiding me.

Hearing me, Trent glanced my way. "I'll leave you to the view, Willow. I have some work to handle."

I reached out and touched his hand. "I actually wanted to

talk to you."

His jaw stiffened, but he remained quiet.

"You can't blame yourself for Dad not saying anything. He trusted you, Trent. He told me so in the letter he wrote me." The hurt flashed across Trent's face as his mask temporarily slipped. I pressed on. "Dad had his reason why he didn't say anything about the ring. For the last few days I've been trying to work through it. But in the end, all I can focus on is he loved me and had my best interest at heart."

It seemed like I penetrated his armor a little.

"But, Willow, I would have dropped everything to help your dad."

Grabbing his hand, I said, "I know and Dad knew, too." With my other hand, I pulled out Dad's letter. I'd had Carson send it to me. It was the same letter Trent gave me in a sealed envelope the day we met. "Read this. It's what Dad thought of you. He trusted you, Trent. Give yourself today and then start to heal tomorrow. You have a family now. Don't hold onto the past. Neither Dad nor your sister would want it."

His brows scrunched and I added, "We're your family. You're stuck with us."

Without warning, Trent engulfed me in a hug. "I'll always be here for you. I promise. You're stuck with me, too."

I hugged him back. After a few moments, he released me. "I think I'm going to go for a walk."

"I suggest the spot over there on top of the hill. It was Dad's favorite."

Giving me a small smile, he took off across the yard toward the hill with the letter in hand.

I watched his retreating figure, hoping he got the peace he deserved.

"You're an amazing woman."

I startled at Gabe's voice. "You scared me. How long were you there?"

"Long enough." Gabe's hair was still damp from the shower. He wrapped his arms around me. "Everyone will be here in two hours. I just got word from the pilot." A long contented breath left him.

"In four days I'm going to be your wife. I like the sound of it."

"Me, too. You'll be Mrs. Thompson."

In his arms, I turned to face him and looped my arms around his neck. "I can't wait."

Chapter Thirty-Three

Six months pregnant

I stood from my adjustable chair and stretched, finishing the last bit of writing on the wall. As a surprise, I had waited to start painting the room until after Francesca finished decorating it. As the godmother, I wanted this to be my gift to the baby. Something to remember me by forever.

I took a Twizzler from the bag as I took it all in. Hopefully, they'd like it. The babies moved and I savored the moment. Each time I felt them was an indescribable experience with my ever-growing belly.

So far, things were progressing perfectly. The babies and I were both healthy, which I was beyond thankful for.

Making it full-term was my next goal.

I cleaned the brushes before heading downstairs. The cheers from the front room brought me up short. Carson and Gabe goaded each other on who was going to win. Not so long ago, I wondered if I would ever have moments like this.

A month ago Rosie had been convicted to a mental hospital. The trial had escalated at an unprecedented rate. As they took her away, she screamed for Carson to save her. She was truly disturbed.

Our friends and Mitchell had been shocked. I truly believed Mitchell had feelings for her. Heartbreaking. It is now Marissa's life's mission to set him up with someone. Last month, I had been a bridesmaid at Marissa's wedding, pregnant belly and all. It had been a beautiful church wedding in New York City.

"Touchdown, Patriots!"

Hearing their dad yell, the babies kicked.

"Motherfucker!" Carson cursed.

A giggle escaped Francesca. I stayed tucked behind the corner as I took the moment in and leaned against the wall.

My wedding ring caught my attention. Gabe and I had married in Italy a week after we were engaged in the same place Dad proposed to Mom. It had been a small affair.

◆———————◆———————◆

"You may kiss the bride."

Gabe's eyes locked on to mine underneath the gazebo. Gardenias hung from the latticework. "I promise I will forever watch over you and our twins. Love you until my dying breath. You have given me the world, Mrs. Thompson."

"Forever, Mr. Thompson."

His lips descended on mine as applauses from our friends surrounded us. The wedding was intimate with only Nonno, Carson, Francesca, Bennett, Marie, Trent, Mildred, and Chris in attendance. They were my family and now Gabe's.

As we stepped apart, Gabe whispered in my ear. "And now we have the honeymoon."

"Yes, we do." Though I had no idea where we were going.

An odd silence grew over the crowd as our family stared at us. Carson and Francesca looked everywhere but at us.

I checked my dress. "What's wrong?"

Nonno looked between us. "Did you say twins?"

Most everyone now knew I was pregnant, but we hadn't disclosed that we were having twins. The plan was to announce it at the reception.

I laughed. We were the worst at slipping. However, it was time. "Yes, Gabe and I found out we're having twins. We were going to announce it at the reception."

With his hands in the air, Nonno rushed forward. "Oh, this does my ole Italian heart good. I have a long list of names I suggested to your mom I'll share with you. They're strong Italian names."

Another giggle escaped. "I can't wait, Nonno. But, we are keeping it a surprise."

"Sei proprio come tua madre," he muttered in Italian. And that's when I realized it. I was just like my mother. Through Mom's pregnancy they had gone back and forth about Italian names.

The congratulations continued as Trent approached. "I'm happy life led you here. Treasure it always."

I sensed the longing in his voice to have what Gabe and I had. The heartbreakingly sad tale of Trent would one day find a happy ending. "Someday you'll find your soul mate."

"Maybe, we'll see."

The wedding had been perfect. Francesca followed suit a month later marrying on the rooftop of the Whitmore Hotel in Florence at sunset. Simply stunning. They kissed as the bells of the Deumo tolled.

Finally, Carson and I had our happily ever afters.

Trent remained close, but he traveled all over the place with his security team, keeping busy. We still had a small security detail with Andre and a couple of other men Gabe knew that Trent now employed. Still, the longing in his voice to one day have love when we spoke at my wedding stayed with me with. Once or twice I tried to broach the subject, but he delicately sidestepped it. I would be forever thankful to Trent, and he would always be like a brother to me.

Because of Alex, I had him in my life. It was the silver lining in the situation, which helped me heal. About two months ago, we had gotten the message from De Luca that Alex and Harley had been dealt with. Their bodies were found on the side of the road... burned. A message had been scrawled on the sidewalk.

They were dead. And I was glad they were out of our lives.

"Yes, take that! Eagles score for the tie!"

"It's only a temporary problem before we kick your ass."

My phone vibrated with a text from Gabe.

Gabe: Are you doing okay?
Me: Yes, I'll be there in a few minutes.
Gabe: Tell the babies I miss them.
Me: They miss you, too. They love hearing you speak.
Gabe: Hurry. I want to feel them kick. Oh and look at the
picture *Apple Blossom sent.*

A picture appeared of Alex Junior. He held a paintbrush and had a smile to his face. Though his father was gone and Candy had left with a new boyfriend to California after Harley turned up dead, Alex Junior thrived.

The first time we met he looked at Gabe and said, "You're not my dad. Who are you?"

We had been worried about confusing Alex Junior, but he had seen the truth all along. Now, we visited him regularly and loved him with our entire hearts. I texted Gabe back.

Me: Such a sweet little boy.
Gabe: I know. Can't wait to see him this weekend.
Me: Me, either.
Gabe: Time's up. I'm missing the babies too much.

I stepped out into the hallway as Gabe stood. The radiant smile took my breath away as he walked to me.

"Hey, sweetheart. Did you finish?"

"I did."

His hand found my stomach as they excitedly moved about.

"They love you."

For a second he remained silent before swallowing hard.

"It's unbelievable the bond I feel with them."

The fact that I had the ability to give Gabe this gift of unconditional love warmed me beyond reproach. After his terrible upbringing, I made sure to shower him with as much love as possible.

For a month, no one found the body of his mother. No one had cared. Two kids out joyriding happened upon her. No words described the depth of emotion I felt for what happened. None.

This was a time for happy thoughts. The past was in the past where the darkness belonged. Only the light and our future remained out front.

Francesca, now in her seventh month, sat on the couch with a bowl of popcorn sitting on her belly. About a week ago her father reached out to her to begin mending the bridges. Abruptly she sat up, sending the popcorn flying.

She looked our way. "Are you done?"

"I just finished."

For the past month, it had driven her crazy not allowing her to go into the room while I painted. I spent a few hours here most mornings, working on the mural that turned into more than I ever dreamed. Luckily, they bought a house right after they married that was ten minutes from ours. They still had the beach house, but wanted to keep it as a weekend getaway. It was wonderful having them so close. Francesca and I were already working out playdate schedules and mommy time.

The pregnancy waddle commenced as Francesca hurried through the main level of the house with Carson right behind her. Throughout the month I had received bribes such as chocolate-covered cherries flown over from Europe, a masseuse who came to my house for a week for massages, and more to let them see the room early. I refused to break but took the bribes in good fun.

Francesca opened the bedroom door and disappeared into the room, but I remained in the hallway. I loved allowing people to take it in without feeling the pressure. Art was meant to be experienced freely.

"Willow?" I walked to the door as she stuck her head in the hallway. "Get in here."

I walked in the room and saw Carson on the opposite side reading the story from the beginning. Each wall was a progression of scenes that told the story of lion whose name was Myles, which also happened to be the name of their son they were having.

The story incorporated the furniture and moved around the room as Myles the Lion rode airplanes, climbed trees, read books, and much more. Even Gabe was quiet as he took in the room, engrossed in the story.

Carson finished first. "I... this is amazing. There are no words."

"You like it?"

He hugged me. "I don't have words to express what this means to me."

Francesca's hand hovered over the lion as he took a swim in the pond. Looking my way tears spilled from her eyes. "I have no words, either. This is amazing. Our child is so blessed."

"Thank you. Gabe and I got Myles a gift in the chair."

The taupe chair had a stuffed animal sewn to match the lion on the walls. "Mildred helped me make Myles's the stuffed lion. Open the box."

The lion paper tore easily as Francesca opened it and gasped, covering her mouth. "I keep thinking I'm going to wake up from this dream."

Carson took her into his arms. "Never, baby. This is real. What did you get?"

She held up the book. "It's Myles the lion's story that Willow painted."

I stepped forward with Gabe. "I sketched and colored the mural. Gabe thought it would be neat to have it bound in a book Myles could keep forever. We had a few extra copies printed that are at the house."

From each side, my two dear friends engulfed me in a hug while whispering their thank-yous. "Check out the bathroom."

Like children on Christmas morning, they scampered to the bathroom. I was overjoyed with what this meant to them as it meant the same to me. Gabe's hand settled on my back and he rubbed it knowing it got sore from time to time.

Carson flipped the lights on as they walked in. Myles the lion had another story in the bathroom. It talked about brushing his teeth and staying clean after he got dirty. I figured any incentive would help the little one. Gabe's arms wrapped around my stomach while they read more of Myles's adventures. "Pretty soon you're not going to be able to wrap your arms around me."

"I think I'll manage. You tired?"

The babies moved as he touched me, eliciting feelings of desire. Even in this state, I craved Gabe multiple times a day. While we were joined, we were truly one with no beginning or end... simply together.

"Very. But I think I can manage sex, ice cream, and a foot massage. Maybe ice cream first."

Gently, he spun me around. "I bet I could change your mind."

"I know for certain you could. And I hope you do."

Chapter Thirty-Four

Eight and a half months pregnant

Our babies were officially full-term. Due to my smaller frame, the doctors suggested a C-section, which we agreed was the best option.

I stood in the nursery and ran my hands along the quilt on the front of one of the cribs. On the blanket, Mildred embroidered half of the willow tree. On the other was the other half of the tree—two halves making a whole... like Gabe and me.

One of the babies kicked. At this point I was ready to serve the eviction notice. I massaged my lower back and shifted as I took the room in one last time before we left.

Warmth filled me. It was more than I ever expected. In a couple of days I would be back here with them in this very room. We were ready to be parents.

Dad's series of three paintings of the willow tree hung between the cribs. Behind them, on the wall, I expanded the painting to cover the entire wall to appear three dimensional as if the cribs sat underneath the boughs of the tree. Within the branches, words of wisdom and love wove throughout.

In the play corner, the wall had been covered with chalk-board paint for the kids to draw on when they got older. A monkey sat on a swing with a marker in hand. Above his head a quote was written:

Over the changing table, birds carried a ribbon with a quote as they flew toward the window:

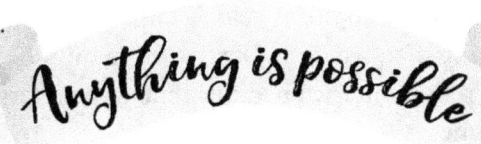

Anything is possible

The entire room had similar designs creating the perfect magical forest for my children. I hoped this allowed their imaginations to flow and believe anything was possible.

Little kicks fluttered inside. "Soon, little ones."

Something changed in the air and I sensed my other half near. I turned and found Gabe leaning against the doorframe with a content smile on his face. "You are absolutely breathtaking."

"And large." Laughing, I walked to him and gave him a kiss.

"No, you're pregnant. I'm going to miss you carrying our kids."

My hand touched where they kicked. "I'll be glad to not waddle, but I'll miss not having them with me all the time."

The sense of loss would be weird. For almost nine months I'd kept them safe.

Gabe checked his phone. "Trent texted and said he landed."

"Good. He sent me a text last night before he took off, excited about meeting his godchildren."

A month ago we asked Trent to be a godfather to our children as well. He had been overcome with emotion for a moment and not able to speak. The honor helped fill a missing piece Trent longed for... a family. I knew it, but after his tragic past, the thought of happiness scared him.

Everything else was set. Our family would be at the hospital this afternoon after we had our time to be a family.

It was time.

"Are you ready?"

"More than ever."

I came to and blinked away the haze. The spinal block hadn't worked, so I had to be put under. My babies. Where were my babies?

Groggily, my eyes searched around me. Gabe sat beside me with a pink blanket in one arm and a blue one in the other. A boy and a girl.

"Gabe—" My voice caught.

He moved closer to me. "You did fantastic, sweetheart."

"Are they okay?"

"They're perfect. The most perfect little babies in the world."

I hated I hadn't been there for the moment they entered the world, but we were all safe and sound. That above all mattered most.

The nurse adjusted my gown. I hadn't realized she was here. "Let's put them skin on skin."

"Yes." Birthing class taught us about the importance. I helped her.

The bed moved up into a sitting position. Our little girl cooed.

"Gabe, they talked."

"They're ready to meet their mother."

Unwrapped from the blanket, my little boy cried in protest until he felt the heat of me. Immediately, he settled. Love at first sight was a poor description for what I felt. Truly indescribable. Little eyes in an adorable scrunchy face meet my stare.

"Hey there my sweet little boy. I've been waiting to meet you." His big eyes closed contentedly. "I love you."

"Meet your daughter, sweetheart."

The nurse placed my sleeping baby girl in my other arm. I brushed my thumb against her leg. Any worry subsided with them in my arms. "I never want this moment to end."

Gabe traced my cheek. "Me, either. Happiest day of my life."

For a moment, we stared at our little blessings.

"You want to try to nurse, Mrs. Thompson?" the nurse in blue scrubs asked.

"More than anything."

On the side of the bed, Gabe watched intently while the nurse helped position each baby for nursing in my arms. The little boy latched on first with almost no help. "He has a perfect latch. Okay, let's get the little girl going."

A little cry left her lips as she searched for me. The nurse helped position her head and she latched on easily, too.

"Oh, she's good, too. How are you feeling?"

"Never better. This is a magical moment."

And it was—having the two babies I'd created with me in my arms. The nurse stepped back. "I'm going to give you some time. If you need me, hit the buzzer. I'll check on you in about thirty minutes."

"Thank you."

"Thank you, Gabe. You came back for me and gave me

all this." My emotions flowed over.

"I will always keep my promise to you. Do you remember when I took you to the tree right before I was deployed?"

The memory of lying under the tree and dreaming of a future together flashed through my mind. "Yes."

"I said… I'll make you my wife. We'll have a little girl and a little boy. That will be my perfect world."

I nodded remembering the words but not able to speak.

"You've now made my life complete. I have it all right here in this room."

Tears brimmed over. At one time, I never thought this day would come. And now I had my happy ever after.

"Which baby was born first?"

"Our little girl."

The pride was evident on Gabe's face. "No one knows our son's name yet. Our family is in the waiting room. No one has seen either baby. I wanted you to be the first." He leaned down and kissed me.

"You truly are an amazing man. What's his name?"

"Antonio Lorenzo Thompson."

I closed my eyes. This moment in time was perfect. One of those to freeze for all eternity in the box of memories. "You named him after Nonno and Dad. Thank you."

"Two men who helped you become the amazing person you are."

Dad would have been so proud. The little boy nuzzled a little closer. "Nonno is going to be ecstatic he finally has an heir with an Italian name."

Throughout the pregnancy, Nonno dropped hints about Italian names. We had random names on cards popping up all over our house. He tried everything in the book to get us to reveal our names, but we held strong. I loved him so much.

"What are you naming our little girl?" Gabe's finger stroked her cheek. He was as helplessly in love with her as me.

Throughout the entire pregnancy, I hadn't been able to decide on a name. I knew Gabe had decided on a girl's name first. Last week, I decided if I had one of each it was meant to be for him to name them both. "I want to use your name for the girl."

"But you don't know what it is."

"I know. But it's meant to be."

This was my ultimate gift to Gabe. Total trust and love. He understood by the look of awe on his face. His fingers brushed our daughter's cheek again as he spoke, "Kendra Loren Thompson. After your mother and you."

In this moment, I felt my parents here with us. "Gabe, the names are so selfless on your part."

"No, sweetheart, they're what gave me the chance at love."

Epilogue

5 years later

We drove to Carson's house down the road. This afternoon the kids had been playing together. Three and half years ago, Carson and Francesca had a little girl named Gabriella. When they told us they wanted to name her after Gabe because of his strength, he had been truly silenced.

Gabriella had been an unexpected souvenir from a trip they took to Fiji. I chortled every time I thought about Francesca blurting out at dinner she thought she was pregnant. Pregnancy word vomit at its finest.

It actually worked out well having them all so close in age. One day a week Francesca had all four and another day I had them. Our children loved each other and were the best of friends, but they created the worst of headaches at time when their imaginations ran a little too free.

A few minutes ago Carson called for us to come over. The kiddos had struck again.

"Did Carson say what happened?"

Gabe chuckled. "No, he wanted us to see for ourselves. He said we'll know it when we see it."

"Oh dear. This is not good at all."

We turned into the driveway and drove toward the house. Tall trees kept the house hidden until we rounded the bend.

I gasped. "What did they do?"

"Oh fuck," Gabe muttered beside me.

The fountain, the major water feature in front of the house, had bubbles multiplying at an exponential rate.

We parked the car and took in the anomaly. They were five. How in the world had they gotten into this? Gabe poked me and I turned. He pointed to the front of the house. Our four children sat in a row on the front steps like Carson and I had so many time when we were in trouble. Why had we been so naughty?

Kendra and Antonio's eyes were wide as they stared at us in the car. Carson stood in front of the children with his back toward us.

It was an adorable scene. I took out my phone and snapped a couple of photos. "For their scrapbook."

"I'm glad we're out of bubbles at our house. This very well could have been us."

"I know."

After Francesca gave me her incredibly thoughtful gift, I started scrapbooking the children's memories. Once a week Francesca and I got together to work on them while we drank wine. The boys watched the children. It gave us a break from all the insanity I wouldn't trade for the world.

While I took in the scene, I texted Trent the picture.

Me: Poor Carson's fountain.

Trent was stateside this week. Last night, he'd been over for dinner. The children loved having him around. When he came over, they received his complete attention. He let Kendra put makeup on him and played pirates with Antonio.

I got a response almost immediately.

Trent: Go easy on my sweet godchildren. I'm sure there's a reasonable explanation.
Me: You're such a softie.
Trent: For those kids... absolutely. We still on for tomorrow?
Me: Yes! Can't wait.

Tomorrow, the entire family planned to gather at my house for Nonno's surprise birthday party. For his present, I painted a series of paintings from all the places he loved.

One day I hoped Trent found love. He had so much to give. I knew he was scared to put himself out there. My heart hurt understanding what all he was missing by not being with his soul mate.

After we stepped from the car, we walked to the front porch. Francesca gave me a wink but kept a serious look on her face. In all honesty, this was funny. But we had to remain firm. Give these kiddos an inch and they took five miles.

Carson put his hands on his hips. "I want the truth, what happened?"

Kendra looked up with her sweet little face. Our children had my eyes and Gabe's hair. They were the perfect culmination of the two of us. "Uncle Carson, don't be mad at Myles."

Under his breath, Carson's little mini me muttered, "Kendra, don't say anything."

She looked to Myles with her head cocked. "Your daddy won't be mad. You were trying to make me smile. Your mommy told us today that we should do nice things for people."

Glancing to Francesca, she massaged her temples and pressed her lips together.

"Myles, what happened?" Carson asked in his no-nonsense tone.

The little boy kicked at an imaginary rock. "Kendra said Aunt Willow wouldn't let her do a bubble bath last night because they were out."

Oh geez.

Antonio chanted, "Myles loves Kendra. Myles loves Kendra."

Gabe's eyes grew wide as he looked to me with terror. Kendra was the apple of his eye. It was nearly impossible to keep a straight face.

Myles looked at Antonio. "Be quiet. I do not."

"You said you loved me, Myles." Kendra's bottom lip quivered. "Why don't you love me now?"

Myles grabbed Kendra's hand and winked at her while whispering, "Shh… it's our secret. We can't let your dad know. He'll be mad."

Oh shit.

The color in Gabe's face drained.

Carson remained stoic, but he fought his smile. "Go inside and sit on the couch. Don't move. We're going to talk and figure out the punishment."

Their little heads hung low. Kendra walked up to me. "Mommy, ask Uncle Carson to not be mad at Myles. Tomorrow, we're getting married, and I don't want my prince in trouble."

I thought Gabe was about to come unglued when he knelt, taking control of the conversation. "Punkin' munkin', you're too young to get married. All boys are yucky still. No getting married until you're thirty."

"You're not yucky, daddy. I heard Mommy say you she wanted adult time with you. I want some kid time with Myles."

My eyes bulged and Carson covered his mouth. Francesca turned the other way while her shoulders shook. Yes, I had needed adult time in a major way. In fact, I had adult time this morning as well while the children were over here. Checking on Gabe, I believed he'd gone catatonic.

I stepped in and said, "Kendra, honey, go inside. We're going to talk."

Running up the stairs, she called from the front door, "I think we're going to live, guys!"

Gabe dragged his hand down his face. "I'm fucking screwed."

Laughing, Carson patted him on the back. "Yeah, you are. I know just the cologne to suggest one day."

Oh no! Francesca and I both tried to censor him. "Carson! Stop!" Gabe knew about the cologne I brought Carson back from Paris. It was the same cologne we joked about and said got the ladies to go crazy for him.

He held up his hands in mock surrender. "What... someday."

I stifled the laugh that came from me and covered it with a cough. Beside me, my poor husband looked lost.

Francesca hooked her arm through Carson's. "It was pretty sweet making her bubbles when she didn't have any."

I turned and the fountain continued to spit bubbles everywhere. "It is." I kissed Gabe on the cheek. "Don't worry. She's still your little girl."

Carson turned my way and closed his eyes before tilting his head back. "How did our parents survive?"

"There were only two of us." I gave him a wink.

"Mommy, I need to go pee-pee," Gabriella called from the front with Gabby, her stuffed horse.

For Gabriella's present, I painted a story for her room, too, but with Gabby the horse as the star. Both children loved their rooms and slept with the stuffed animals every night. Myles the lion had to visit the stuffed animal vet to be re-stitched last year.

"Coming, sweetheart." Taking the stairs two at a time, Francesca hurriedly took Gabriella.

As the bubbles kept spitting, Gabe kept staring. Only when Carson clasped him on the shoulder did he come back to the present. "I'll let you gather yourself and head inside to talk with the kids."

"Gabriella is next."

Gabe's words stopped Carson, but then he smiled. "Nah, she's going to be a nun."

"Riiiight," I said and got the censored looked myself before he turned to head inside.

When the front door closed, Gabe looked a little frantic. "Willow, she's too young to start that shit. We need to remove all princess books. No more fairy tales. I wasn't expecting this at least for... for... twenty more years."

On my tiptoes, I leaned up and kissed him, hoping to ease some of his worry. "Carson and I used to get pretend married when we were five. And then, I would help him defeat evil empires."

This eased him marginally. He wrapped his hands around

my waist.

"I think you need a little more adult time."

He touched his lips to mine. "I think a lot more adult time is needed."

Playlist

Below is a list of songs that remind me of
White Lies and Black Truth

Unsteady – X Ambassadors

Hello World – Lady Antebellum

Yours – Ella Henderson

Close – Nick Jonas

Jar of Hearts – Christina Perri

Everytime We Touch – Cascada (Yanou's Candlelight Mix)

Jet Black Heart – 5 Seconds of Summer

Listen to Your Heart – D.H.T., Edmee

For You – Demi Lovato

Stone Cold – Demi Lovato

Black Magic – Little Mix

Stay – Rihanna

Should've Been Us – Tori Kelly

Far Away – Nickelback

You Ruin Me – The Veronicas

Heart of Stone – Iko

4 In The Morning – Gwen Stefani

PILLOWTALK – ZAYN

Let It Go – James Bay

Say Something – A Great Big World

Hurt – Christina Aguilera

Take A Bow – Rihanna

Beneath Your Beauty – Labrinth

Never Say Never – The Fray

Cry – Rihanna

Heaven – DJ Sammy

Can't Help Falling in Love – Haley Reinhart

Say You Love Me – Jessie Ware

Please Don't Say You Love Me – Gabrielle Aplin

Wild Horse – Natasha Bedingfield

Poison & Wine – The Civil Wars

Salvation – Gabrielle Aplin

Concrete Angel – Christin

Thank you from the bottom of my heart

for making this journey possible

It's because of you I get to submerse

myself in the magical word of writing.

Thank you infinity factorial

Xoxo

Kristin

Other Books by Kristin Mayer

Available Now

The Trust Series

Trust Me
Love Me
Promise Me
Full-length novels in the TRUST series are also available in
audio from Tantor Media.

The Effect Series

Ripple Effect
Domino Effect

The Twisted Fate Series

White Lies
Black Truth

Stand Alone Novels

Innocence
Bane

Co-Written Collaborations

Finding Forever (co-written with Kelly Elliott)

Coming Soon

Whispered Promises
Untouched Perfection
Flawless Perfection